"This isn't love,"

Nicholas said, lifting her into his arms.

"I know," Molly whispered, burying her face against his neck.

"It's only lust."

She nodded, her hair drifting across his chest and arms.

"Do you understand this, Molly?" His voice was a low growl. "This isn't about love."

"It isn't about love," she repeated, the words sounding softer, sweeter, as she said them.

The bed shimmered in the gentle glow of the gas lamp. Soft and inviting, the beginning and the end and all that there could ever be....

"In another minute there can be no turning back."

Dear Reader,

Welcome to Harlequin Historicals and to a world of adventure and romance where almost anything can happen.

This month we bring you Barbara Bretton's debut novel for Harlequin Historicals. *The Reluctant Bride* is the delightful tale of the battle over a dilapidated hotel between a stubborn American woman and a cynical Englishman.

Rose Among Thorns is Catherine Archer's first published work. This talented newcomer is sure to delight with her story of a conquering knight and the proud Saxon woman who meets his every challenge.

In *The Naked Huntress* by Shirley Parenteau, a society columnist finds herself at the mercy of a notorious saloon keeper when she unwittingly poses for a scandalous portrait.

Kit Gardner's *Arabesque* was one of our 1991 March Madness promotions. In her second novel, *The Dream,* straitlaced schoolteacher Elizabeth Burbridge must match wits with the dashing Lord Alec Sinclair. Those of you who recall the author's fast-paced, lighthearted writing will not be disappointed.

Next month look for new titles by June Lund Shiplett, Isabel Whitfield, Suzanne Barclay and Mary Daheim.

Sincerely,

Tracy Farrell
Senior Editor

The Reluctant Bride

Barbara Bretton

Harlequin Books

TORONTO • NEW YORK • LONDON
AMSTERDAM • PARIS • SYDNEY • HAMBURG
STOCKHOLM • ATHENS • TOKYO • MILAN
MADRID • WARSAW • BUDAPEST • AUCKLAND

Harlequin Historicals first edition August 1992

ISBN 0-373-28735-6

THE RELUCTANT BRIDE

Books by Barbara Bretton

Harlequin Historicals
The Reluctant Bride #135

Harlequin Intrigue
Starfire #18

Harlequin American Romance

Love Changes #3
The Sweetest of Debts #49
No Safe Place #91
The Edge of Forever #138
Promises in the Night #161
Shooting Star #175
Playing for Time #193
Second Harmony #211
Nobody's Baby #230
Honeymoon Hotel #251
A Fine Madness #274
Mother Knows Best #305
Mrs. Scrooge #322
All We Know of Heaven #355
Sentimental Journey #365
Stranger in Paradise #369
Bundle of Joy #393

BARBARA BRETTON

Barbara Bretton's published works range from stories in Katy Keene comic books—written when she was ten years old—to articles in the *New York Times,* not to mention numerous contemporary and historical romances. The author, who was born and raised in New York City, now makes her home in suburban New Jersey with her husband, Roy.

In memory of Tom E. Huff,
who believed even when I didn't

Chapter One

Cape Charlotte, Delaware
July 1887

The oak banister beckoned in the morning sunlight that streamed through the window on the second floor landing. Molly Hughes, her arms piled high with bed linens, paused at the top of the staircase. She shouldn't do it. She was three weeks past her eighteenth birthday and it was high time she put aside the pleasures of girlhood for more adult responsibilities. But that sleek curve of wood was so inviting and it was so long since she'd done anything for the sheer fun of it.

Lately it seemed that everything about her life had been conspiring to remind her that she was no longer a child, and she wasn't entirely certain she liked the change. The Pemberton Arms was the oldest hotel in Cape Charlotte, and unfortunately the years had not been kind to it. Taxes, unpaid bills, the endless stream of repairs necessary to keep a roof over their heads—she couldn't pinpoint when it had happened, but Molly was reasonably certain adulthood, with all its attendant problems, had arrived when she wasn't looking.

Quickly glancing about, Molly dropped the bundle of laundry on the landing, hitched up her voluminous skirts, then swung herself up onto the banister with ease born of practice. The lobby floor seemed a long way down from where she sat, but she took a deep breath and loosened her grip.

Faster and faster she flew, her thick red hair breaking free of the network of pins and combs that held it neatly in place. She felt giddy as a child caught stealing sugar kisses when the cook's back was turned. She was tempted to race up to the top floor and sample all the banisters, but reason prevailed. Besides, she had only two pairs of cotton hose to her name and she couldn't afford to sacrifice one of them to her high-spirited whim. As it was, the snags and ladders would take her hours to mend and even longer to explain.

She scurried back up the stairs to gather the laundry, stumbling over a frayed runner on the third step from the bottom. Truth to tell, sliding down the banister was safer than navigating the creaky main staircase. Arthur, the Pem's elderly jack-of-all-trades, had given the staircase a lick and a promise a few months ago, but Molly knew it was near impossible to keep up with the problems of an aging hotel when there was no money to make repairs.

At least there was one benefit to growing older, she thought as she crossed the lobby and headed toward the kitchen. Each year brought her closer to her twenty-first birthday, when she would inherit the treasure trove of jewels her mother had left in trust for her then infant daughter. Not that Molly gave a fig for diamonds and pearls. She couldn't imagine anything sillier than spending more time than necessary tending to her toilette. Those jewels were her nest egg, the proceeds of which would enable her to turn the Pem into the most wonderful hotel on the Cape Charlotte boardwalk.

Tossing the laundry into the chute near the end of the rear hallway, she strolled into the kitchen. Her earliest memories were of sitting propped up on one of the maple chairs while Fritzie fed her oatmeal and her father told her stories about his boyhood in England. It was hard to imagine her father living anywhere but Cape Charlotte. "Loved the town the first moment I saw it," he once told her. "Same as I loved your mother." When he died, almost ten years ago, Molly had smiled through her tears at the thought that her parents were finally together for eternity. She might have lost them, but she still had the Pemberton Arms, the place that had meant the world to them.

She paused in the doorway, her gaze roaming the familiar room with its maple wainscoting and red brick fireplace. Sunny yellow curtains framed the wide window where pots of showy mums rested on the sill. And, of course, there was Fritzie in the center of it all. Darling, wonderful Fritzie with her hair piled up on her head and skewered in place with the tortoiseshell pins Molly had given her for Christmas ages ago. Fritzie was a medium-size woman with a bosom made for cradling a frightened child. She always smelled of vanilla and roses in springtime, and she was a mother to Molly in every way that truly mattered.

"Too late for breakfast, girl," said Fritzie, shaking her finger at Molly from across the room. "And good oatmeal it was."

"Don't be a grump, Fritzie," said Molly, blowing her a kiss. "Toast is fine for me."

"Skinny as a fence post you are," said Fritzie as she chopped onions for the stew pot. "You shouldn't be missing meals the way you do."

"If I get fat I won't be able to fit into my dresses and then where will I be?"

Fritzie's round face darkened and Molly wished she could retract her words.

"Himself with all his money and he cannot spare a dollar for this child to buy new clothes. Three gowns and two of them threadbare..."

"Pish!" said Molly with a snap of her fingers. Mention of her father's brother, Jonathan, always tumbled Fritzie and the staff into black moods. "One day I'll have a satin gown for every day of the week and slippers to match."

"Can't say I can imagine you in velvet," said Arthur, who was polishing what remained of the silver service. Arthur, who was as skinny as Fritzie was round, claimed three score years and ten, but his head of thick hair belied that fact. "Don't see too many ladies in velvet dresses splashing in the waves."

Stella laughed as she gathered her mop and bucket. "Never know when a gal might need herself a satin gown to scrub the bathroom floors."

Molly smiled good-naturedly as her beloved friends laughed at the thought of their Molly in silks and satins. Molly was their girl, their special pet. She no more belonged in expensive ball gowns than did Fritzie or Stella. Molly had been the focus of their lives from the day she was born, and it was thanks to these fine people that she had clothes on her back and food in her stomach.

Her Uncle Jonathan was her nominal guardian, but he saw fit to do nothing more than send a monthly stipend for her care—and not even that since before Christmas.

He had never even sent her good wishes on her birthdays, much less sailed across the ocean from England to see to her welfare himself. It wasn't that it bothered her particularly; it was difficult to miss someone you had never known. Still, Molly was accustomed to loving and being loved, and it hurt her that she'd never had the chance to know her beloved father's brother.

She sniffed the air appreciatively. "Is that fresh coffee I smell?"

Fritzie nodded. "Arthur bartered a night at the Pem for five pounds of beans. Sheriff Walters and his wife will be spendin' Saturday night with us."

Molly laughed out loud. "Well, at least we'll have guests to look forward to," she said, reaching for the iron pot resting on the wood stove. "I would hate to think I made up all those beds for nothing." She poured herself a cup of coffee and added two lumps of sugar. She debated a third lump but decided against it. She would dearly love the bacon, as well, but life was all about choices. Truth was she had a prodigious appetite, but there simply wasn't enough food to go around since her uncle had stopped sending her monthly stipend.

The tax man had been around twice, nosing into their business, and making dire predictions about the fate of the Pem if the current quarter's taxes remained unpaid much longer.

"Don't you worry," Molly had said with great bravado. "Has my uncle ever failed us?" There's always a first time, a small inner voice had whispered. Not long after that confrontation, her monthly stipend had stopped arriving.

The thought that the Pem might be endangered was too terrifying to contemplate.

She took a sip of the dark brew, savoring the sweet richness of such an unexpected luxury. Luxuries were rare at the Pem and now they would be rarer still. Someday, she thought, as the usual Friday morning activity bustled around her. The minute she collected her inheritance she would see to it that no one at the hotel had to pinch pennies ever again.

Fritzie had already started to prepare the evening meal. The smell of sizzling beef and onions made Molly's mouth water in anticipation. Local residents made it a habit to drop in for one of the cook's hearty stews or thick soups, and the revenue they generated helped keep the Pem afloat. Despite her carefree ways, Molly worked as hard as anyone else: polishing, changing bed linens, chopping vegetables and stirring soup pots while she waited for her beloved Pem to be discovered.

And it would happen one day. She was certain of that. The day would come when the Pem had to turn away visitors. People would travel from New York and Philadelphia and as far away as Chicago to enjoy the convivial atmosphere, the beautifully appointed rooms, the delicious—and plentiful!—food.

How wonderful it would be to have fresh coffee every morning and all the bacon you could eat. Her mouth watered as she thought of juicy roasts of beef and ice cream bombes like the ones she'd eyed longingly at the King George farther up the boardwalk.

Oh, if only she had money...

Stella bustled into the room, her gray hair wreathing her head like a silvery corona. "Trouble," she said, her voice lowered dramatically. "Trouble coming right up the street in the fanciest suit you ever saw."

Molly met Fritzie's eyes across the room.

"The tax man," said Fritzie knowingly. "Lord help us, but we've told him twice already that you can't get blood from a stone."

Molly pushed aside her teacup, her hunger forgotten. "It can't be the tax man," she pointed out. "He promised to give us more time." She tried to push aside the knowledge that another quarter's taxes would be due in less than a month.

The expression on Arthur's kindly face struck fear into her heart. "Tax men don't always do what they say they're gonna do, Molly."

Stella gestured toward the front of the hotel. "Mark my words, whoever that gent is, he's comin' this way."

Molly pushed back her chair and rose to her feet. "It's my day to man the front desk," she said. "I'll take care of him."

"Mind your manners," cautioned Fritzie with a stern shake of her finger. "We can't afford to be makin' any more enemies than we already have."

"I'll be as sweet as apple pie," said Molly. "He'll be so charmed that he'll forget all about those blasted taxes."

Their hoots of laughter followed Molly as she walked through the back hallway and into the lobby. Her quick-silver temperament was legendary around the Pem. Even as a baby, so the story went, she had been exceptionally high-spirited. "Knew exactly what she wanted, right from her first breath," the staff liked to say, "and let us know about it, too."

The truth was, she could charm the birds from the trees if she put her mind to it, and most of the citizens of Cape Charlotte doted upon Molly. Unfortunately she was as unpredictable as the winds off the ocean. Certainly she was nothing like her parents with their sweet dispositions and calm demeanors. Molly had her mother's coloring and her father's wit, but there any resemblance to her parents quickly ended. She was all fire and storm, crashing headlong through life with more energy than sense.

She positioned herself behind the registration desk and smoothed down her flyaway hair. If ever she needed an infusion of common sense, it was right now. She'd heard enough tales about the infamous tax man and his uncaring ways to know that one untoward remark could very well mean the end of the Pem. She hated feeling vulnerable and needy, but there was no escaping the fact that she needed the tax man's understanding much more than he needed hers.

Voices floated over the open transom. She couldn't make out the words but at least one of the voices sounded familiar, although she couldn't imagine what Old Jake would be doing on their doorstep. Old Jake operated the only coach that ran between the railway station and Hotel Row, and he guarded his route with fierce determination. It was ages since Jake had delivered a paying guest to the Pem.

Despite the tug of curiosity, she remained where she was. If it was the tax man outside, she didn't want to appear anxious. She tilted her head at the sound of the second voice. Definitely male. Deep, dark, vaguely growly but not in an unpleasant way. He didn't sound quite like anybody she'd ever heard before. Once Arthur had imitated an Englishman who'd spent the night in their very best suite and, while this man's tone was rougher, there was something of that rhythm in his words. A faint shiver ran through her at the sound of his voice, a voluptuous ripple of sensation that caused her to feel as if her heart was too big for her chest.

She fiddled with the registration book that rested near the edge of the leather-bound blotter. He couldn't be the tax collector, not with that accent. Could he possibly be a real live guest with money to burn? The very thought made her spirits soar with hope and she raced to the window to take a peek at the mystery man.

The sign above the building read Pemberton Arms, but there all resemblance to any hotel in Nicholas St. George's experience ended. How it managed to stand upright was beyond his comprehension. A strange assortment of towers, porches, wings and chimneys, the building looked more like a deck of cards about to topple than a fine hotel.

"Took you long enough," said the driver of the coach that had carried his valises from the railway depot. "Could've told you walkin's no picnic." When Nicholas, cramped and hot after the long trip from New York City, had opted to send on his luggage and walk to town the coach driver had acted as if Nicholas had decided to fly under his own power.

"I needed to stretch my legs," he said easily, amused by the man's outspokenness. The man obviously had him pegged as a wealthy Englishman, more accustomed to dimly lit libraries than the great outdoors.

"Well, you got yourself to the Pem, same as me," the old man observed. He grinned, exposing a few empty spaces where teeth used to be. "Somethin', ain't it?"

"This can't be the right place."

The driver, a man with skin tanned the color of burnished walnut, laughed. The sound did not augur well. "Ain't but one Pemberton Arms in Cape Charlotte, mister, and this is it."

There was no denying the truth. He'd walked past establishments beautiful enough to tempt Queen Victoria herself. Manicured lawns, elaborate flower gardens, trellises laced with climbing rosebushes heavy with crimson blooms. Unfortunately, this yellow monstrosity before him was the Pemberton Arms. He could imagine Jonathan Hughes laughing from beyond the grave.

"Stay where you are," he said to the driver. "I'll fetch my own valises." Before the older man could protest, Nicholas swung the two heavy leather bags up and out of the coach.

"Got yourself a set of muscles," the driver said with a whistle. "Didn't think you Englishmen did much liftin' and carryin'."

"Depends on the Englishman." Nicholas reached into the pocket of his jacket and removed an array of American currency. "What's your pleasure?"

The driver grinned around his cigar. "That big one on the end is my pleasure, but it ain't my fare." He extracted a smaller bill from the array. "This'll do fine."

Nicholas folded the bills but not before withdrawing one to match the driver's choice. "With thanks for your courtesy."

The driver whistled low, then pushed his cap farther back on his head. "You English gents are real generous," he said, pocketing the money. "When it's time to go home, you ask for Old Jake. I'll be here in two shakes of a lamb's tail with the railroad schedules from Cape Charlotte to anywhere."

With a wave of his hand Old Jake rode off, leaving Nicholas standing at the foot of the steps. He'd only been in the United States for less than two days and already he'd met more eccentric characters than in the past two months in London. While he wasn't naive enough to believe class distinctions didn't exist in the United States, he did find the blurring of social boundaries intriguing.

This sorry excuse for a hotel, however, was anything but intriguing. A flutter of white curtains at the window drew his attention. He thought he saw the vague outline of a female form, but it disappeared before he could be certain. The slate walkway meandered up an incline toward the front door, bordered on either side by weeds that threatened to overtake the path. A cluster of half-hearted tulips drooped near the porch steps. Not even their vivid red blossoms managed to dispel the air of abandonment about the place. Three windows on the second floor were broken while the whitewashed shutters on five others dangled by a thread. The kindest thing anyone could do for the hotel would be to light a match, then toss it through one of those broken windows and let the laws of nature take their course.

The front door creaked open and Molly ducked her head, pretending to be engrossed in the guest register. Valises! A wonderful sign. She was reasonably certain the tax man wouldn't arrive with a change of clothing. Thank God the guest's back had been turned when she peeked out the window. It certainly wouldn't do for the owner of the hotel to appear so appallingly eager for patrons.

"Good morning," the man said, his voice even more intriguing than she'd first thought. "Where do I put my bags?"

She looked up and found herself staring at the most handsome man she'd ever seen in her life. He was everything wonderful she'd ever imagined a man could be. His dark chestnut hair was combed back from his forehead and his eyes were as blue as the ocean should be but never was. Even from across the room she could see the shad-

ows his thick eyelashes cast upon his prominent cheekbones. She loved the fact that, unlike most gentlemen, he
was clean-shaven. Without a camouflaging beard or
mustache, the strong line of his jaw was quite apparent.
He certainly didn't look like anyone she'd ever met before. And his clothes! You didn't have to be a tailor to
recognize quality yard goods when you saw them. The
wool in his fawn-colored tail coat probably cost enough
to pay the taxes on the Pem for an entire year. Even
tossed over his arm the way it was, it still held true to its
construction. She immediately noted that his trousers
were cuffed and creased and that he wore boots instead
of the toothpick-toed shoes that were so popular among
the vacationing men who visited Cape Charlotte.

He was tall and handsome and obviously rich, and
Molly could only wonder what on earth he was doing at
the Pem. It didn't occur to her that she was staring at him
in a most rude fashion. She had simply never seen such a
splendid-looking man before in her life, and she found it
difficult to gather her wits about her again.

He stepped up to the desk, carrying two huge valises as
if they were as light as feather pillows. On the rare occasions they had guests, Arthur huffed and puffed his way
up the stairs with the valises as if he had the weight of the
world upon his shoulders. Oh, what a difference there
was between Arthur and this... this Adonis.

Suddenly she found her heart beating more quickly
inside her chest and she had to take a deep breath to calm
her nerves. *Goose,* she chided herself, annoyed by her
reaction. You'd think he really was the tax collector, she
was so jumpy.

He offered her a smile bright enough to light the sky.
"I said, where do I put the bags?"

She blinked, embarrassed to be caught in her reverie. "Next to the divan."

She watched as he strode across the room and deposited his valises at the appointed spot. He walked the way she imagined a king or an emperor might walk, as if he owned the world and could claim it any time he wanted. She cleared her throat. "Would you like a room or a suite?"

"You have suites?"

"You needn't look so surprised. Bedroom, sitting room and bath. Best we've got and reasonable, too. No doubt it'll be taken before nightfall." She sounded like a carnival barker but at least she had found her voice. Truth was, there were five suites on the third floor alone sitting empty right that minute begging for a taker, but he didn't have to know that. From the looks of him, she could up the standard price a few dollars and he probably wouldn't bat an eyelash.

"Fine," he said, not even asking about the price. Molly's spirits soared even higher. This would be like taking candy from a baby. "I'll take it."

"It's expensive."

His blue eyes twinkled with amusement. "I can afford it."

"I daresay you can," Molly murmured beneath her breath. She'd noticed those gold cuff links, big as a baby's fist, winking at her from under the sleeves of his coat. Better take care or she'd sound greedy and grasping. She pushed the register across the blotter, then dipped her pen in the inkwell and handed it to him. "For one night?"

"Longer." He met her eyes and something odd happened deep inside her stomach, a ripple of sensation that brought a flush to her cheeks. "Is that a problem?" he asked.

"Of course not. Just sign the register and I'll have Arthur show you to your rooms." If he stayed a full week she could actually pay the staff at least part of their wages. If he stayed for the season, her tax woes were over. *And he would be such a pleasure to look at each and everyday....*

She watched as he signed his name at the top of the blank white page then pushed the register back to her. *Mr. Nicholas St. George of London,* she thought. *You might be the answer to my prayers.*

Chapter Two

"Best suite in the house," the elderly porter said as Nicholas carried his own valises up the winding staircase to the third floor. "You can see the ocean like it was in your front yard."

"Which it probably will be any day," Nicholas muttered as he looked out at the ocean a few minutes later. The porter hadn't lied. The Atlantic, in all its glory, was there for him to admire. Trouble was it wouldn't surprise him if the Atlantic ended up rolling through the front lobby during the night and washing them all out to sea.

What in hell had he gotten himself into?

He turned from the view and glanced at his suite of rooms. If this was the best in the house, he understood why the hotel was as quiet as the Australian outback on a hot day. He had wondered why the young woman at the front desk had seemed so flustered when he said he'd need a suite for a few days. Now he realized she hadn't been flustered; she'd been amazed.

On his walk from the railway station, he'd taken careful note of the magnificent buildings that beckoned to Americans on holiday—fine structures with wide front porches and wicker chairs and impeccably manicured front lawns worthy of an English country estate. He'd even seen the unmistakable signs of electric light fixtures strung along the porches. He'd heard laughter from inside those buildings and seen the unmistakable signs of a thriving clientele in the constant flow of serving girls carrying pitchers of lemonade to guests on the beach.

Not so at the Pemberton Arms. He hadn't heard or seen a single other guest anywhere. No serving girls in starched uniforms bustled about. There was nothing about the Pemberton that wasn't old, dilapidated or totally unsuitable. A gas lamp with a cracked globe rested atop a dark pine table. The table butted up against a narrow bed that boasted a pillow as thin as a soda cracker and a coverlet whose moth holes were barely covered by embroidery.

The staff tried, though. He had to grant them that. The wooden floors were bare but they'd been polished to a high gloss. The furniture smelled of lemon oil and not a mote of dust marred the scarred wooden surfaces. The windows might be broken, but what glass there was sparkled in the sunshine. And, to his amazement, the savory aroma of beef stew tantalized his nostrils. Someone obviously cared enough to keep what little they did have in the best condition possible.

Still, it was all so much less than he had imagined it would be.

Nicholas sat on the edge of the bed and yanked off his boots. A wave of bone-deep fatigue washed over him but he fought against it. Only forty-eight hours ago, his ship had docked in New York Harbor. He'd quickly collected his belongings and rented a coach to take him up to the Convent of the Sisters of St. Clare in a place called Tarrytown. There he had made arrangements for Maureen Alice. She would have a room overlooking the Hudson

River with her own closet and reading light. The curriculum was strict but he took a measure of comfort in knowing the orphaned child would have a roof over her head and food to eat.

There weren't many things in life toward which Nicholas harbored sentimental feelings. Abandoned children, however, ranked high on his list. He knew full well how it felt to be alone in the world with nothing but your wits to protect you.

And—damn his thieving soul to hell for eternity— Jonathan Hughes had reminded him from beyond the grave of exactly that.

"This won't take long I trust, Franklin," Nicholas had said as he took a seat in his solicitor's office on that warm June morning just three weeks ago. "I have important business to see to."

Franklin Morris had smiled knowingly. "Another assignation, Nicky? Our good Queen Victoria frowns upon daytime dalliances."

His response to that was simply to change the subject. "Now what is this most urgent matter you spoke of in your message?"

"It's about your late stepfather's will."

His jaw muscles tightened. "Jonathan Hughes's will is no business of mine."

"I'm afraid it is," said Franklin, his tone even. "It appears there was a codicil that concerns you that has only now come to light."

Nicholas listened in amazement as Franklin told him that he was now the proud owner of the Pemberton Arms, a small hotel in the American state of Delaware.

"I want nothing to do with it," he said flatly. Jonathan Hughes had done nothing for him in life and Nicholas would accept nothing from him in death. "Sell it."

"There is a staff to consider."

"One month's severance and good references."

"Some of the staff are rather advanced in years."

"An extra month's wages."

"It seems there is also a child."

Nicholas sat up straighter. "A *what?*"

"A child." Franklin read from the legal document before him: "Maureen Alice Hughes."

"Good God!" Nicholas exploded. "Had he a bastard hidden away somewhere?"

"Nothing quite so dramatic. Maureen Alice Hughes is the orphaned daughter of Jonathan's brother, William, and William's wife, Sarah."

"Sounds as convoluted as the plot of a penny dreadful."

"Be that as it may, I'm afraid Maureen Alice lives at the hotel."

Nicholas shrugged. He refused to be drawn into a mess of Hughes's making. "Then it is up to her mother to find alternative shelter, is it not?"

"You are not listening to me, Nicholas. The child is an orphan." Franklin glanced down at the stack of papers on his desk. "Has been for almost ten years since her father died."

His solicitor explained what he knew of the situation and, unbidden, an image of a wide-eyed little girl appeared before Nicholas and tugged at his heartstrings. A blood relative of Jonathan Hughes was not high on his list of concerns, but it was hard to imagine an innocent child left in the care of a man as cold and uncaring as his late stepfather. "Damn his hide to hell for eternity,"

Nicholas swore, his hands clenched into fists, as the whole ugly mess swept in on him again like a primal tide. "What in the name of God was he thinking of?"

"Jonathan Hughes was not the kindest of men."

"You are a master of understatement, Franklin." He tried to gather his thoughts. "You are certain that this child comes with the hotel?"

"As far as I can ascertain, she does."

"Like the divans and the gas lamps?"

"Exactly, my boy."

"Sell it all," he muttered as the bright promise of the morning darkened. He helped himself to a brandy from the ever-present decanter on Franklin's desk. Again the vision of a wide-eyed little girl appeared before him, bringing with her painful memories from his past, and he stubbornly willed her away.

"We cannot sell a child," said Franklin.

"But my stepfather can bequeath her like a piece of furniture?"

Franklin handed him an envelope of ivory parchment. Nicholas's name was scrawled across the front in large, ink-smeared letters. That handwriting was as familiar to Nicholas as his own face in the mirror.

"The answer may be in there," said Franklin.

A smart man would burn the blasted thing and be done with it. There was nothing Jonathan Hughes could say to him now that would erase the memory of years of neglect and hatred.

Eschewing Franklin's offer of a sterling letter opener, Nicholas ripped open the flap, scattering forest-green sealing wax across the carpet. "I commend the Pemberton Arms Hotel and Maureen Alice Hughes to your attention," the letter read. "Sell one or both as you see fit. Responsibility lies in the eye of the beholder. I trust the irony of the situation amuses you as it does me. (Signed) Your loving stepfather.''

Nicholas swore as he crumpled the stiff parchment into a ball, unmindful of Franklin's concerned curiosity. That coldhearted bastard had once again found a way to twist the lives of others into bizarre shapes of his choosing. Anger, scalding and fierce, rose up inside his chest, burning away the pain.

"I don't want a child, Franklin. I don't even want the blasted hotel." He rose from the chair and paced the length of the office in an attempt to outdistance his conscience.

"I could send my assistant, Murdock, over there to settle things to your satisfaction," Franklin pointed out. "You're not her guardian. In truth you are not legally responsible for her welfare in any way."

...*Not legally responsible*... Where had he heard those words before?

Nicholas rose from the narrow bed at the Pemberton Arms and stripped off his coat and tie, then began to unbutton his shirt. Try as he might, he was never very far from the thirteen-year-old boy who had stood on Hughes's doorstep, hating himself for his vulnerability and yet praying for a home with his wayward mother and her husband.

Staring out the window, he saw not the Atlantic Ocean but his father's ebony coffin as it was lowered into the waiting earth. His childhood innocence had been buried with the man. He'd felt such a sense of terror and loneliness that he wondered how it was his heart continued to beat. He could still taste the fear, metallic and cold, upon his tongue.

And he'd been better than halfway to manhood at that time. How must it feel to be a little girl, cast adrift in a world that paid scant heed to children? Legally she was no concern of his. But morally—that was another story entirely.

How well Hughes had known him to understand that.

"You're nothing to me, boy," Hughes had said that first night while his mother drank glass after glass of sherry in the far corner of the room. "You have a grandmother. Let her take care of you."

"My grandmother is in India," he'd said, struggling with tears of exhaustion. "I thought—"

"You thought!" said Hughes with a laugh. "I do not believe you've thought of anything but yourself your entire life."

Nicholas had cast a pleading look toward his mother, but she continued to drink her sherry and gaze out the window at the gardens beyond the glass.

Hughes had an idea, however. He'd sent Nicholas up to Scotland, to a boarding school so cold and forbidding that Newgate seemed cozy by comparison. Three weeks later Nicholas escaped through a broken window and had signed on to a merchant ship before anyone realized he was missing.

Hughes had guessed right when he said Nicholas's conscience would be his jailer, but he'd be damned if he allowed his stepfather's machinations to turn into a life sentence. Children were more resilient than people realized. Wasn't he proof of that? Sometimes he suspected that the notion of happiness was a fairly modern invention, conjured up by lovers of fairy tales to console mortals faced with the harsh truth of the human condition.

He couldn't offer the orphaned girl a home or a family, but he could offer her shelter with the good sisters in

New York State, and that was far more than had ever been offered to him.

On the voyage across the Atlantic, he'd entertained the notion of keeping the Pemberton Arms and using the profits to help refurbish Merriton Hall, his family home in England—the home Jonathan Hughes had all but destroyed through pointed neglect. Now that he'd actually seen the hotel, however, he realized that in the unlikely event there were profits, those profits would have to be plowed right back into the hotel, simply to keep it standing. The Pemberton made Merriton Hall look like Buckingham Palace.

His solicitor had recommended he sell the hotel once he'd bundled up the child and placed her safely in the care of the good sisters of St. Clare. Maybe that was the right course of action after all.

He divested himself of his shirt, tossing it onto a ladder-back chair near the washstand. The sea breeze felt cool against his heated skin as he stood at the window, gazing out at the ocean. He wanted to strip down to his skin and plunge himself into the water, then swim until he was exhausted. He couldn't remember the last time he'd pushed himself to the limit and beyond. His life in Australia, the years in the South Seas and aboard ship, all seemed as if they had happened to somebody else.

"Your towels."

He spun around at the sound of the tremulous female voice. The pretty desk clerk with the dimples and stubborn chin stood in the doorway, her slender arms piled high with linens and a look of shock upon her face.

"Come in," he said, as casual as you please. "Put them on the bed."

Molly stood in the doorway, unable to move. The man was practically naked. Not even on the beach, where vacationers threw propriety to the four winds, had she ever seen such a display of unclothed male flesh. Had he no shame? Nobody stood shirtless in the window in broad daylight. Certainly nobody decent.

"Well, come in, girl." He folded his arms across his chest and stared at her with a look she could only describe as brash.

She forced herself to put one foot in front of the other, but her mind was occupied by the sight of his muscular torso, backlit by the sun that streamed through the window.

He was beautiful. The thought brought color to her cheeks as an odd heat suffused her limbs. Who would think a man could be beautiful? Once years ago Fritzie had taken her to a museum in Philadelphia, where Molly had stood, transfixed, before a statue of a Greek god. This man was every bit as pleasing to the eye as that statue had been, but with one very significant difference. The statue had been made of marble, while this man was definitely flesh and blood. "Sorry," she mumbled, hurrying to the bed. She deposited the towels and quickly turned around to head for the door.

"Just a minute."

She hesitated in the doorway. "Yes?"

"Soap," he said. "I don't see any by the washstand."

"I'll find some for you."

"What time is dinner?"

She looked at him over her shoulder. "Dinner?"

"The main meal," he said with a slow grin. "I'd say it's beef stew."

Her eyes widened. "You want to eat dinner at the Pem?"

"You sound surprised."

"I am."

"Where do your other guests dine?"

"We have no other guests." She bit her lip in annoyance. What an idiotic thing to say. Now he'd probably grab his valises and march out of there, taking all of his lovely money with him. "Six o'clock," she said after a moment.

"Do you dress for dinner at the Pemberton Arms?"

"Of course we do. Don't be thinking you can come to dinner like that."

His laugh was as big as he was, and it set off her temper like a Roman candle on the Fourth of July. He made her feel foolish somehow—and unbearably young.

"I'll thank you not to laugh at me," she snapped. "How am I to know what you intended by that question? Most guests have the decency to remain dressed in broad daylight."

"Most chambermaids knock, unless they wish for an even bigger surprise."

It had been so long since they'd had a real live paying guest that Molly had forgotten how to treat one. "I won't make that mistake again."

"Don't forget the soap," he said with a most annoying chuckle.

"You'll get your soap."

"And make sure to knock first. I'd hate to upset you."

"I'll send Arthur. He won't care if you're buck naked."

She closed the door behind her then leaned against the wall. The sound of his low male chuckle floated over the transom. Why had she said such a stupid thing? Now he'd think she was spending her time thinking about him without his shirt and trousers on. Fritzie had told her time and again to think before she spoke. Would she never learn?

Placing her hand on her chest, she listened to her blood pounding in her ears. Full of himself, he was. She'd read about Englishmen and their peculiar ways, although she had to admit this Nicholas St. George certainly didn't seem typical of Queen Victoria's subjects. She'd always imagined the English to be terribly proper, all decked out in fancy clothes, certainly not strutting about half-naked at high noon. She had no doubt that there were probably other things he did at high noon, as well, things that decent young women didn't dare contemplate.

There was something vaguely uncivilized about this man, as if he didn't operate by the same set of rules everyone else did. His eyes were the eyes of a sailor, clear and blue and gazing off toward the horizon as if he could see things mere mortals could not. And he certainly didn't lack for money, if his clothes were any indication. Yet the impressive musculature of his chest and shoulders belied a life of luxury and indolence.

Well, no use thinking about it. Whatever he was doing in Cape Charlotte was his business, not hers. All they had to do was keep him content and well fed while he was at the Pem, and make sure he paid his bill before he left. Other than that, he could go to the devil for all she cared.

Nicholas listened to the sound of her footsteps on the staircase. What a short-tempered little chit she was. He hadn't meant anything by his laughter, but her anger had been sparked just the same. She hadn't hesitated to give him a piece of her mind, and he grudgingly admired her disregard for conventional propriety. He recognized a fellow renegade when he saw one, and that redheaded maid was surely that.

Or was she a desk clerk? Apparently employees performed multiple chores at the Pemberton. He laughed at

the thought that she might also be the cook responsible
for the beef stew simmering in the downstairs kitchen. It
seemed highly unlikely that the Pemberton, downtrod-
den as it was, could afford to keep a full complement of
staff in its employ. He hadn't paid her much heed earlier, save to notice the mass of titian hair that framed her
heart-shaped face. She'd had the look of the school-
room about her and he preferred his women more sea-
soned.

That was why it had come as a surprise to see her
standing in his doorway. She was taller than he'd imagined and more voluptuous, her body that of a woman
and not the schoolgirl he'd believed her to be. Her blue
cotton dress was worn threadbare in spots, and he could
see the hem had been lowered more than once. An attempt had been made to camouflage the stitches with a
thin line of rickrack, but it fooled no one. A blind man
would have noticed the way the bodice pulled tightly
across her rounded breasts, straining the fabric in a dangerously provocative fashion. Unlike the other women he
knew, however, the girl seemed oblivious to the effect she
had upon the opposite sex.

Her innocence and naiveté had been painfully obvious in the way she'd blushed red as her hair at the sight
of him without his shirt. There was nothing coy about the
lovely maid. Nothing false. She wore her feelings on her
sleeve the way other women of his acquaintance wore diamonds and pearls, and for some strange reason he found
the contrast most appealing.

It was a shame he wasn't a connoisseur of girls on the
brink of full flower, because he suspected that she would
be an experience he would not soon forget. He had met
some beautiful girls on the brink of womanhood, all
dewy and fresh, but although he'd been tempted as he

was now, Nicholas had neither the patience nor the inclination to woo a trembling virgin, one who believed in true love and happily ever after. He didn't believe in fairy tales any more than he believed in the concept of forever. As a child he'd seen the power a faithless wife could wield over a man, and that power had altered the course of Nicholas's life.

"He's a pretty one," said Stella, bustling back into the kitchen after the first course. "If I were thirty years younger..."

"You'd be stealing my own thoughts," said Fritzie, fanning herself with her snowy-white apron. "If my Will and I hadn't a history, I'd be invitin' the young man to park his boots under my bed."

"What do you think, Molly?" Stella asked, dishing up a plate of beef and vegetables for their guest. "Ain't he a sight for sore eyes?"

"I wouldn't know," said Molly, feigning rapt interest in her bowl of stew. "I'm afraid I didn't notice."

"Didn't notice!" Stella's voice scaled new heights. "That boy puts the angels to shame and you didn't notice."

"Aren't you being a trifle dramatic?" she asked. "He's only a man."

"She's just a child," said Fritzie with a laugh. "When she gets as old as we are, she'll understand."

Molly busied herself with buttering a piece of day-old bread. Oh, she understood, all right. She understood way more than they knew. All afternoon she'd been plagued by the image of him half-naked in the sunlight. When Arthur took the soap upstairs to the Englishman, she had been tempted to casually stroll past his open door in hopes of catching another glimpse of his magnificent torso.

"And he smiled at me like I was a young girl in a party frock...." Fritzie was saying as she prepared the strawberry shortcake for his dessert. She sighed dramatically. "Oh, would I love to see that boy in a bathing costume."

Molly's cheeks flamed and she ducked her head. She'd seen him in far less than any bathing costume she'd ever noticed on the beaches of Cape Charlotte. Why, she'd probably be married before she ever gazed upon such a display of masculinity again. *Oh, he looks splendid, Fritzie,* she thought. *More wonderful than you could possibly imagine.* The kind of man she'd dreamed about.

"Our girl's blushing," said Stella with a hoot of laughter. "Why, I do believe she's sweet on our handsome guest."

"Go on with you," said Fritzie. "Molly hasn't an eye for the fellows—at least, not yet." Fritzie stepped around the worktable and bent down until she looked Molly in the eyes. "He wouldn't be making eyes at you, would he?"

"Good grief!" Molly shoved back her chair and rose to her feet. "Why is everyone so interested in that stupid Englishman? You would think we'd never seen a man before, not one of us."

The look on Fritzie's face was shrewd and knowing. "Don't go gettin' any ideas, miss. There's the likes of us and the likes of him and that's the way it always will be."

"Oh, do be quiet," Molly snapped. Why was it that Fritzie knew her thoughts before Molly did? "I haven't the slightest interest in him or anyone else. The Pem is the only thing I care about." She paused, contrite. "And you, of course."

Fritzie patted her arm. "'Tis normal to be drawn to a handsome face. At your age I had my head turned a time or two myself before I married."

"Married!" Molly almost choked on her tea. "That's the last thing on earth I'm thinking of."

"Your time will come," said Fritzie with a nod of her head. "Not when you expect it or want it, but it will come."

The only time Molly had ever seriously considered marriage was when the tax collector had showed up at their door, breathing fire and brimstone and dire predictions of the end of the Pemberton Arms. Marriage seemed as unattainable as the moon. Why, she had never even danced with a young man in the moonlight, much less fallen in love.

If only some kindly young man would come along, one who understood the situation and how badly she needed her inheritance, a man who was willing to wed without expecting anything...physical from the union.

Unbidden, thoughts of Nicholas St. George came to mind. He would never stand for such a thing. The woman who married him would have to expect a great deal of physical intimacy. There'd been something sensual, almost pagan, in the way he'd stood bare-chested at the window, reveling in the sun and sea air. A man like that would expect a lot from his wife, things that went beyond being a helpmeet.

Maybe he had a wife, she mused, not asking herself why that thought made her feel so melancholy and alone. A beautiful, accomplished woman who gave wonderful parties and understood the mysteries of the bedroom. On Molly's fifteenth birthday, Fritzie had gulped down some cooking sherry, then tried to explain the facts of life to the equally embarrassed girl. It had taken Molly weeks be-

fore she could look at Fritzie's husband and not want to
disappear into the ground. After three years she still
wasn't entirely sure people actually did those things that
Fritzie had mentioned—or, more amazing, that some of
them actually enjoyed it. How it was possible to enjoy
such acrobatics amazed her. All that poking and prod-
ding seemed rather foolish to her.

But still she had seen the glow on Fritzie's face on Saturday mornings, and she hadn't missed the twinkle in
Will's eye when he strutted into the kitchen behind his
wife, smiling like the cat that ate the canary. Well, to each
his own. Some people liked lima beans; some people
hated them. It was simply a matter of taste.

For a third-rate establishment, the staff at the Pemberton Arms had turned out a first-rate supper. No cav-
iar or French wines, to be sure, but fresh food perfectly
cooked and served with enthusiasm if not élan. All in all,
as he finished the last of his strawberry shortcake, then
leaned back in his seat to light a cigar, Nicholas had no
complaints.

True, it had been a bit quiet in the dining room as he
ate his meal, but it wasn't as if solitude was a new commodity. For six months he had been at a station in
Queensland, Australia, at the back of beyond with only
his own thoughts for company.

"More coffee, sir?" The jovial woman named Fritzie
popped up at his elbow.

He nodded, then watched as she refilled his cup. Fritzie was one of those robust women whose full figures and
girlish complexions belied their age. Only her hands,
gnarled and speckled with liver spots, gave her away. The
hands of a woman who had worked hard all her life. He

could tell her hair had once been an ebony hue, but it was faded now, silver strands outnumbering the black.

"Dinner was splendid," he said, offering up his best smile. "My compliments to the cook."

The woman beamed. "I'd be pleased to accept those compliments, sir."

"You're the cook?"

"One and the same. You should try my chicken pot pie," she said, forgetting about the cream for his coffee. "I make it on Saturdays—" She stopped, looking at him closely. "Will you still be here on Saturday?"

He thought for a moment. That was three days away. Three days at the Pemberton Arms was hard to imagine, but he doubted if he could put the wheels of sale in motion any more quickly than that. "I'll be here," he said.

Her smile grew broader. "'Tis a pleasure to feed a man with an appetite," she said with that open manner of hers. "No offense meant, but I didn't think Englishmen cared much for simple fare."

Apparently Americans harbored as many misconceptions about the English as he had maintained about the Americans. "I can't speak for most Englishmen, but I spent time in Australia, where I learned the pleasures of good food, simply prepared."

"Australia," she said with a knowing wink. "Rough-and-tumble country. No wonder you're so—" She stopped in midsentence. "Listen to me, talkin' to beat the band and you without cream or sugar." She bustled over to the sideboard, then returned with sugar bowl, tongs and creamer. "If you be needin' anythin' else, sir, just ring the bell. One of us will be with you directly."

She turned to head back to the kitchen, but Nicholas stopped her. "There is one thing, Fritzie." He might as well put his plan in motion without delay. He had stayed away from England for too many years; he didn't want this trip to keep him from home any longer than necessary. "I'd like to speak with the manager, if you would find him."

"The manager?"

It seemed a simple enough request. "The owner," he said, rephrasing it. "The man in charge of things."

"Beggin' your pardon, sir, but are you displeased?"

"Not at all, Fritzie." Obviously the boundaries between guest and servant were made of gossamer wings at the Pemberton Arms. "I simply have some business to discuss."

She started to say something but then caught herself. "I'll—I'll see what I can do, sir."

"Thank you, Fritzie. You can tell your employer that I'll be on the front porch awaiting him."

Fritzie disappeared into the kitchen, and Nicholas leaned back in his chair and finished his second cup of coffee. A man-to-man discussion over cigars and brandy—assuming the Pemberton Arms had a decent bottle. Little Maureen Alice would be bundled off to school in New York. The employees would be well taken care of. He'd even help the manager find a position elsewhere. And the Pemberton Arms would be sold for scrap.

A simple plan and a fair one.

He went out onto the front porch to wait.

"I still don't understand," said Molly. "Why does he want to see me?"

"Not you, dearie," Fritzie explained for the third time. "He wants to see the owner."

"Which happens to be me," Molly pointed out. Her stomach suddenly knotted.

"It's a trick," said Arthur, who was enjoying a piece of leftover shortcake. "The man means trouble. I could smell it from the first."

"Don't you go gettin' our girl upset," Fritzie barked at him. "'Tis nothin' to be worried about. Perhaps he's lookin' for a companion over a game of cards."

Molly grabbed at that explanation and clung to it like a life raft. The man had had such a profound effect upon her equilibrium earlier that she feared she might actually swoon at his feet. "Maybe that's it. He looks to be the kind of man who would enjoy a game of chance, doesn't he?"

Stella giggled behind her apron. "Wouldn't mind takin' a chance with him," she said, ignoring Fritzie's warning glance.

Fritzie gave Molly a swift hug. "He loved my beef stew, if I do say so myself. Full of compliments, he was. Maybe he wants to tell the owner what a treasure I am." That statement made everyone laugh, even Molly. Fritzie had no modesty whatsoever where her cooking was concerned. "Now go smooth down your hair and see what he's about."

Molly gave her hair a lick and a promise with the back of her hand, trying to ignore the way her fingers shook.

"I have a pretty plaid ribbon in my nightstand," said Fritzie. "Maybe you could—"

"He'll take me as I am," said Molly with more courage than she was feeling, "or he can keep his comments to himself."

"That's our girl," said Arthur. "No one will get the better of the Pem while Molly's around."

Molly walked slowly through the quiet halls with the measured pace of a prisoner en route to the guillotine. She could just imagine his face when he discovered she was the owner of the Pem. He'd probably throw back his head and laugh that rumbling laugh of his until she would want to toss him into the ocean and let him swim back to England.

She stood in the doorway and gazed out toward the boardwalk. Dusk was descending over Cape Charlotte, a bluish-violet haze that softened the edges of life and made everything seem all glowing and romantic. Lights twinkled in the distance, and if she listened hard enough over the pounding of her heart, she could make out the strains of music and laughter. How wonderful it must be to—

"Nice night, isn't it?"

She jumped at the sound of the now-familiar voice. There, at the far end of the porch, stood Nicholas St. George. His jacket was slung over the railing, and she immediately noticed that he'd undone the collar of his starched white shirt and rolled up his sleeves to the elbow. Good Lord, why did the man find it so difficult to stay clothed?

Taking a deep breath, she glided toward him as if her gown were made of the finest silk instead of well-washed cotton. "Fritzie said you wanted to speak with the owner."

"The manager," he said. He glanced over her shoulder. "Is he detained?"

"No, he isn't. He's right here." She lifted her chin and met his eyes. "I am the owner of the Pemberton Arms."

Chapter Three

"My name is Molly," she continued to his astonishment, "and I run this place."

"That's impossible."

"And why is it impossible?" Her tone was sharp. "Am I not intelligent enough?"

He wondered if the brandy had been more potent than he'd first thought. "You're a child," he stated flatly. "You're still wet behind the ears."

"I am not a child. The Pemberton Arms is my responsibility, and if you have any complaints, you can make them to me or find yourself another place to stay."

She wheeled and was about to flounce back into the hotel when he regained his power of thought.

"I'm looking for somebody," he called. She turned back to meet his eyes. "A child."

She glared at him, all fiery indignation. "Like me?"

"Even younger," he said. At least he had assumed so. "There is no child at the Pem."

"Have you sent her off to school then?"

"Arthur's children are already in service at the Eastwind Hotel in Atlantic City and Stella's girls are married." *He's up to something,* she thought, eyeing him with suspicion. "Maybe you have the wrong establishment." Handsome rogues with money to burn rarely found their way to the Pem. She should have known better than to think he would stay.

"I assume there's but one Pemberton Arms in Cape Charlotte."

She nodded, an odd feeling of dread building inside her. "Does this child have a name?"

"Maureen," he said. "Maureen Alice Hughes. Do you know of her?"

Dear God, she thought, heart pounding. *No one has called me Maureen in years.* "I might."

He hesitated. His business with Maureen Alice wasn't any of the chit's affair, but it was patently obvious she wasn't about to give an inch without an explanation. "I bring news of her late uncle, Jonathan Hughes."

"Uncle Jonathan is dead?" That would explain so much: the unpaid taxes, the missing stipend. The world started to spin around Molly and she leaned back against the railing.

"Uncle Jonathan?" Nicholas stared at her as comprehension dawned. "You're Maureen Alice Hughes."

Her head snapped up and she glared at him. "And what's it to you if I am?"

He had to hand it to the girl. She'd recovered her equilibrium faster than he had. "I'm your—" He paused. What in hell was he anyway? Guardian seemed absurd when the "child" in question was obviously a young woman. Besides, he wasn't her guardian at all. "I'm here to help you."

"Oh, I'm sure," she said, her voice heavy with sarcasm.

There was something about her that brought out the worst in his temper. Surely there was a better way to break the news to her, but the words were out before he could find it. "I don't have to steal the Pemberton, Molly. I own it."

She came at him then with her fists raised, and he had to move quickly to the side to save himself from a pummeling. Her green eyes flashed fire and he couldn't remember the last time he'd seen so much rage in such an attractive package. And she was cagey. She ducked beneath his outstretched arm, then landed a punch a man would have been proud of. It was, however, the last straw for Nicholas.

Before she realized what he was about, he swept her off her feet and deposited her in the rocking chair at the far end of the porch. She whimpered once as her bottom hit the cane seat but she didn't cry out. He admired her for that. Another woman would have been awash in self-righteous tears, but not Maureen Alice Hughes. Her stubborn jaw was set and her eyes were defiantly dry.

"You're despicable," she said as he towered over her. "Pretending to come here like a regular guest."

"You don't *have* guests. That should have been your first clue something was amiss." She looked as if she would like to hit him again, but he grabbed her wrists and held them tight.

"Consider your actions," he warned. "Not even a woman can strike me twice without consequence."

"I don't need a guardian," she said heatedly. "You might as well go back where you belong."

"Trust me, Miss Hughes, when I say I have no desire to be guardian to anyone, much less a foul-tempered brat such as yourself. I have other plans for you." Although he wasn't entirely certain that even the good sisters in Tarrytown would welcome this hellion with open arms.

"You're a horrible man! No one makes plans for me but me."

"Perhaps if you'd received some criticism earlier in life you would know how to behave."

He released her wrists and Molly fought down the urge to rub the red spots. She knew he had used only a fraction of his strength to hold her fast. That fact should have given her pause; instead it only served to infuriate her. Bested at every turn. It was almost more than she could bear.

"And what kind of plans did you make for me, Mr. High and Mighty?"

"A convent school," he shot back, "but I doubt if even those God-fearing women could make a lady of you."

"How dare you talk to me like that!"

"If you can control your temper, there are a number of things we need to discuss."

"I have nothing whatsoever to say to you. The Pem belongs to me and you'll have to kill me with your bare hands in order to get it."

"Not necessary," he drawled, reaching into his shirt pocket. "I have the documents here to prove my ownership."

She held out her hand. "I'd like to see these so-called documents, Mr. St. George."

"You may look," he said, still holding on to the papers, "but they remain in my possession."

He didn't trust her, thought Molly. That fact was one of the few rays of sunshine in this whole bleak encounter. She peered at the papers but found them to be a confusing hodgepodge of legal phrasing and convoluted claims. The one thing that seemed clear, however, was the fact that her Uncle Jonathan and this handsome stranger were somehow connected.

"Are we related?" she asked as he put away the papers.

"No." He didn't have to look quite so relieved. "Your late uncle was my stepfather."

"Did you know him?"

His handsome face settled into a mask of steel. "I did."

Again it hit her that Jonathan Hughes was dead. She had never met her uncle so she didn't feel the usual sorrow associated with death, but mingled with her apprehension over her future was a sense of loss for the last member of her father's family. "I can't believe he's gone. Surely he must have provided for me somehow."

"He did. He handed you and your hotel over to me."

Stay calm, Molly. Even though she longed to grab those papers from his breast pocket and tear them into confetti, she knew she would never get away with it. He would overpower her in the blink of an eye, and she shuddered to think what measures he would take to ensure that she not try a stunt like that again.

"Now what on earth would you want with a place like the Pem, Mr. St. George?" she asked, all sweetness and light. "What with you living in England, how could you possibly oversee its care? Unless your wife . . ."

"I have no wife, but even without one I could do a better job than the one that has been done thus far."

"And I daresay if I had your money I could do a better job, as well." She tried to ignore the frisson of excitement she'd felt at the revelation that he had no wife.

"Money," he said. "Now we reach the heart of the matter. I have money. You have none. Even if I handed you the Pemberton Arms, how could you keep it running?"

"The same way we have for years," she retorted, overlooking the stipend her uncle had sent each month. "Through hard work and a touch of good fortune."

He glanced at the broken railing and the rickety porch steps. "Good fortune has been absent lately, hasn't it?"

To her horror, her eyes filled with tears and she turned away before he could notice the telltale shimmer. "You shouldn't have come here," she said. "Everything was fine until you showed up."

Everything, of course, was not fine and it hadn't been so for a long time. The Pem was on the brink of collapse and it would take but one more visit from the tax collector to bring about that collapse. St. George was merely hastening the process.

How frustrating to know that her inheritance lay collecting dust in a bank vault when that money could be put to good use right there. Three years until she turned twenty-one. It might as well be a lifetime. She knew in her heart of hearts that long before that magic birthday, the door to the Pem would be nailed closed and her beloved makeshift family cast to the four winds.

"You have problems," said St. George. "Surely you must realize that."

She felt as if all of her emotions were right there at the surface of her skin, ready to burst forth.

"Why don't we postpone further discussion until tomorrow?" he asked. The girl wasn't ready to see reason, at least not yet. The hour was late and it was clear that she was in danger of losing her composure. Of course, compared to the Englishwomen of his most recent acquaintance, Molly Hughes had more than likely lost her composure on the day she was born and never recovered it.

"How can you expect me to sleep with you hovering over me, plotting to steal my home?"

"It's your home," he persisted, growing tired of her insistence. "But it is my hotel. Do not forget that one most important fact."

She glared at him, her eyes shooting off sparks in the soft haze of evening. "Listen well, Mr. St. George—you'll never get this hotel away from me. I'll fight you with my dying breath."

"It needn't come to that, Molly."

"Don't call me that!" she snapped. "Only my friends call me Molly." She drew herself up to her full height, which for a young woman was considerable. "And you most definitely are not a friend."

"God Almighty!" he roared, his patience coming to an abrupt end. Did American girls learn none of the gentle arts at their mothers' knees? What happened to flirtation, to sweet coercion? "Don't you understand the matter at hand?" He gestured broadly, too angry to care if the whole of Cape Charlotte heard him. "This belongs to me. Your beloved hotel is mine to do with as I wish. Did it never occur to you that you might present your case more effectively without the female hysteria?"

"If you're implying I should have batted my eyelashes at you like a simpering cow, then you are sorely mistaken, Mr. St. George. I'd rather fight you with my fists."

"You'd lose, Molly," he said, his voice a threatening whisper.

"I don't care!" Her voice was high and tight, and he wondered if she was on the verge of tears. "I don't care about your stupid papers or your fancy clothes." She swallowed a sob and he almost felt sorry for her. How must it feel to want something with the passion and intensity with which she wanted this pathetic excuse for a

hotel? He couldn't imagine. He had never wanted anything or anybody in his life with that kind of heedless
fervor. Only anger had triggered that type of response in
him. Anger toward his mother for bolting. Toward his
father for lacking the courage to press on. And toward
Jonathan Hughes for having had the capacity to change
a child's life but choosing to do nothing instead.

In that regard, both he and Molly Hughes had a great
deal in common. Much more than she would ever know.

Molly wished the earth would open wide and swallow
her whole. To show weakness in front of such a man was
tantamount to waving the white flag of surrender. She
silently cursed her wild emotions for getting the better of
her. But there was nothing she could do to erase the
damage already done to her cause.

He was a hard and selfish man, this Nicholas St.
George. Oh, his name was all bluenosed and terribly
English, but she recognized the look of the outlaw in his
eyes and it was her response to that look that terrified her.
Unlike her sweet-tempered parents, Molly was a fighter.
Fritzie liked to say that all of William and Sarah's more
contentious family traits had bypassed those gentle peo-
ple and taken root inside their red-haired daughter.

She didn't remember her mother, but her father had
been a man who lived his life in a cotton-candy world of
memory and dreams. Molly saw her world for what it was
but chose to do her level best to mold it into the world she
wanted it to be. She knew she was annoying at times,
impossibly arrogant at others. Spoiled by the loving
concern of Fritzie and her other friends. Yet despite it all
Molly somehow realized that their future, their welfare,
depended upon her. She was the glue that held the
framework of their lives together.

Get hold of yourself, girl, whispered the tiny voice of reason. This wealthy Englishman held all the cards in his large, surprisingly work-roughened hands. She needed time to think. In the space of a few hours, her entire life had been turned bottom for top.

If this man was telling the truth—and she had the most terrible feeling he was—she and her beloved family could expect to find themselves sleeping on the boardwalk any day now. She took a long look at St. George. There was nothing about him that suggested patience or great generosity of spirit. He said he had come across the Atlantic to see to the well-being of little Maureen Alice, but grown-up Molly didn't believe that for an instant. It was the hotel that had brought him there and the prospect of even greater riches.

What she needed to do was find a way to convince him that keeping the Pemberton—and its staff—would accomplish that goal far better than divesting himself of his unexpected inheritance. And for that she would need more time.

The girl was transparent as glass. The inner workings of her mind were as obvious to Nicholas as the moon rising over the ocean. Like a good chess player, she had recognized her vulnerability and was moving to protect her position. A damn shame he couldn't offer her any encouragement, but in this instance he deemed it kinder to be cruel. What point was there to false hope when the situation was patently obvious?

Besides, it was late and he was not at all interested in prolonging this discussion. He wished there was some easy way to cut short this encounter. She was clearly the emotional type and he hadn't the energy to deal with a scene at this late hour. Emotional scenes were better played out in daylight when a man could see what he was up against.

From somewhere up the boardwalk he heard the sounds of music and laughter, and an idea formed. With one swift movement, he vaulted the porch railing to the ground and headed for the pathway leading to the boardwalk.

Molly stared at his departing figure. "And where do you think you're going?"

"Out to sample the charms of your Cape Charlotte, Maureen Alice."

"Of all the rude things to do," she said, her voice huffy. "We were in the middle of an important conversation."

"It can wait," he said, as casual as you please. "The music, however, cannot. We'll continue this discussion in the morning." He swept her a mocking bow. "Good night, Molly. Sleep well."

Stunned, she watched as he strode off down the boardwalk. Everyone knew the English believed themselves to the manner born, but this Nicholas St. George certainly took the prize. She fought the urge to race after him and slap his arrogant face. The only thing that stopped her was the growing certainty that he would toss her over his shoulder and fling her into the ocean if she dared to try it. But her stomach was tied up in sailor's knots and the palm of her hand itched to make contact with his cheek; if she didn't break something into a thousand pieces right this very minute she would go absolutely crazy.

She glanced around the front porch, searching for something suitable. A jardiniere stood near the rocking chair, complete with a drooping potted palm. The majolica container would make a satisfying racket when it shattered, but unfortunately she couldn't lift the blasted thing, much less throw it over the railing. Well, no matter. The best breakables were inside. Glassware. More plants in ceramic pots. Mismatched chinaware. Candlesticks heavy enough to knock a certain pigheaded Englishman from here to kingdom come.

That notion brought a smile to her face for the first time in hours. How lovely it would be to see him lying at her feet, all helpless and needy. She'd show him how it felt to have your fate resting in the hands of a stranger. Not an easy thing for man or woman.

She stormed back into the hotel, letting the front door swing shut behind her with a bang. If she were married, this whole idiotic situation would never have come about. Surely the Englishman could have been bought off with a king's ransom of rubies and diamonds.

Of course she couldn't marry just anyone. She didn't want some calf-eyed fool trailing her around, declaring his undying devotion. What she needed was someone as steely and uncompromising as she was, someone who understood that this marriage would be one of convenience—*her* convenience—only, with none of the usual rights and privileges associated with holy wedlock. Someone who didn't love or desire her any more than she loved or desired him.

Someone like Nicholas St. George. The notion of marrying her number-one enemy made her laugh out loud at the absurdity of this whole line of thinking. If she was looking for the antithesis of romance, that would certainly be it. When she found the true man of her dreams, her heart would be as untried as it was today.

She reached for the pewter candlestick that rested atop the piano in the main parlor. Better to smash the candlestick against the fireplace than entertain idiotic fantasies about marrying for money. Temper tantrums, like slides down the banister, had always been infinitely satisfying—no matter how grown-up she was supposed to be.

"You all right, girl?" Arthur's voice sounded from back in the kitchen, moments after the candlestick crashed against the brick mantel.

"Just fine," she called out, lying through her teeth for the second time that night. "I knocked over a candlestick."

Arthur mumbled something about taking care, while Molly stood in the middle of the parlor and waited for the glow of satisfaction to bloom. Nothing. She considered tossing the candlestick's mate against the fireplace, as well, but suddenly it seemed to require more effort than it was worth. The only thing that would help diffuse the anger inside her breast would be the sharp crack of her hand against the Englishman's cheek.

But there had to be something she could do, some course of action that would force Nicholas St. George to see reason. Fritzie, she thought, heading toward the kitchen. Maybe Fritzie would be able to make sense of this mess and help Molly draw up a battle plan. In times of difficulty, Molly had always turned to her surrogate mother for help and comfort, and not once had Fritzie failed her.

Arthur was seated at the scarred maple table, polishing the hotel's motley assortment of cutlery. He looked up as Molly entered the room.

"Where's Fritzie?" asked Molly without preamble.

"She turned in early," said Arthur. "Said her rheumatism was acting up."

"I have to talk to her."

"I don't know about that," said Arthur, in his careful way. "Fritzie also said something about Will—"

Molly didn't wait for him to finish his sentence. She dashed through the kitchen and took the back staircase two steps at a time. Fritzie and her husband had a tiny two-room suite on the third floor beneath the eaves. It was very hot up there in the summer, and terribly cold in the winter, but Fritzie loved that apartment the way Mrs. Vanderbilt loved her estates. Most of the staff preferred the first floor rooms, but not Fritzie. Molly's nursery had been on the third floor, and Fritzie had spent the first years of Molly's life caring for the motherless girl with the same devotion she would have shown to her own children, had she and Will been blessed with any.

Fritzie would have the answers, thought Molly as she ran toward the rooms at the end of the hall. Fritzie would be able to put Molly's chaotic emotions into order and help her figure out a way to deal with Mr. St. George.

She skidded to a stop in front of the closed door. Fritzie never closed her door before midnight in the summer. Usually Will sat in front of their open bedroom window with a glass of lemonade while Fritzie caught up on darning. Molly hesitated a moment, then reached for the doorknob when the soft sound of laughter brought her up short.

"Go on with you, Will...." Fritzie sounded young and flirtatious, not at all like her brisk self.

Will's reply was too low for Molly's straining ears.

"Oh, you're a wicked one, you are...." Fritzie's words dissolved into girlish laughter and Molly backed away, cheeks flushed and hot. She thought of how the Englishman had looked with his torso bare and gleaming golden in the sunlight, and she wondered if even Will with his glasses and thinning hair seemed beautiful to Fritzie.

Last night she would have swung open that door, oblivious to everything but her own distress. Now she found herself slipping quietly back down the hallway to her room near the stairs, her heart beating an uncomfortable tattoo inside her chest. It was St. George's fault, all of it, barging into the Pem and disrupting everything.

She closed her door behind her, not even bothering to light the gas globe. Fully clothed, she sprawled across her bed, her mind a kaleidoscope of conflicting emotions. If only he hadn't come into their lives. He should have stayed in England where he belonged.

His claims were ridiculous. No matter what she had seen written on those fancy papers of his, she absolutely refused to believe that the Pem could possibly belong to anyone but her. She was her father's daughter. He had owned the hotel before her, and she had no doubt that he had left it to his only child.

But you never questioned it, did you? that infernal voice of reason asked. She'd never once thought to make certain that her position was secure. All of her plans to restore the Pem to its former grandeur were ashes in the wind if the hotel belonged to someone else.

She buried her face in her pillow, hot tears scalding her cheeks. Thanks to the Englishman and his arrogant claims, her world was no longer the safe place she had believed it to be, and she suddenly had the feeling that she might never find it so again.

Chapter Four

The next morning Fritzie seemed happy and girlish, almost like a new bride on her honeymoon. Despite her morose mood, Molly found herself casting curious glances at the woman across the breakfast table.

"And what is that look on your pretty face, girl?" asked Fritzie as she served up another portion of eggs to the assembled staff. "Your cheeks are as red as apples in September."

"Look who's talking," crowed Stella with a bawdy laugh. "Don't think we haven't noticed the smile on *your* face, Mrs. Rafferty."

"You watch your tongue, old lady," said Fritzie with a wicked smile. "Our girl doesn't need to hear any of your bawdy notions."

"I don't mind," said Molly. "I'm not a child any longer."

That statement gained Fritzie's full attention. "And what brought about that statement, miss?"

She shrugged, feigning interest in her toasted white bread. "I'm too old to be wrapped in cotton wool, Fritzie. I know about...marriage."

Fritzie sighed. "I remember sayin' the same thing myself at your age." She fixed Molly with a look. "It's that

Englishman, isn't it, that be puttin' the bloom in your cheeks."

"Ridiculous!" said Molly with a snap of her fingers. "The only thing interesting about him is his wallet."

"I may be old but I'm no fool," Fritzie shot back. She narrowed her eyes. "And what was it he wanted with you last night, missy?"

"It wasn't me he wanted," Molly said. "It was the manager of the Pem."

"Would that be all?"

"Of course," Molly said, crossing her fingers behind her back. "You know those fancy Englishmen—he wants clean sheets twice a day and beef roasts for dinner every night."

Fritzie was having none of it. "You have a crush on him, missy, and don't you be tellin' me otherwise."

"Don't say that! I've never had a crush on anyone in my entire life." She hated him with every fiber of her being. He had come to town for the sole purpose of taking from her the only things that mattered: her home and family.

"Then it's high time you did."

"What a thing to say! I have no interest in nonsense like that."

"I say what needs to be said. You should be knowin' that by now. 'Tis nothin' to be ashamed of." Her gaze grew stern. "He wouldn't be toyin' with your innocence, now would he?"

"He doesn't know that I exist."

Fritzie nodded, satisfied. "We wouldn't be needin' troubles like that. Not with the sheriff and his wife comin' tomorrow night. We'd be doin' the Pem a disservice if everything wasn't as fine as we can make it."

Fritzie launched into a list of chores to be divided among the staff and Molly's head swirled. If she had to spend the day scrubbing floors and beating rugs, she wouldn't be able to keep her eyes on Nicholas St. George.

"I'll do the marketing," she volunteered, careful to keep her tone innocent and unconcerned. "Why should Stella have to walk from one end of town to the other in all this heat?"

"Bless your heart," said Stella, who would rather do anything than be out in the midday sun. "Floors ain't half the bother."

Molly breathed a sigh of relief. She was fleet of foot and extremely organized. She could manage to do the marketing and still have time for what was important. She had no doubt Nicholas St. George would be out and about Cape Charlotte today and she intended to force him to speak with her, if she had to follow him from one end of town to the other.

She hadn't the heart to tell the others what manner of trouble they were in. She harbored the faint hope that she would be able to dissuade the Englishman of his plan to sell out the Pem from under her before it became necessary to upset everyone else.

With their breakfast over, the staff dispersed to attend to their various chores. St. George had left word that he would not be eating breakfast at the Pem and, as she raced through the dishes, Molly kept an ear out for the sound of his footsteps on the staircase.

She was drying the last platter when she heard the front door squeak open. Wiping her hands on her gingham skirt, she tore through the hallway and reached the foyer in time to see the door swing shut behind that skunk of an Englishman. She flung open the door, not even noticing as it banged sharply against the wall.

"Where do you think you're going?" she demanded.

"You're repeating yourself, Maureen Alice," he said, drawing out her given names in a most annoying manner. Once again his suit coat was slung over his arm. Why couldn't the man stay properly dressed?

"You said that same thing last night," he continued. "I don't believe my comings and goings are any of your affair."

"We have to talk." She hurried down the steps after him. "We *need* to talk."

"I own the Pemberton Arms. You do not. There appears to be little to talk about."

"You hateful thing!"

"Name-calling is seldom the best way to promote fellowship," Nicholas drawled. "I would think you'd be more polite to your employer."

"You are not my employer," she raged. "You are nothing to me at all, save trouble. I wish—" She stopped, struggling with her ever-volatile temper.

"Don't stop now. Say whatever is on your mind."

"I wish you'd go back where you came from and leave us alone."

"Is that the best you can do, Molly? You disappoint me. I thought surely you would consign me to the devil in no uncertain terms."

"Oh, how I would love to do exactly that," she said, "but in truth I would settle for consigning you to England."

Molly stared in amazement as he threw back his head and laughed loud and long.

"At times they are one and the same thing, Molly."

"But you're English," she said. "I thought all Englishmen loved England. My father never stopped talking about England until the day he died."

"England is all things to all people," said Nicholas with a shrug of his broad shoulders.

"Am I supposed to know what that means?"

"It doesn't matter if you do or do not," he said evenly. He put his hands on her shoulders and moved her aside. "This has been most entertaining. Now if you'll excuse me . . ."

Before she knew what he was about, he was halfway up the path heading to the boardwalk. She hurried to catch up with him.

"Oh no, you don't," she said, falling into step with him. She would worry about the marketing later. This was more important. "You got away with that last night, but I refuse to let you disappear on me today."

The chit wouldn't give up. Nicholas had never met a woman as single-minded. Not even the marriage-hungry women he'd met since his return from Australia had the same intensity of purpose as Maureen Alice Hughes. He'd spent much of the previous evening attempting to figure out how the Pemberton Arms managed to stay open, but now it occurred to him that the answer to that conundrum was marching right beside him with all flags flying.

"You're an annoying brat," he said mildly as they reached the boardwalk then headed toward the Pavilion.

"I know," said Molly. "I've heard that before."

"I would imagine so," he muttered under his breath. It was hard for him to picture anyone spending time with the red-haired spitfire and not coming away with that selfsame opinion.

"I would like to talk about the Pem."

"And I would like to stroll in silence."

"Well, isn't that just too bad," she said in a pert tone of voice. "In America rich men don't always get what they want."

He looked down at her, trying not to notice the swell of her breasts in that damned skimpy cotton gown. "Neither do obnoxious young girls who do not know when to talk and when to keep still."

"If you'll listen to my argument, I promise to leave you to walk in peace."

He sighed loudly. He had the feeling he had no choice in the matter. The wide and welcoming boardwalk stretched as far as the eye could see. The sun was bright and only a few wispy white clouds marred the vivid blue of the sky. Waves crashed against the pale, pink sandy beach, then receded, leaving a silvery foam along the shore. About a mile ahead the midway beckoned. Last night a dancing companion had told him of the unbelievable sights to be found there: fire-eating men, tattooed ladies, pigs that could add and subtract better than many earls and ladies of Nicholas's acquaintance.

If he didn't give the girl a chance to speak, he would never have the opportunity to explore any of it before he went back to New York. As it was, he had an appointment at the Pavilion with a delightful woman who had promised to introduce him to townspeople of importance, one of whom was bound to be a realtor.

"Five minutes," he said, glancing at his pocket watch, "and then you are to leave me in peace, as promised."

"Ten minutes," said Molly, chin thrust outward in defiance, "and you are to listen to every word."

"God Almighty," he exploded, not caring who heard him. "I'm of a mind to fling you across my knee and spank some manners into you."

Again that flash of danger in her green eyes. "Don't even consider it," she warned, standing her ground. "I don't fight fair."

"Somehow that doesn't surprise me."

"Why, you dreadful—"

"Molly!" The woman called Fritzie bellowed from the front porch. "You forgot the list for the market."

"Oh, drat," muttered the troublesome child. She glared up at him. "Stay here," she ordered, as imperious as Queen Victoria. "I haven't finished."

Only a magician could have disappeared so completely. Moments later Molly stood at the point where the path met the boardwalk and looked for Nicholas St. George. She could have stood there until doomsday for all it mattered, because the Englishman with his fancy clothes had walked away from their confrontation without so much as a by-your-leave.

Righteous fury pounded inside her breast. Oh, he was a smart one, she thought as she reluctantly headed off to market. As smart as he was glorious to look at. This was no helpless fop, incapable of fending for himself. Where another man might feel cowed being in a strange town in a foreign country, she had the notion he relished the challenge. She had no doubt that Nicholas St. George would make it his business to speak with every realtor in town about the Pem's future.

Thank God the Pem was the dilapidated white elephant everyone thought it to be, for she had no doubt he wouldn't rest until he stumbled upon a buyer. For once she was thankful so few people saw the potential in the rambling old hotel.

Two hours later, lugging baskets filled with lettuce and onions and neatly wrapped packages of the butcher's cheapest cuts, Molly trudged back toward the Pem. Fast as she was, it had still taken an unconscionable length of time to gather up all of the things on Fritzie's list. She'd been dreadfully distracted at the market. Once she had actually stuck her thumb through the fragile skin of a ripe tomato, and all because she thought she spied Nicholas St. George near the pickle barrel.

If she wasn't in such a mean frame of mind, the thought of him plucking a penny pickle from the pungent barrel would have been laughable, but right now Molly wasn't finding much humor in anything. She hadn't seen hide nor hair of that wily Englishman anywhere, and she could only hope he'd had as miserable a morning as she.

The sun was approaching its zenith and not even the breeze off the ocean promised much relief. Her arms ached from the heavy bundles and she wished she'd thought to pin up her hair before setting out to market. The heavy mane felt as oppressive as a winter cloak as it drifted across her shoulders and down her back.

"Mornin', Molly." Rachel Tuttle nodded as she passed by with her two daughters. "Hot, ain't it?"

"The devil's weather," Molly said, winking at the younger of the two girls. "I'm counting the days until Christmas."

She continued on, wondering if Rachel Tuttle ever wore anything but that black bombazine dress with the outdated bustle, when the flutelike sound of ladies' laughter drifted toward her from the Pavilion. She knew all about that kind of laughter. It was the way Stella and Fritzie sounded when the milkman with the big blue eyes showed up on their doorstep with a quart jug of sweet cream.

He's in there, she thought, moving toward the Pavilion to take a peek. Flirting and laughing with the ladies and treating them like they were made of spun sugar. Hah! She could tell them a thing or two about the handsome stranger in their midst. He was arrogant and cruel and altogether too interested in his own petty concerns to have any regard for the consequences of his actions.

The maître d' stopped her at the door, a look of disdain upon his face. "May I help you, miss?"

She became aware of her faded skirt and skimpy blouse, of her flyaway hair brushing against her cheeks. Everything she owned was either too old, too tight or too threadbare to pass muster anywhere but in her own home. "I'm looking for someone."

He stepped back as if she had forgotten to bathe recently. "I doubt if there is anyone you know in here."

She hesitated, torn by the overwhelming desire to push his smug face into a soup bowl. Rising on tiptoe, she looked over his shoulder toward a bouquet of women at a table near the window. They were all clad in afternoon gowns of rose pink and periwinkle blue and all the colors of the garden. And in the center of that crowd was Nicholas St. George, looking like a fox let loose in a henhouse.

"Miss, I must ask you to—"

"Don't worry," said Molly, turning away. "I'm leaving." She walked away from the Pavilion, aware of the sharp scrutiny of the maître d'. She didn't particularly care about the opinion of that glorified waiter, but she did care about her own dignity and she knew nothing good could come of storming into the restaurant dragging her bounty of produce behind her. Molly was certain she could hold her own anywhere, but she also realized she would be at a distinct disadvantage in front of those old cows. Clothes might not make the woman, but they certainly did a good job of impressing some of them.

That didn't mean the Englishman had been granted a reprieve. There were other ways to beard a lion and it didn't always have to be in his own den.

She disappeared around the corner of the building, then settled down on a wooden bench to wait. He had to come out sometime, and when he did she would be there to greet him.

"Mr. St. George!" The wife of a prominent Cape Charlotte landowner tapped him on the wrist with her fan. "You haven't been listening to a word I said."

"On the contrary, Mrs. Spencer," he said, pulling his glance from the glass doors. "I heard each word about the Jubilee."

"Royalty is so romantic, don't you think?" Delphine Reynolds, wife of another important man, sighed deeply. "I told Charles I would do anything to be in London for the Jubilee galas."

It seemed to Nicholas that American women were more enthralled with English royalty than the royal family itself. Queen Victoria's Golden Jubilee had been the main topic of conversation for the past two hours, and at the moment he could cheerfully have upended the sovereign from her throne. He had the feeling that the female half of the population would gladly trade in their American independence for an invitation to just one of the galas Delphine had mentioned.

Where were the businessmen he'd been expecting to meet? So far the luncheon had been nothing more than a waste of time. He was doing his level best to maintain an acceptable level of interest in the women's conversation when a slight commotion at the door caught his eye. There, shoulders squared for battle, stood Molly Hughes. The maître d's scornful appraisal of her mended dress and scuffed boots had been palpable from across the room, and a spurt of anger on her behalf took him by surprise. That supercilious bastard was looking at her as if she weren't fit to wash his knickers and Nicholas would have enjoyed knocking him on his judgmental bum.

She'd looked young and determined and more than a little scared as she juggled her parcels, and a new emotion rushed in to take the place of his anger. Damn it to hell, he swore to himself as his table mates chatted on. Don't go feeling protective of the chit. Molly Hughes was nothing to him. As soon as he found a buyer for the Pemberton Arms, he would settle a sum of money on her staff and bundle her off to the convent school and be done with it.

Of course, considering the way she had looked last night in her clinging blue dress with her eyes all wide and filled with fire, a convent school might not be the logical place for all that passion. The thought passed through his mind that there might be other ways to take care of her future, but he quickly pushed them away. Only a man with a penchant for turmoil would get involved with a young woman like Molly Hughes.

While the convent school certainly didn't need Molly as a boarding student, they might be able to train her to be a governess or some such thing. He had little idea what young women without means did to keep soul and body together. He hated the thought that she might one day end up careworn and old before her time, beaten down by hardship.

Other than the oldest profession of them all, it seemed to him that women either cared for their own home and children or the home and children of other people. Here and there you'd meet a seamstress or milliner, but more often than not women made their way in the world bartering their domestic skills—in one way or another.

He wasn't a man given to sentiment. His protective instincts ran more toward self-preservation than altruism. It occurred to him yet again that what he was feeling might be a simple case of lust for the red-haired hellion. Whatever it was, it didn't give the girl the right to spy on him as she was doing now from the entrance to the Pavilion.

"I daresay we must be boring you, Nicky." The eldest of the quartet of ladies fixed him with a look. "You're too young to spend so much time gathering wool."

He glanced toward the door again to discover that Molly had disappeared. Scraping back his chair, he rose to his feet and with a nod of his head, offered his apologies. "It has been delightful," he said, his voice laced with the proper degree of regret, "but I'm afraid I have an appointment."

He quickly settled the bill with the maître d', arranging for a bottle of champagne to be delivered to the table with his compliments, then exited the Pavilion. The boardwalk was alive with merrymakers. Little boys in short pants rolled enormous hoops, growing giddy with laughter each time a hoop tapped the derriere of a strolling vacationer. There was no sight of Molly anywhere, but Nicholas wasn't fooled. The brat was probably hiding behind a rosebush, watching his every move.

He started at a brisk pace toward the Carousel, and before he'd gone ten feet Molly popped up at his side.

"Predictable," he said as if being stalked by a wild-eyed young woman with vegetables was an everyday occurrence. "You're nothing if not predictable."

"You think you're so smart," she said, temper hotter than the midday sun. "How dare you disappear on me the way you did!"

He kept on walking.

She grabbed at his sleeve and he shook her off like a burr.

"Don't you ignore me," she snapped. "If you think you're going to show up here and turn my life upside down, you have another think coming."

"'Another think coming'?" He shook his head. "The American idiom is filled with surprises."

"I'm not one of those simpering cows at your luncheon table, Mr. St. George. Changing the subject will not deter me from my goal."

"I doubt if a regiment of foot soldiers could deter you."

"I shall take that as a compliment."

He looked down at her and laughed out loud. "It wasn't meant as one, Molly."

"No matter," she said, dismissing him with a wave of her hand. "I want my fifteen minutes of your undivided attention."

"Ten minutes," he corrected. "Only eight of which remain."

"Good day, Molly!" called out a tinker, as his wagon jingled its way along the path that ran adjacent to the boardwalk. "Having troubles?"

The whole town, it seemed, knew Molly Hughes.

She turned and waved at the rotund old man. "Hello, Jimmy. Don't worry—everything's fine."

Turning back to Nicholas, she pointed toward stairs that led down to the beach. "There are benches beneath the boardwalk, where we can talk privately."

Amused—and more than a little curious—he followed her down to the sand, then took a seat next to her on the narrow bench. It was shady beneath the boardwalk and private, as she'd said, the perfect place for a rendezvous. He cast a curious glance at her. Could that possibly be what she had in mind? So far he'd discovered American women to be amazingly direct and, God knew, she was a delectable, if prickly, bundle of womanhood. It wouldn't surprise him if her passions ran as quick and hot as her temper. Perhaps he'd been hasty in his judgment of her virtue. She might have known the pleasure of many a man's kisses.

His reaction to that thought was decidedly mixed.

The bench had been a terrible mistake. Molly realized it the second he sat down next to her, his muscular thigh pressed against her leg in a most unnerving fashion. She had simply wanted to make certain nobody interrupted her presentation of the facts, not invite such intimacy. She caught the scent of soap about his person and a strange tingling sensation ran up her spine. She had never sat so close to a man in her life, and the unfamiliar feelings his nearness awakened inside her were as seductive as they were frightening.

If she knew what was good for her she would stand up and put some distance between them, but he might construe that action as weakness, and she would rather have died than let him think her weak.

"Seven minutes," he said, glancing again at that infernal pocket watch of his. "Use them well, Molly."

There was no time for subtlety. "I want to know what your plans are."

He arched a dark brow. "My plans?"

"For the Pemberton."

"I have no plans—"

Her spirits rose.

"—save for putting it on the market."

They plummeted. "You cannot."

"I can do anything I want to, Molly. I'm the owner."

"What do you want with the hotel anyway? You look as if you have a great deal of money—you don't need to sell it," she blurted. "Why don't you just go back to England and forget you ever met us."

"Are you blind, girl? The place is an unmitigated disaster. You're lucky it hasn't fallen down around your pretty ears. The kindest thing I could do would be to close it down."

"You can't do that!" Her voice rang out across the sun-swept beach.

"I'm not a total scoundrel. I would see to it that the employees found new situations."

"New situations! Stella is seventy years old, and Arthur nearly that. They deserve pensions, not new positions."

"Impossible."

She shook her head, despairing of ever being able to make him understand. "The Pem is their home."

"Do you mean to tell me that they live at the hotel?"

She named ten other employees and eight permanent guests who also had no other place to call home. "And Fritzie and her husband, as well."

The situation was even more absurd than the hotel itself. Twenty-two pathetic souls—twenty-three if he included Molly—actually lived in the monstrosity. Nicholas cursed Jonathan Hughes yet again for leaving him with the most ridiculous excuse for an inheritance anyone had ever had the misfortune to receive. Now the fate of a score of hapless individuals rested in his hands.

He glanced over toward Molly. She met his eyes. She didn't look away or smile or do any of the things he would have imagined a young woman in her situation might do. She met him as an equal, and somehow that made her more desirable than any woman he'd ever met. She managed to keep him off balance, and he didn't care much for that feeling at all. Another woman would have turned this intimate situation to her advantage, using flirtation to sweeten the dealings between them.

But not Molly. Those fiery green eyes of hers were unflinching in their gaze, and he found himself possessed of a grudging admiration for her tenacity, if not her charm. He'd never met a female who cared so little about using her feminine wiles. And yet there was no denying the fact that she was a woman. Her alarmingly direct manner was coupled with a form as ripe as a sweet peach ready to be plucked.

The fact that he'd even noticed disturbed him.

Ridiculous that this annoying chit should have any effect on him whatsoever. He found it amazing that he'd considered, even for a moment, how she would feel in his arms. She was nothing but trouble and a sane man would make certain he kept his distance.

The moment he saw that the Pemberton was a disaster and that she was well past the age of reason, he should have boarded the next train back to New York and said good riddance. But, no. He'd felt the tug of responsibility despite the fact that the responsibility, in truth, was not his. He owed the late Jonathan Hughes nothing—and this girl even less. The Pem was a sinking ship, and the inhabitants, survivors clinging to a life raft.

If he had half the sense with which he'd been born, he'd see to it that his soft spot for orphans did not extend toward hot-tempered redheads who believed they could bend one and all to their will without offering compensation of a romantic nature. Still, there was something about her that called to him in a way he didn't understand.

He'd been with women more beautiful in his time, women who understood the nuances of seduction and the pleasures of the boudoir. Once again he doubted if Molly Hughes had ever known the touch of a man's lips against hers. A vision of her, breathless and wide-eyed in his arms, gave him pause.

Damnation, he swore silently. What in hell was wrong with him? He sounded like a pubescent schoolboy instead of a man of experience. It was thoughts like this that led a man down the garden path and into trouble. Just because she seemed both guileless and straightforward was no reason to let down his guard.

He should sign the hotel over to her this very afternoon and be done with it. What should it matter to him if next month or next year they all found themselves out on the street with that hotel a pile of rubble? Or if Molly ended up scrubbing floors for a living or pleasuring old men with money to burn. He would be back in London by then, at Merriton Hall with an inventive mistress or two, and this whole ridiculous episode would be nothing more than a topic for conversation at dinner.

"For heaven's sake, will you *say* something?" Patience had never been Molly's strong suit, not even now when her back was against the wall. "We've been sitting here for ages and you haven't said one single word."

He turned to her, his blue eyes betraying nothing at all.

She sighed in exasperation. "I brought you here to talk, not to commune with nature."

He leaned back on the bench and clasped his hands behind his head. "Has it never occurred to you that most men do not care to be hectored?"

Her feathery brows slid together in a fearsome scowl. "I'm not looking to become your friend. I'm simply trying to hold on to what is rightfully mine."

"A debatable issue, that."

"Moral rights are vastly more important than legal rights," she said with certainty, "but perhaps you wouldn't understand that." She eyed him with disdain. "Why, that shirt you're wearing would pay Fritzie's wages for a week."

His grin was slow and sardonic. "Then perhaps you aren't paying Fritzie what she's worth."

"Unfortunately I cannot afford to pay Fritzie what she's worth." Or anyone else, for that matter.

"That should tell you something."

She leaned toward him, so intense was her need to make him understand how much this mattered to her and to those she held dear. "It tells me I must do anything within my power to keep the Pem."

"You realize another man might take that as an open invitation."

Her stomach muscles tensed. "You wouldn't."

"You sound uncertain."

"You're a gentleman," she said, not entirely convinced of that fact. "You wouldn't take advantage of the situation." She paused, heart thundering inside her chest. "Would you?"

"What do you think?"

"I do not think there are many things you would not do."

"Smart girl. You've paid attention." He rose to his feet, towering over her as she sat on the bench. "If you put your mind to it, you might be able to come up with a way to convince me the Pemberton Arms isn't entirely a lost cause."

"You're vile."

"And you're blushing."

"Is it any wonder?" she mumbled, feeling her cheeks with the back of her hand. She was beginning to understand all about the dangers to be found on—and beneath—the boardwalk.

He reached for her hand and drew her to her feet. He did not, however, allow her space to breathe. No one should be allowed to stand so close to another human being without benefit of clergy.

"How old are you, Molly?"

"Eight—eighteen." A simple question and yet she stumbled over it like a backward child working on a slate of sums. If she kept on like this, all would be lost before the day's end. She lifted her chin and met his eyes. "How old are you?"

His teeth flashed white and dangerous in the shadows. "Much older than you."

"I answered your question," she persisted, aware that she was pushing the limits of his endurance. "The least you can do is answer mine."

"Twenty-eight." He reached out and drew his thumb along the swell of her lower lip. "Has anyone ever kissed you?"

The question was bold and improper, and it made her tingle from her scalp to her toes. "That," she said primly, "is none of your business."

"As I thought," he said. "It's written all over that innocent face of yours." He withdrew his hand and she felt bereft without his touch. What on earth was happening to her?

"We—we should be talking about the Pem."

"We are," he said, his deep blue eyes searching her face. "We're trying to figure out what you have to offer in exchange for the hotel."

"You filthy—" She raised her hand only to have him grasp her wrist and hold it fast behind her back.

The dangerous glitter in his eyes told her she had made a dreadful mistake.

"If I am to be punished," he said, grabbing her other wrist and pulling her up against his broad chest, "at least let the crime fit the penalty."

Chapter Five

Tension shimmered in the air between them. She was lighter than air in his arms, trembling with age-old yearnings that were as new to her as springtime. Her eyelids fluttered closed once again, while her lips were moist and slightly parted, lush and inviting and his for the taking.

And, damn it, he wanted to take her. Right there on the sand while the rest of Cape Charlotte strolled past them on the boardwalk above. He wanted to be the first. He wanted to feel her legs wrapped tightly about his waist, hear her cry out when he entered her, rid himself of the ridiculous feeling that he would never again meet a woman who could give to him what she could.

She was everything he was not—hopeful and innocent and filled with a passion for life that he'd never known even on the best of days. He saw the darkness while she embraced the light. What other explanation could there be for believing she could salvage the Pemberton Arms with nothing more than the power of her will? She had no money, no education and no family. But still she believed, and he knew if he let himself, she might be the woman who could make him believe, too.

Dangerous stuff, that. He knew better than to believe in happy endings.

He also knew she would do anything to hang on to the Pem, but not even that fact made him doubt the reason she trembled in his arms. She was too young, too untried, to feign desire where there was none. She wanted him, although she might not understand why, and if he cared anything at all about self-preservation, he would let her go now before he found it impossible to stop.

But not before he'd tasted her lips. He wasn't generous enough to forego that pleasure.

She gasped as his mouth covered hers, drawing her breath from her body and leaving her weak with longing. His lips were hard and insistent and she feared she would faint as his tongue darted into the cavern of her mouth and sought to draw her own tongue into a sensual battle. He tasted vaguely of wine and heat, a combination that only added to the light-headed feeling that had her clinging to his muscular shoulders for support. He pressed her against him, his hands insistent against the small of her back, urging her closer.

She felt hot and cold, terrified and exultant—a swirling mass of anger and submission that made her fear for her sanity. This was all wrong. Her first kiss should have been given in love, not anger. The man whose mouth claimed hers should have whispered sweet nothings in her ear, wooed her with flowers, taken her dancing beneath the stars.

Nicholas had done none of those things. He was practically a stranger to her—a stranger who wanted to take all she owned and leave her with nothing.

And yet there was this powerful magic, this breathtaking longing that made everything else fade into nothingness before the heat of his kiss.

When finally he ended the embrace, she felt as if she'd been cast adrift on an alien sea.

"Go home, Molly," he said, his voice gruff. "Go away."

She struggled to regain her senses. "Wh-what?"

The sound he made was low, almost a growl. "You don't know what's happening here. Go home before I do something you're not ready for."

To her everlasting embarrassment, her eyes brimmed with tears. "How dare you even suggest that you . . . that we . . . that I would ever—"

"You would," he said softly, touching her mouth, which was swollen from his kisses. "You would have done whatever I said."

And to prove it, he kissed her again, more fiercely this time, as if he was trying to convince himself instead of her.

"You have nothing I want, Mr. St. George," she managed as she broke the kiss. "Nothing except the Pem."

"Then we have a long hard battle ahead of us, Molly Hughes, because that's the one thing you can't have."

Molly waited near the porch of the King George Hotel until she'd managed to calm down—and until her kiss-swollen mouth lost its telltale ruby hue. That sense of being a stranger in her own body lingered. Who would have imagined a simple kiss could engender such a hurricane storm of feelings inside her breast?

She felt like a traitor, as if she had somehow gone over to enemy territory and revealed a secret battle plan. She hated the fact that the Englishman had the upper hand over her now. That kiss beneath the boardwalk had changed everything. He'd seen her vulnerable and yearning, two things she had never thought she could be, and now she would have to work twice as hard to make him take her position seriously. The Pem meant nothing to him and everything to her. It was as plain as that.

Fritzie was waiting on the porch when Molly came up the walk, lugging the bags from the market.

"I'd be thankin' the Almighty you're home," Fritzie said, grabbing Molly's arm. "The worst has happened, my girl, the very worst thing of all."

Molly found it difficult to put thoughts of the Englishman's kisses from her mind, but the look on Fritzie's face quickly brought her to the matter at hand.

"Is everyone all right? Has there been an accident?" Gruesome images of runaway coaches or nasty spills down the staircase popped into her head, pushing aside the more sensual—and confusing—daydreams that had followed her home from the boardwalk. Everyone at the hotel still remembered the day Will had had the accident that cost him the use of his leg.

"Worse than an accident," moaned Fritzie, wringing her hands in a most uncharacteristic fashion. As a rule Fritzie was the essence of calm, even when no one could say if Will would live or die.

Molly's stomach clenched in alarm. "If you don't tell me what is going on, Fritzie, I shall—"

"The tax man!" Fritzie's voice went deep and dramatic. "He came back."

First the appearance of Nicholas St. George and his claim of ownership; now the return of the dreaded tax man. Was there to be no end to the woes besetting the Pemberton Arms? "I hope you had Arthur send him away."

"He tried, but the man is a monster."

Molly glanced toward the door. "The tax man is inside?"

Fritzie nodded. "Waitin' for you, he is, and this time he means business."

Horrified, Molly listened as Fritzie laid out the man's complaints for her.

"Thirty days," said Fritzie, dabbing at her eyes with a cambric handkerchief. "Come the middle of August we are all to be booted out on the street without so much as a good riddance."

Molly wanted nothing more than to bury her face against Fritzie's motherly bosoms and be hugged and petted and told that there was nothing to worry about. But she knew better. She had only to look in Fritzie's eyes to recognize that the older woman was looking to Molly to guide them out of this disaster in the making. Thank the good Lord Nicholas St. George hadn't returned to the Pem with her. How he would gloat over the mess she had gotten them all into.

She squared her shoulders and reminded herself that she had never faced a problem she couldn't solve. She might not have been blessed with privilege as had their English guest, but she had a clever mind and strength of character and with those qualities she intended to dazzle the tax collector.

Unfortunately, the tax collector proved to be immune to Molly's best attempts. She begged, pleaded, demanded, but he would not be budged.

"Thirty days," he said, slipping his crisp papers into a battered leather portfolio. "We have been as lenient as we are able to be. The time has come to render unto Caesar that which belongs to him."

Molly's retort was both biting and profane.

"You're too clever by half, my girl," said Fritzie as the front door slammed shut behind the angry town official. "That quick tongue will be gettin' you in trouble one of these fine days."

"I'm afraid it already has." She gave Fritzie a sheepish look. "We now have only fifteen days to find the money."

Fritzie's shoulders sagged as if the weight of the world rested upon them. "King Midas himself couldn't conjure up all that money in just fifteen days."

"It's a disaster," said Molly, ashamed of her temper. She followed Fritzie through the back hallway and into the kitchen. "If I were a man, I swear I would be tempted to rob a bank." Anything to find a way out of this mess. She chuckled grimly. "I could steal back my own inheritance."

"The bank!" Fritzie brightened. "There's a notion. My Will was sayin' that old Mr. Garron of Langston Bay would be gettin' a mortgage from the First National Trust Company, enough to spruce up his hotel and buy a coach and four."

"Mortgages have to be repaid, Fritzie. I doubt if the bank president would look upon weekends at the Pem as payment." She sank onto a chair and rested her elbows on the tabletop. "Besides, Mr. Garron owns a farm in Baltimore County and his own hat company, to boot. Money goes to money. That's the way it is and the way it always will be."

"I'd be thinkin' it's worth a try, girl," said Fritzie sternly. "With only fifteen days to our name, we can't be stickin' up our noses at opportunity, now can we?"

"You don't understand. There's more to this whole mess than you know."

Fritzie put a kettle to boil, then sat down opposite Molly. "Then perhaps it would be time you're telling me everything. I can't imagine anything worse than the tax collector."

Molly hung her head in despair as she thought about Nicholas St. George and her late Uncle Jonathan and the mess her life had suddenly become. "It's worse than the tax man, Fritzie. It's worse than you can possibly imagine. . . ."

By the dinner hour Stella and Arthur and all the others had heard the bad news. Molly thought she would go mad if she saw another pair of weepy eyes or heard the question, "What *are* we going to do?" one more time.

Hard as it might be to contemplate, she would be able to make her way in the world if she had to. She was young and strong and clever and even if it meant scrubbing floors for a living, she would be able to survive.

It was a very different story for these beloved souls who comprised her family. The tax collector, for the moment, was forgotten. Nicholas St. George had taken his place as the enemy of the Pemberton Arms.

"You have to make him understand," bellowed Stella, seventy years old and going deaf, as Molly washed the dishes. "What would an Englishman do with an American hotel anyway?"

"Sell it," Molly answered, hands deep in the soapy water. "He doesn't want a hotel, Stella. All he wants is money."

That brought a bitter laugh from Arthur, who stood near the back door smoking the pipe her father had given him upon Molly's birth. "Don't make much difference either way, much as I can tell. Tax collector or fancy gent—either way we get the heave-ho."

A pall settled over the kitchen. There was no arguing his words. Will, his bad leg propped up on a stack of pillows, sat at the table with Fritzie. A deck of playing cards rested on the table between them, their nightly game of rummy forgotten. Laughter rang out from the front room, where a few of the steady boarders were indulging in charades, but in the kitchen there was nothing but silence. Molly had sworn them all to secrecy. There was no use throwing the entire household into turmoil a moment before it was necessary.

"We'll find a way to stay together," she vowed as she washed the last glass and turned it upside down on the counter to drain. "I swear to you I won't fail you."

Fritzie sighed and pushed back her chair. The look on her face made Molly want to cry. "You mean well, girl," she said kindly, "but you know it won't be happenin' the way you'd like it to be." They were old, Fritzie went on, and without family. More than likely to end up living their lives in the poorhouse in Chambers County.

"I can work," Molly said, all bravado and bluster. "We'd find a tiny house to rent someplace and—"

Fritzie rose to her feet and walked toward Molly. "You've done your best by us all your life, girl, same as your da tried to do. This time I'd be thinkin' the odds are stacked too heavily against even you."

Edward Dunellen was a gregarious sort, the type of man Nicholas had always considered to be quintessentially American. Plainspoken and jovial, the rotund man managed to turn a business dinner into a social occasion with little obvious effort. As he watched the realtor signal the waiter for brandy, Nicholas was again struck by the similarities between America and Australia. There was a certain lack of convention that he admired, a joie de vivre that extended into all avenues of endeavor and all walks of life. He could live in a place like this and enjoy it.

The waiter brought over a bottle of good brandy and two snifters, then disappeared into the shadows. Dunellen did the honors.

"I do believe I can help you with the sale of the Pem," said Dunellen as they finished their second brandy each. "Maybe not in the way you imagine."

Nicholas lifted a brow. "And what does that mean exactly?"

"I know the place," said Dunellen bluntly. "It needs more work than most folks are likely to put into it."

"Then how do you propose to sell it?"

Dunellen looked like the cat who'd devoured the cream. "Have you seen the Abercrombie Hotel next door?" Nicholas nodded. "The owner is looking to grow. The only thing standing in his way is the Pem."

"Meaning he would raze the hotel and use the land as he saw fit?"

"You're a smart man, Mr. St. George." Dunellen leaned back in his chair and crossed his hands over his ample belly. "Can't get you much for the building but I can help you with the land."

Nicholas said he would like to sleep on the proposition, and after some more convivial conversation, Dunellen bade him goodnight.

"If you're in need of female companionship I can be of service," Dunellen added after the two men shook hands in farewell. "Cape Charlotte is small but some of our ladies are quite friendly."

"Thank you, no," said Nicholas. "I'm enjoying my solitude tonight."

Dunellen laughed and tucked his gloves into the pocket of his suit coat. "As you wish." With a bow, he made his exit.

Nicholas lingered over a cigar and what was left of the brandy, letting his thoughts follow their own path. There was no doubt in his mind that Cape Charlotte was a town on the way up. Dunellen had explained a little of the geography of the seaside resort, and even Nicholas, unfamiliar with the region, quickly grasped the fortuitous placement of Molly's hometown. Washington, the nation's capital; Philadelphia, the nation's birthplace; and New York City, the nation's heart—each of those cities was within reach of Cape Charlotte. The town possessed a beautiful shoreline and an adequate harbor and Nicholas had no doubt it could easily become a first-rate port for an enterprising importer.

The town had already attracted its fair share of bureaucrats and their families from Washington and Baltimore, fat and prosperous men with money to burn. Dunellen mentioned three hotels on the boardwalk that had doubled their profits last month alone. The Pem, unfortunately, was not one of them.

Nicholas puffed on his cigar, trying to shake away the feelings of guilt that came over him each time he thought of selling the hotel out from under the girl. Not that there was an alternative. Even if he handed over the hotel to her and took the next train back to New York, it wouldn't be long before she found herself out on the street with nothing to call her own but a sheaf of unpaid bills and a dismal future. The Pem needed more than she could provide—and certainly more than he was *willing* to provide.

But, damn it, there was the way she had felt in his arms. That soft sigh of surrender. The unexpected pleasure of discovery.

Maybe he should have taken Dunellen up on his offer of female companionship. Not that Nicholas couldn't have found such companionship on his own. The redoubtable Mrs. Spencer had made it perfectly clear that she was available, yet he had turned her down as well.

Something was happening to him, something he neither liked nor understood, and he wanted to put as many miles between himself and trouble as he possibly could. This was an impossible situation, one in which he could only lose. He hated losing at anything, whether it be games of chance or the game of love. And the stakes this time were far greater. This afternoon beneath the boardwalk he had come close to losing his edge.

Holding Molly in his arms, he had found himself prey to feelings he'd spent the better part of his life avoiding. Desire was present, as he had known it would be, but that had been only part of the equation. Mingled with desire was admiration and curiosity and a sense of recognition that scared the hell out of him. She was as innocent as spring rain, as guileless and forthright as it was possible to be.

He'd never met anyone like her before. He doubted if there were many women like her anywhere. What had made her this way? he wondered. What combination of traits and experiences had fashioned the mercurial creature he'd kissed beneath the boardwalk? There was nothing devious about Molly Hughes, nothing underhanded or deceitful. She laid her cards on the table for the world to see and fought for what she believed in, traits rarely seen in the men of his acquaintance.

Damn these thoughts. He didn't want to understand her—or any woman. Sex for its own sake had always been more than enough to satisfy him. Love muddied the waters, and more than one man had drowned while searching for shore.

Which wasn't to say he didn't believe in the game of love. He'd cut a wide swath through elegant boudoirs and humble shacks. The Englishwomen he'd met had seemed intrigued by the life he'd lived. His years in places like Australia and Tahiti had taught him many things about pursuit and seduction that stood him head and shoulders above his Oxford-educated peers. He was stronger, larger, less civilized and more inventive by half, and his reputation among the ladies of London had grown by leaps and bounds since his return to England.

There was something of the black sheep about Nicholas. He'd heard some of the whispers, even encouraged a few of the more interesting rumors about his past, his present and his future. He'd discovered early that women responded ardently to a man about whom clung the scent of scandal, and he wasn't fool enough to lose his advantage. There were some who said he was a selfish bastard, only looking for a woman of position to help him restore Merriton Hall to its former glory, and he didn't argue the point.

He wanted what belonged to him. He wanted the house and the title and the respect that came with both. When his mother had bolted from her marriage, running off with Jonathan Hughes, Merriton had become a curiosity—and his father an object of pity, until the night Edward St. George put a pistol to his head and pulled the trigger as thirteen-year-old Nicholas struggled in vain to stop him.

While Jonathan Hughes lived, Nicholas had stayed away from the country of his birth, and his family's estate had suffered for it. There had been no other way. His stepfather had deserved to die, but Nicholas hadn't been willing to spend the rest of his days in prison for the privilege. And so he had waited until Hughes drew his last breath before coming home to claim all that was rightfully his.

He'd discovered Merriton was older, smaller, darker than he'd remembered—and that the memories that had waited for him over the years were as vivid as they'd been in his nightmares. Merriton was no longer his home, if it ever had been, but it had been his father's. It belonged to his family—or, rather, to the memory of the family he'd never had—and even if he always felt like a stranger in the country of his birth, he would see to it that he reclaimed everything that Jonathan Hughes had stolen from him.

He would never end up like his father, broken and humiliated, clinging to the hope that the woman he loved would return to him. He sought pleasure where he found it and moved on before an affair had the chance to ripen into something deeper. Two weeks . . . a month . . . it varied with the woman and the circumstances. He made it a point of honor to end each affair before any hearts could be broken.

Franklin Morris, his solicitor, had said that Nicholas needed a wife. Merriton needed a woman's touch and Nicholas was painfully aware of his shortcomings when it came to dealing with servants and society alike. Since his return to England, his life had become a series of entanglements predicated on the very fact of his bachelor status. "All women believe in romantic fidelity," Franklin had said, "but only wives understand how quickly that ideal crumbles before the reality of marriage."

Marriage was about property, about heredity. It opened up the doors to society in a way nothing else could. Family was everything to his countrymen. Who you were, where you came from, the intricate plaiting of bloodlines and history were the stuff of which success was made. More profitable liaisons of a financial kind were struck over brandy and cigars in the library of a baronial mansion than had ever been conducted in the dim light of a solicitor's office.

Nicholas was shrewd enough to know that the fortune he'd accumulated in Australian gold needed constant attention if it were to increase. He'd been blessed with a sharp mind and a keen business sense, but without the connections of family and friends, his place in society would never be as secure as he would like.

And although he would never admit it, not even to himself, at the center of his being was an emptiness that nothing could fill. It had never occurred to him that such a thing was even a possibility.

Until now.

With Molly Hughes.

"Sir?" A waiter appeared at his side, all solicitude. "Another brandy?"

He shook his head. He could drink a bottle of the stuff and not come close to blocking out the memory of the way she'd felt in his arms. The way she'd made him feel. There were no rules with Molly, no dance steps, or familiar patterns to follow. He wasn't seeing the shadow of another man in her eyes or hearing the echo of words said many times before. Everything to her was new and fresh, from the magic of a first kiss to the discovery of the pleasures yet to come. He wouldn't have imagined a woman's awakening to be as powerful an aphrodisiac as it had turned out to be. He couldn't remember the last time a simple kiss carried with it so much wonder.

The wonderment, however, belonged to her.

The danger was his alone.

He reached in his pocket and pulled out some American currency, then tossed it on the table. Let the waiter figure it out. Tomorrow he would tell Edward Dunellen to approach the owner of the Abercrombie and put the wheels of sale in motion.

And then he would track down Old Jake and buy himself a ticket out of Cape Charlotte.

Back at the Pem, Molly found she couldn't sleep. The hours ticked by and still she tossed and turned in her narrow bed. Each time she closed her eyes she saw the stricken look on the faces of Fritzie and Will and the others as she told them of the double-edged sword that hung over her head.

Pushing away the covers, she sat up in bed and wrapped her arms around her knees. There was no point trying to coax sleep from hiding. Her thoughts were tangled, her emotions close to the surface. The memory of the Englishman's kiss was painfully clear, reminding her of how terribly she had failed the people who mattered. Nicholas St. George was out to do her in, same as the tax collector. He wanted to take away her home, strip Fritzie and the others of the only security they had.

Her face burned at the memory of the interlude they'd shared beneath the boardwalk. To think she had come so close to being in league with the enemy.

Money, she thought, swinging her legs from the bed then walking to the window. In the end it all came down to money. Money to pay the taxes. Money to spruce up the Pem. Money to convince the Englishman that he didn't need a hotel in Cape Charlotte.

She leaned against the window and peered out at the moon-swept beach. If only she were older and wiser—just three more years would make a world of difference. If she were twenty-one she could march down to the bank and demand her inheritance right on the spot. There would be money enough to make her master of her own fate, not forced to bow to the will of others.

Not a one of them would have another moment's worry. They could have bacon and fresh coffee every morning and roast beef for dinner and never once have to hide behind a tree when the grocer stormed up the street, waving another unpaid bill. The Pem would be the grandest and most popular hotel on the beach, catering to travelers from as far away as Chicago.

She wasn't twenty-one, however, and her inheritance would remain locked away for another three years unless she suddenly found herself a husband. The very idea made her laugh. The only men she knew were Will and Arthur and both of them were old and married. Maybe she should put an ad in the *Cape Charlotte Gazette*. WANTED: One Temporary Husband. She imagined herself standing in front of the Carousel on the boardwalk, asking eligible gentlemen to volunteer their bachelorhood to aid her cause.

"Just for a day or two," she would say, "then we can have the marriage dissolved." And no romance, thank you very much. A business proposition, plain and simple, one that would last only long enough for her to claim her fortune and then they would both go their separate ways as if the wedding had never happened.

All of which only proved how young and foolish she was. She was looking for a miracle when there were none to be found. There wasn't a man for a hundred miles who could fill those requirements.

She paused as a movement on the beach caught her eye. She parted the curtains and looked out. A man was striding across the dunes, his imposing figure backlit by the silvery glow of moonlight. The Englishman, she thought, not without a touch of anger. Who else would be parading about at this hour as if it were a normal thing? His shoulders were as wide as the landscape, his waist and hips narrow. He made her think of the conquering warriors she'd read about in school, men who took what they wanted, the consequences be damned.

As he started up the walkway toward the Pem, she noticed that his torso was once again bare, his skin damp from the ocean. His pants clung to his powerful legs in a way that left little to her imagination. What was there about the man that he found it so infernally difficult to keep his clothes on? Even the conquering heroes of her imagination somehow managed to keep on their suits of armor.

She wondered if he had gone swimming with his trousers on or merely stepped back into them after leaving the water. The fact that she would even entertain such a question should have shocked her, but this had been an evening of so many surprises that she feared she was beyond embarrassment. If ever there was a time for plain thinking, this was assuredly it.

She stood quietly by the window and stared at him in a most blatant fashion. She hated him for what he was doing to her. Blessed by the gods with money and position, he believed himself above the problems of ordinary people. He had as little concern for her problems as he had for those of the fishmonger at the pier. She was certain Nicholas St. George was counting the days until he could flee Cape Charlotte and return to the more cosmopolitan pleasures to be found in New York and London.

You'd never catch him building a life in a seaside town like Cape Charlotte. The thought of his spending more than a week there was laughable.

"No," she murmured as he came up the path, "you'd never want to stay in a place like this, now would you?" If the train was late, a man like Nicholas St. George would probably buy the railroad in order to get where he was going.

He stopped suddenly, as if he'd heard her or somehow sensed her presence. She didn't move from her position at the window, nor did she close the curtains. He looked over his shoulder, toward the azalea bushes looming in the darkness, then up toward where she stood. Neither said a word. Their gazes locked and it seemed to Molly as if the ebb and flow of time ceased while each took the other's measure.

Finally he was the one to break the impasse. With a deep bow, he disappeared onto the porch and she heard the front door creak open, then shut. She wondered how many more nights she would hear his footsteps on the stairs as he climbed the steps to his room. Two more nights . . . maybe three. He would either find a buyer for the Pem or he wouldn't. Whatever the outcome, she knew it wouldn't take much longer.

And that was when the idea took hold.

It was risky and not without an element of danger, but Molly had never believed life came with guarantees. She couldn't just sit back and let her fate be decided by a stranger. She had one chance to influence her future and, come hell or high water, she was going to grab opportunity with both hands before it left Cape Charlotte.

Chapter Six

Molly came downstairs the next morning filled with resolve, only to find the kitchen in a state of turmoil. Although it was only eight o'clock, both the stove and the oven were burning and it seemed as if every cook pot in the house held something savory.

"What on earth is going on?" she asked as she made herself a cup of tea and grabbed a slice of toast from a platter of leftovers. "You look as if you're preparing to greet President Cleveland."

Fritzie, who was up to her elbows in bread dough, cast Molly a look. "Company tonight," she said, kneading the dough with strong, sure movements of her capable hands. "Drink up, girl, there's lots to be done."

Molly took a sip of tea, grimaced and reached for the sugar bowl and treated herself to two lumps. The time for frugality would soon be over. "All this for Sheriff Walters and his wife?"

"And where have you been, girl, sleeping the day away?" Fritzie pounded at the dough, then stretched it like an elastic rope. "We have thirty for dinner and all of them stayin' the night."

"What?" Molly leaped to her feet, splashing coffee on the skirt of her mint-green cotton dress. "Where on earth did you scare up thirty guests?"

Fritzie explained that the train from Baltimore to Philadelphia had run into problems five miles from Cape Charlotte and the seaside town now had an overload of hungry and tired travelers.

"It won't solve our problems with the Pem," Fritzie went on, "but the extra money will be helpin' us move on when the time comes."

Molly nodded, biting her tongue against the urge to share her plan with her beloved Fritzie. At first she had panicked at the idea of the hotel swarming with strangers on the most important night of her life, but the more she thought about it, the more the idea appealed to her. The greater the number of witnesses, the stronger her position. The sheriff would make certain the Englishman did the noble thing.

She gestured toward the dining room as casually as she could manage. "Has His Nibs had breakfast yet?" He'd come in so late the night before that she would be surprised if he was up and about.

Fritzie shrugged.

"Too early for the likes of him, no doubt," Molly said evenly, as if it didn't matter one whit.

"Too late is more like it," said Fritzie, turning the dough and beginning again from a new angle. "Stormed out of here first thing as if the devil himself was on his tail."

"Did he say where he was going?"

"He asked where he could find Old Jake."

Molly leaned forward in her seat, hands trembling as she clutched her cup of tea. "Did he—did he take his valises with him?"

"No valises, but it wouldn't be takin' a genius to see the man is ready to move on."

God must be watching over her. The next train to New York was due in tomorrow afternoon and she couldn't imagine that he would be heading anywhere else. "Seemed angry, did he?"

Fritzie nodded. "You wouldn't be havin' an argument with the man now, would you?"

"Me?" She was all wide-eyed innocence. "I haven't spoken a word to him since before supper yesterday." Which was true enough, if not entirely forthcoming.

"You're nervous as a cat," Fritzie observed as she divided the ball of dough and shaped it into three perfect loaves. "Would there be somethin' you're not tellin' me?"

She put down her cup and pushed back her chair from the table. "A million things, Fritzie. My mind feels like the pieces of a crazy quilt."

Fritzie wiped her hands on her apron, then gave Molly a hug. "Don't be worryin' about things you can't change, girl. It just makes life harder than it already is."

"But I *can* change things!" The words burst forth of their own volition. "It's not too late for me to—" She stopped, horrified by how close she had come to revealing her secret. If Fritzie had any idea what Molly was planning, the woman would lock her up in the attic and throw away the key.

Fritzie took Molly's face in her hands. "Look at me, missy."

Molly's gaze focused on Fritzie's ears, her nose, her hairline.

"As I feared," said Fritzie with a shake of her head. "It's hidin' something from me you are."

Molly gathered up her courage and met Fritzie's eyes. "There's nothing to worry about," she said, wishing it were twenty-four hours later and the whole episode over and done with. "I'm . . . distracted, that's all."

"'Tis more than that."

"Truly, Fritzie." She forced a small laugh. "It's just that the Englishman has upset me more than I realized."

"And that's all?"

Molly whispered a quick prayer for forgiveness. "That's all," she lied, crossing her fingers behind her back. "There's nothing more to it than that."

Old Jake lived at the opposite end of town in a run-down house that looked as if it had once been used as a barn. Behind the house was a ramshackle stable where Nicholas found the old man currying his roan.

"Leavin' town so soon?" Old Jake looked up from his work. "Would've figured you for another week at least."

"My business is finished," said Nicholas, laying a hand along the horse's muzzle. "How soon can I board a train for New York?"

Jake put down the currycomb. "I'd say you're mostly in luck. Tomorrow we got the five o'clock headin' up New York way."

"Can you tell me how to find a ticket agent?"

"You're lookin' at one." Jake walked over to a pile of wooden crates near the haystack. He lifted the lid and withdrew a stack of tickets. "You tell me where you're fixin' to go, and I can git you on your way."

"You're an amazing man, Jake." Nicholas pulled money from his pocket. "And, as I remember, an honest one. If you'll help yourself to the fare, I will be in your debt."

Chuckling, Jake took the correct number of bills, folded them and placed them in the wooden crate with the remainder of the tickets. "Wish there was more of your kind around here, mister. You do make my life easy." He eyed Nicholas with open curiosity. "Did you do whatever it was you came here to do?"

"Afraid not. Nothing was as I'd expected it to be." Not Molly or the Pemberton Arms or this eccentric little town that had somehow managed to charm him despite himself.

"Not much in life is what we expect, far as I can see." He reached for a blade of straw and stuck it in his mouth. "Thing is, you got to learn how to accept what is and quit worryin' about the rest."

There was truth in Old Jake's words, Nicholas decided as he strolled back into the heart of town, but he'd never been much good at accepting life on its own terms. If he had, he would have let his late stepfather wreck his life the way he'd wrecked the lives of everyone around him. Nicholas had always been good at recognizing danger in whatever form it sought to present itself, and Molly Hughes had danger written all over her.

Damn her pretty hide to hell. He'd seen her last night standing at the window on the third floor, looking down at him with those big green eyes of hers. He'd spent most of yesterday doing his best to erase the memory of that kiss beneath the boardwalk. When good brandy didn't work, he'd stripped off his shirt and trousers, then plunged into the ocean. He swam until his lungs burned with the effort, but still he couldn't manage to outdistance the feeling that he was in trouble.

As soon as he'd seen her framed in the window, it had all come rushing in at him again. Lust. Uncertainty. Anger. An unexpected tenderness that hit him like a blow to the gut. He'd spent the better part of his life believing tenderness and vulnerability were two sides of the same tragic coin, and the fact that he was capable of such weakness scared him.

He knew all about the ways in which a woman could destroy a man. His father's descent into hell had left scars that would never disappear and Nicholas had no intention of baring his heart to new scars, all because of a girl with green eyes and a sharp tongue.

This afternoon, after he saw Edward Dunellen, he would see the president of the Cape Charlotte Bank to arrange for a modest settlement to be made on the residents of the hotel to help them find new accommodations. Whatever happened to them after that wasn't his concern.

The thirty railroad passengers arrived in late afternoon, tired, hot and understandably irritable. Molly manned the front desk, fielding requests for ocean views and private baths with as much cordiality as she could muster.

"We're under renovation," she said to one guest, stretching the truth just a tad when asked why the rooms were so Spartan. "Come back next year and you'll be surprised."

The guest wandered off, muttering something about wishing there'd been room at the King George Hotel up the boardwalk, but Molly chose not to be offended. When she had her inheritance she would make it her business to see to it that the Pemberton Arms boasted the fanciest baths this side of Washington, D.C. She would tear out the old windows and put in the biggest, showiest ones her pocketbook would allow.

She was grateful for the hustle and bustle involved in getting the travelers settled, for it helped keep her mind off what was coming up. It also made it easier for her to make certain everyone was situated exactly where they should be. Come hell or high water, she was going to see to it that the sheriff and his wife occupied the room next to Nicholas St. George.

Fritzie had her suspicions that something was wrong, but Molly put up a valiant front.

Every time she heard a noise she looked up, heart in her throat, but it was never St. George. He couldn't have left because his valises were still in his bedroom, but she'd bumped into Old Jake at the depot and he'd told her about Nicholas's visit. Tomorrow afternoon he'd be leaving for New York. If things didn't work out now she wouldn't have a second chance.

The terrible thought that he might only return to retrieve his luggage made her weak with anxiety. Short of her borrowing the constable's pistol and demanding her money from the bank at gunpoint, this was her last chance. This had to work. She couldn't bear to contemplate the alternatives open to her if it didn't.

Luncheon was a hectic parade of plates, spilled food and crying children.

"Maybe we wouldn't be wantin' the Pem to be busier," moaned Fritzie as she cut into an apple pie and placed slices on dessert plates. "A body needs eight hands like an octopus to keep up with things."

"I'm too old for this," said Stella, rubbing the small of her back.

Arthur smothered a yawn while he stacked coffee cups and saucers on a tray.

Molly, however, was filled with energy. "Don't you worry," she said blithely. "When we're successful, we'll hire a nice young staff to do the work."

"And be puttin' ourselves out of work?" asked Fritzie with a toss of her head. "Not very likely."

"You'll be supervisors," said Molly, "able to boss everyone else around while you do nothing more strenuous than pour yourself a cup of coffee and eat bonbons."

"Oh, those are fine words you're speaking," said Fritzie, "but you shouldn't get us so excited about things that can't be."

But it *was* going to happen. Each hour that passed brought Molly closer to her goal. Her plan was so simple that it almost frightened her. Surely God must be watching over her to have handed her this opportunity on a silver platter. In a way she almost felt sorry for the Englishman. When he went back to London, he would be older and wiser—

And married.

Sheriff Walters and his wife appeared shortly before dinner, and Molly made certain she was the one to show them to their accommodations.

"Best room in the house," she'd said blithely, ignoring the fact that the only thing in its favor was that it was adjacent to the Englishman's.

"What a cunning sampler," said Mrs. Walters, admiring a faded needlework on the wall. "All those tiny little stitches."

The sheriff himself was more interested in the mattress on the double bed than in the wall hangings. "Hard as a rock," he said, bouncing his big behind up and down on the sagging springs. "You got anything more choice than this, Molly?"

Molly knew a moment of utter panic. Summoning up a guileless smile, she hurried to the window and flung open the curtains. "More choice than this splendid view?" she asked, although the view was nothing new to the sheriff and his wife, any more than it was to Molly.

"The missus and I have a party to go to tonight," he stated, clearly unimpressed. "If I wanted to sleep on a bed of nails I could do that at home."

His wife placed a hand on his forearm. "Now, Harry," she said in a soothing tone of voice. "You saw how busy they are here today." She offered a big smile to Molly, who was too scared to breathe. "I think this is more than adequate compensation for a few pounds of coffee beans."

The sheriff relented and Molly silently blessed the woman for her tact.

"You're just going to love this room," she went on, turning down the coverlet and smoothing a pillow slip. "Nice and quiet this end of the house...far enough away from the kitchen noise... a quiet neighbor who's hardly ever here..." She paused for a moment. "You may have seen him about town... a tall Englishman?"

The response was even more than she had hoped for.

"Oh, dearie!" Mrs. Walters rolled her eyes heavenward and placed a hand upon her bosom. "I've seen him in town...oh yes, I have." She lowered her voice conspiratorially. "I had no idea Englishmen were so... rugged."

Molly glanced toward the sheriff but he was busy in front of the glass, smoothing selected strands of hair across his balding pate.

"Quite an eye for the ladies," Molly offered up more loudly. "I saw him myself at the Pavilion with Mrs. Spencer and looking just as bold as brass."

"The handsome ones are like that," Mrs. Walters noted. "They march through life taking anything they please. A young girl can't be too careful."

Molly nodded, wishing she could summon up a maidenly blush at command. "When he looks at me there are times I feel as if he can see right through my—" To her delight a fierce blush appeared of its own volition as she recalled their kiss beneath the boardwalk.

"Don't let him turn your head, girl." The sheriff tore himself away from his own reflection. "I can't tell you how many marriages got themselves started when a foolish girl believed a man's stories and got herself compromised."

Molly could scarcely conceal her delight. This was far better than her wildest dreams. "Thank you, Sheriff Walters," she said demurely. "Without a father to protect me, I've always looked toward Arthur and fine men like you to guide me. All I have is my good name. . . ."

The sheriff preened at the compliment. "Don't you worry, Molly," he said gruffly. "Nobody'll take advantage of you. Not while Harry Walters is still breathing. Your good name is safe."

The Englishman didn't show up for dinner.

Not that Molly had expected him to, but the fact was nobody had seen Nicholas St. George since sunup and she found her nerves growing more tightly drawn with each hour that passed. Where could he be? she wondered, as she waited tables during the main meal. Had he found himself a willing woman down by the Carousel, one who returned his kisses with more ardor and expertise than Molly had shown the day before?

She brushed the thought from her mind the way she would have chased away a pesky fly. So long as he hadn't seen fit to marry anybody, what did it matter if he'd found some shameless hussy with whom to spend the time? It was nothing to Molly. Absolutely nothing.

The only thing she was concerned with was making sure that her scheme worked the way she had it planned. Unfortunately, she couldn't brush away her pangs of conscience as easily as she had her worries about the Englishman. She had always prided herself on her direct and honest manner. Who would have imagined she could find it in her heart to be duplicitous?

But when it came down to a choice of her conscience or saving the Pem for the people she loved, she knew she would do it all over again.

Shortly after nine o'clock Molly excused herself and went upstairs, ostensibly to check on the guest rooms. Most of their impromptu visitors had decided to walk off their hearty dinners with a stroll up the boardwalk toward the Carousel and the Pavilion. Stella had retired to her room. Fritzie and Will were playing cards in the kitchen while Arthur readied the dining room for tomorrow's breakfast.

"Good night, everybody," said Molly, heading for the staircase, as casually as she could manage.

"Early, isn't it?" asked Fritzie, looking up from the game.

"Busy day," said Molly. "I'm not as young as I used to be, you know."

They were still laughing as Molly went to her room to prepare for her wedding night.

Once safely behind locked doors, Molly stripped off her clothing and poured water into her washbasin. The water was cold but she gritted her teeth and managed to finish bathing. She didn't dare go back down to the kitchen and heat up a pot of water. Fritzie frowned upon wasting good wood to heat bathwater in the summertime, and the woman would be instantly suspicious if Molly suddenly demanded a warm scrub. She shivered her way through her ablutions, doing her best to concentrate on the bath itself and not the reason for it.

But as she briskly rubbed herself dry with a towel, she caught the faint lavender scent of the soap she'd used and a feeling of light-headedness came over her. The feeling was so intense that she sank to the edge of her bed and, towel clutched to her chest, lowered her head to her knees.

"What am I doing?" she whispered as the reality of it all finally sank in. Preparing herself like a real bride on her wedding night for the unsuspecting groom. She must have been out of her mind, totally daft, to believe this scheme of hers had even a ghost of a chance to succeed. She laughed, a small sound in the quiet room. Robbing the bank suddenly seemed easier—and a great deal safer than what she had in mind.

But she had no other choice. Time was slipping away and an opportunity as perfect as this one was unlikely to appear again.

With great deliberation she slipped a freshly laundered chemise over her head, smoothing it across her breasts and stomach, letting it fall free over her hips and thighs. Her skin was unbearably sensitized; soft as it was, the cotton material made her nerve endings tingle. She stepped into her faded blue dress, then struggled with the long line of buttons. Her fingers refused to obey her commands and she had to stop, draw a deep breath, then begin again. *My wedding dress,* she thought with an odd little flutter inside her chest.

Once she'd seen a paper pattern for a real wedding dress at the yard goods store. All frills and ruching and yards of lace. A bride couldn't help but be beautiful in a dress like that. Why, her groom would fall in love with her all over again just at the sight of her.

Sighing, she dismissed the thought. How silly to suddenly go all soft and sentimental like a foolish schoolgirl. You would think she wanted something like that for herself.

Dispensing with stockings, she slid her feet into a pair of calfskin slippers that Fritzie had presented to her for her eighteenth birthday. The leather was soft and supple, molding itself to her feet like a second skin. Such a sinful luxury made her feel like a princess in a fairy tale. She knew it was foolish, but somehow the slippers gave her confidence and she knew she would be needing as much of that commodity tonight as she could muster.

Standing before the mirror, she drew her tortoiseshell comb through her wild mane of red hair, wincing as the teeth of the comb encountered snarls. As always, her hair stubbornly refused to submit to her ministrations and, with a sigh, she gave up and simply tied the mass of waves back with a length of blue velvet ribbon.

Straightening her shoulders, she took one last look at her reflection, then opened her door and headed down the hallway toward the Englishman's suite.

Footsteps echoed on the stairwell and, heart thumping, she pressed herself against the wall and waited until they continued down toward the lobby. Harry Walters and his wife had returned from the Carousel an hour earlier, and she heard their voices through the door as she passed. "Do stop fussing in front of the glass, Harry, and come to bed," said the sheriff's wife. "You're bald now and bald you'll stay."

What on earth would she do if they decided to pop out to venture downstairs for a glass of lemonade on the front porch? She knew it would be virtually impossible to explain her presence at the Englishman's bedroom door and still bring her plan to a successful conclusion. Moving swiftly, she grasped the latch, then turned it, slipping inside his bedroom and closing the door behind her as quietly as she was able.

There was no need to light the gas lamp on the night table, for she knew each and every room in the hotel like the back of her hand. She knew exactly where the bed was, pushed up against the wall, with its sheets and coverlet all neatly turned down and waiting. The wardrobe was against the far wall, the private bath through the door to her left. A door to the right led to a tiny sitting room, big enough only to hold an escritoire and chair.

But it was the bed that drew her. He had left his window open with the curtains drawn back, and it seemed to Molly as if all the starshine in the world was centered right there on that narrow bed.

There was no time to be wasted. She pulled down the shade and released the curtains, plunging the room into total darkness. She hesitated for a moment, debating the wisdom of removing her gown, but decided against it. Her courage would only go so far. Instead, she unbuttoned the first three buttons of the bodice, then slid between the covers to wait.

The pillow slip was cool against the heated skin of her cheek. She pulled the covers over her shoulders and burrowed more deeply into the bed, willing herself to become invisible. Her heart beat so loudly she wondered how it was that the sheriff and his wife in the next room didn't hear it pounding inside her chest. The bed smelled like the Englishman, like his skin, a subtle spice and sunshine smell that made her almost dizzy with sensation.

The notion that he had lain between these sheets, his hard and powerful body naked in this very spot, made her tremble even as the fever inside her burned hot. She was jumpy, that was all. The reason was clear as day. Her plan was so audacious, so dangerous, that an attack of nerves was perfectly understandable.

And that was all this was, a simple attack of nerves. This wasn't about the way he'd kissed her beneath the boardwalk or the strange sensations rushing through her body. This was about her inheritance. About the Pem. About her future and that of the people she loved.

Fate had dealt her an impossible hand, but she refused to fold her cards and admit defeat.

Not without a fight.

Chapter Seven

At last Molly heard the sound of the Englishman's footsteps coming down the hallway. There was no mistaking the heavy drumbeat of his boots against the wooden floor and Molly found herself matching her breathing to the rhythm of his step. She knew an instant of panic as the latch squeaked, and she considered making a run for the window. The thought of leaping three stories to the ground wasn't nearly as frightening as the notion of staying exactly where she was.

In his bed.

The door swung open and she dived deeper under the covers, making certain the blankets were over her head. She made herself lie as flat against the mattress as she possibly could and prayed she didn't have to sneeze.

"Damnation," she heard him mutter as he bumped into the foot of the bed. "Dark as bloody hell in here."

If he lighted the gas lamp, all would be lost before it began. She scarcely dared to breathe as he stumbled around in the dark. Moments later his heavy boots hit the wooden floor, first one and then the other. The sound of his trousers sliding down his leg made her shiver. He mumbled something under his breath and she felt faint when the bed dipped with his weight.

She caught the faint smell of whiskey when he yawned. He punched at the pillow, rolled over, and she found herself a heartbeat away from him, clinging to the side of the mattress to keep from sliding toward him.

Was he naked? The question danced before her in the darkness as she struggled to keep her distance. It didn't seem as if he'd had time to divest himself of all his clothing, but Molly knew he had a most unusual penchant for various stages of undress. Why, he might as well have been naked as the day he was born the other night as he walked up from the beach with his clothes plastered to his muscular frame and the moonlight—

Stop this! she warned herself. If she followed this line of thinking any further, she would surely lose her nerve and her last chance to save the Pem would go with it.

His breathing slowed, grew deeper. Molly listened in amazement as she realized he was asleep. Would nothing go as planned? She couldn't lie here all night, waiting for him to discover the visitor in his bed.

Scarcely breathing herself, she inched slowly, cautiously, toward the middle of the mattress until she thought she would swoon from his nearness. *You don't have to get any closer, Molly. Do it now!* All she had to do was scream at the top of her lungs in order to put the next part of her plan into action, but she felt as if she were suspended in a pool of warm and silky water, soft and weightless and infinitely yielding.

He murmured something low and moved toward her, his breath hot against her cheek. His words were unimportant. She understood his meaning in every fiber of her being. Her mind cleared of everything but pure sensation. His hard chest was pressed against hers, the heat of his body making her yearn toward him, moth to a flame.

None of her midnight conversations with Fritzie had come close to explaining this longing deep inside, in a place she hadn't known existed. Only once before had she felt anything close to this dark magic—under the boardwalk when he had taken her in his arms and kissed her.

He *was* naked! Gloriously. Miraculously. She wished the room were flooded with sunlight so she could take in the sheer beauty of his form.

He grew hard against her, an insistent and powerful force, and the shock of his heat and power ricocheted through her body. She'd heard ... suspected ... wondered ... now she understood. This was the secret women whispered about. The reason why men pursued and women deflected until both fell, willing victims to the ancient call of blood and destiny.

She felt as if she were caught in a maelstrom, being pulled down into the seductive, swirling darkness. She couldn't think or breathe or—

He reached out and cupped her breast, his fingers tendrils of fire against the skin bared by her open bodice, burning away the soft, sensual haze that had surrounded her.

Listen to your head, Molly, not your heart! He didn't even know who she was, whose body was pressed up against his. How many women had tumbled into bed with him and been soon forgotten?

This wasn't a dream. It wasn't romance. And if she didn't do something right now, this minute, all would be lost. She took a deep breath, then screamed for all she was worth.

Nicholas sprang from the bed like a shot. Naked and aroused, he stared at the wild-eyed apparition glaring at him from the other side of the bed.

"Stop that yowling!" he roared. "You'll wake the dead."

She wouldn't stop. She stood there, hands over her face, shrieking.

He rounded the foot of the bed, visions of an irate staff bursting in on them. Grabbing her by the arms, he shook her.

"What in the name of hell is going on here?" he asked as she mercifully stopped for breath. "What were you doing in my bed?"

The mention of the word *bed* triggered a new spate of caterwauling the like of which he'd never heard before.

"Let go of me!" she yelped like a scalded cat. "Don't you dare lay another hand on me!"

His arousal was by now only a memory and, painfully aware of his nakedness, he reached for the sheet, then wrapped it about his waist. He glanced around the room, as if to assure himself he was, indeed, in the right suite. He'd been so damned appreciative of the brandy offered at the Pavilion that it might have clouded his judgment. It looked like his room, but then that wasn't saying terribly much at the Pemberton Arms. He'd consumed a prodigious amount of brandy. Anything was possible.

The only way to be certain was to look inside the wardrobe. She was standing directly in front of it, a wailing bundle of woman. He stepped toward her. She stumbled backward. He reached out to steady her, but she mistook the motive of his action and fell back against the door of the wardrobe, causing it to topple sideways and land with a crash against the hardwood floor.

What happened next would always remain a blur. Molly, still wailing, sat on the floor in a heap, looking pathetic and wide-eyed amidst the clothing dislodged from the fallen wardrobe. The next instant—or so it seemed—all hell broke loose. The door to his room swung open, hinges squeaking in violent protest, then slammed into the wall. A bear of a man, clad in a nightshirt, burst in. His left hand was curled into a fist. His right hand was curled around a gun. Behind him a round-faced woman with a headful of rag curlers peered at the scene with almost as much amazement as Nicholas himself.

"What in the name of—?" The man approached him menacingly. "What did you do to that child?"

It occurred to Nicholas that the woman he'd discovered in his bed was many things; a child, however, was not among them. Wisely he kept that observation to himself and stood his ground.

"Ask her," he snapped. "This is my room, not hers. She's the interloper."

"Don't you think you can smart-mouth me just because you're English," said the man in a stunning non sequitur. "I want answers and I want 'em now."

They all turned to Molly, who was beside herself with the enormity of what she had set in motion. She tried to speak, but her sobs made it impossible. This wasn't the clear-cut, impersonal plan she had dreamed up. It was as messy as the fallen wardrobe, a great and awful tangle of emotion that she'd never once anticipated.

"Say something!" roared the Englishman, glaring down at her with more fury than she had ever seen in anything short of a hurricane. "Explain this whole damn thing!"

Mrs. Walters gasped as the sheriff trained his gun on Nicholas. "Maybe you foreigners curse in front of women, but we frown on that here in America, and I'll thank you to hold your tongue."

There's no way out of this now, Molly thought wildly as a crowd formed in the room. It was clear that the entire wretched situation was out of her hands. The whole thing was sordid and ugly—the direct opposite of the way she had felt in his arms. *But you'll get the Pem, Molly. And that's all that you want.*

A puzzled Fritzie bustled in, followed by a yawning Will. Stella and Arthur stood in the doorway, wringing their hands, while a score of overnight guests milled about, eager for a front row seat for the excitement. Fritzie clasped Molly to her capacious bosom and stroked her hair and rebuttoned the top of her bodice. *I did it for you and Stella and Will and everybody else, Fritzie. It's time I took care of you the way you've cared for me all these years.*

An intense wave of shame washed over her, and she buried her face against Fritzie's bosom to wait out the storm.

Nicholas fixed Molly with a murderous glance that would have felled a lesser enemy. As the minutes wore on, the effects of the prodigious amount of brandy he'd downed wore off, and he faced the situation at hand with almost stunning clarity.

From the gun-toting man in the nightshirt to the plump cook he'd talked with just the other day, they all were of similar mind: he was a rapacious monster, bent on stealing the virtue of an innocent young woman. Doubtless he would have taken that innocence had it been offered, but he'd never been a man to take what wasn't given willingly.

Truth was he didn't even remember being in bed with her.

Of course he didn't expect them to believe that. If he had heard the uproar emanating from his room, then walked in to see the lovely Molly cowering near the up-ended wardrobe, he would have reached the same conclusion that everyone else had apparently reached.

"Back home we have names for men like you," said a matron near the doorway.

"They're all alike," said another woman emphatically. "Take what they can with not even so much as a how-do-you-do."

"Her reputation's ruined," added a third in a voice of doom. She clucked sadly. "Only thing the poor girl's got and now it's gone."

At that Molly began a fresh bout of sobbing, which only seemed to make the man with the gun angrier with Nicholas.

"Aren't you overstating the case?" Nicholas ventured. He wanted to grab this situation by the horns without being gored in the process. "The young woman's honor is intact, I can assure you."

"Listen to him, talkin' so big," said Fritzie, anger flashing from her faded blue eyes. "Himself all high and mighty while my girl faces ruin—and to think I believed your uncle to be the heartless one...."

"Don't know too much about your country," said the man with the gun, "but 'round Cape Charlotte we don't take a woman's honor lightly."

Nicholas thought about the bejeweled and bedecked ladies who had made their vocation obvious as they strolled along the boardwalk last night. Honor certainly hadn't entered into any of their dealings, yet somehow the constabulary of Cape Charlotte had managed to look the other way. Mentioning that fact, however, seemed unwise given the circumstances.

"We need to talk about this," he said, directing his words to Molly, who had ceased wailing for the moment.

She looked as if she wanted to say something.

"Speak up," he ordered, more harshly than he might have. "If you have something to say, then say it."

The man with the gun stepped between them.

"Can't say I like your tone of voice, mister."

"Can't say I like much of anything about this situation," Nicholas shot back. "If you would all leave, perhaps Miss Hughes and I could make some sense of it."

Molly gasped at the thought. "No," she managed. "Please, no..." She'd never be able to keep up this charade if she were alone in the room with him. Her response to his nearness in the bed had been so fierce, so overwhelming, that she feared she would be putty in his hands if he decided to seduce the truth from her. And now that her conscience had added guilt to the equation...

There was safety in numbers and she needed as many people about her as possible.

"Shaking like a leaf she is," said Fritzie, smoothing Molly's hair with loving hands. She glowered at the Englishman, who looked as if he might be contemplating murder.

In the corner of the room Stella was weeping, her face buried in her gnarled hands. "Ruined," she keened. "Ruined and nothing to be done about it."

Mrs. Walters stepped forward. "There *is* one thing that can be done," she ventured. "Something that *should* be done."

Molly held her breath. She couldn't broach the topic of marriage. All along she had believed the words would tumble from her mouth like spring water over stones, but they were stuck deep in her throat and refused to be dislodged.

It was out of her hands now. Whatever happened from this point on, she would somehow learn to live with it.

Mrs. Walters straightened her shoulders and commanded center stage. "Marriage," she intoned with the ringing clarity of a traveling preacher. "Marriage would save her good name."

"Marriage?" The word tore from Nicholas's throat like buckshot through lace. "Absolutely out of the question."

The room fell deathly silent. All eyes turned toward him. The man in the nightshirt aimed his pistol at Nicholas's heart. You would think he had announced the end of Western civilization.

"Put down the gun," he said, bristling with anger. He wasn't about to be intimidated by a man in a candy-striped nightshirt.

The man said nothing, just stood there with that infernal pistol pointed at him. Nicholas had heard stories of men who got themselves into ridiculous predicaments like this, but he never thought he'd be one of them.

"You're in our country now," said the man in the nightshirt. "You'll obey our laws."

"Willingly," said Nicholas, "but I think we would all be better served if we had a representative of the law here to handle things."

"Pleased to oblige you, mister." The man in the nightshirt smiled wide and cocked the pistol. "The name's Harry Walters and I *am* the law."

The wedding of Nicholas St. George and Molly Hughes took place one hour later in the lobby of the Pemberton Arms Hotel. Fritzie and Will served as witnesses. Stella wanted to play the piano while Judge Lane performed the ceremony, but Nicholas said if he heard one note of music he would take an ax to the upright. Everyone in the room believed he would do exactly that. There was no music.

Judge Lane seemed a bit perplexed by the nocturnal nuptials, but Sheriff Walters assured him that, despite appearances to the contrary, both the bride and groom were eager for the ceremony to begin.

"But the young lady is crying," he pointed out, staring at Molly.

"She's weeping for joy," said Nicholas dryly. "Can we begin?"

"Take your places, please," said the judge, perching his spectacles upon his nose and peering at Molly and Nicholas.

Molly took up her position to the Englishman's right. She was still wearing the pale blue dress with the white collar and cuffs. Her wedding dress. Why was it her imagination had never taken her quite this far? She'd worked out the plan, figured out how to get to this point, knew exactly what she would do the moment the wedding was over and she was legally entitled to her inheritance.

But somehow she had never considered how it would feel to actually take those vows. She cast a glance at Nicholas, trying to ignore the way her heart did an odd flip-flop inside her chest.

Husband. A simple enough word. Who would have imagined how complicated it could become? Certainly Molly never had. In a matter of minutes, this man would be her husband in word, if not in fact. She would be Mrs. Nicholas St. George, a married woman free to claim her inheritance.

And to share his bed.

She was ashamed of the ripples of pleasure that forbidden thought set into motion, but her blood would not be denied. From the very first moment when she saw him standing in front of the Pem with the summer sunshine gilding his dark chestnut hair, she had been possessed of the need to be close to him. That kiss beneath the boardwalk had been her first . . . no matter what happened after tonight, the memory would be with her always.

She glanced about the room, trying to bring herself back to the matter at hand. Fritzie's face was set in lines of worry, and Molly couldn't help but notice the way she fingered her rosary in a manner more nervous than devout.

"Are we ready?" asked Judge Lane, looking from Molly to Nicholas.

Molly nodded, wishing she had a nosegay to hold to hide the trembling of her hands.

"Get on with it," said Nicholas, taking a long, shuddering gulp of whiskey.

Molly looked pointedly at the glass and, to his credit, he handed it to Sheriff Walters, who polished off the rest of the liquor himself in one loud swallow.

Judge Lane cleared his throat, then began. "We are gathered here together in the eyes of—"

"Spare us the pious pronouncements," snapped her bridegroom. "Just the essentials."

The judge shot Molly a questioning look. Her eyes brimmed with tears as she forced a smile. "Whatever he wishes," she managed.

Judge Lane's voice was carefully flat, almost as flat as the unadorned vows. Stripped of the flights of poetry, the promises were stark. If this had been a real wedding, Molly would have been struck speechless with the enormity of giving over her entire life to the man she loved. She belonged to him now, body and soul. She was his to do with as he wished. A married woman existed only in the shadow of her husband, and Molly knew the Englishman's shadow was long indeed.

She should be grateful that this was a marriage in name only, one that would be dissolved as soon as she had accomplished her goal.

But there was still something so beautiful about the words, something so hopeful and wonderful about the promises, that she found herself crying softly as the judge pronounced them man and wife, wishing her wedding had been born of love and not convenience.

Chapter Eight

The silence in the lobby of the Pem was thicker than the early-morning fog rolling up from the beach outside. The judge looked around the room but no one was brave enough to step forward to congratulate the newlyweds.

"Under normal circumstances, this is the moment when I suggest that the husband kiss his new wife, but all things considered . . ." His words trailed off mercifully.

Still no one moved or uttered a sound. Molly wondered if this was her punishment: doomed to stand there like a statue for the rest of her life with all of those sad-eyed gazes trained upon her. *Say something, please!* she pleaded silently. She didn't care who spoke first or what they said, only that this terrible stillness be ended.

Finally it was Nicholas who broke the awkward spell they had fallen under with a terse "Good night." Turning on his heel, he headed for the front door.

Molly stared after him. They had just been pronounced husband and wife and he was marching out the front door as if he'd stopped by for supper and a game of whist. She sprang to life, catching up with him on the top step of the porch. "Where are you going?"

"To get drunk." The expression on his face could best be described as deadly. "Given the situation, I can think of no companion I'd prefer to a bottle of brandy."

She squared her shoulders and faced down his anger with anger of her own. "I don't like being married any more than you do, Mr. St. George. Believe me when I say I look forward to the moment when we can rectify this situation."

He towered over her, blocking out the moon. "And when will that be?" If the whole episode weren't so preposterous, she would be scared out of her wits. "Is there a time schedule built into this code of morality of yours?"

"We can see a lawyer tomorrow about dissolving the marriage."

"A twenty-four-hour marriage? Your virginal sensibilities are easily placated." He arched a sardonic brow. "Why not forty-eight hours? Seventy-two? Or twelve, for that matter. I didn't realize morality was so easily regulated in America."

"Oh, do be quiet about morality. These people care for me. They worry about my future. You had no business manhandling me as you did, and they saw to it that my honor was upheld."

"And I suppose you had business in my bed?"

"That was a mistake." Her cheeks flamed with embarrassment and guilt. "I had moved you to another room and Fritzie gave my room to another guest and—" She was making a dreadful hash of things. Better to stop before it grew any worse.

"You can do better than that," he said with that foreign twist to his words that managed to make the simplest statement sound fraught with undercurrents. "If you had moved me to another room, why were my clothes still in the wardrobe?"

She fell back upon illogic to cover up her guilty tracks. "I hate you!" she declared in self-righteous passion. Leave it to a man to notice such an unimportant detail.

"As you wish," said her husband, starting down the porch steps. "It matters little in the scheme of things."

She laughed in his arrogant face. "You're a stranger here. Nobody cares about you. If I screamed right now, the whole town would be out here to defend me."

He remained unconvinced. "That works one time only, Molly. You're a married woman now. There is no longer the question of honor to defend."

Instinctively, she moved back a step and it was his turn to laugh.

"Don't worry," he said as he turned once again to leave. "You have nothing of interest to me, Mrs. St. George." He paraphrased her words of that afternoon beneath the boardwalk and she didn't miss his intent. "Not one damned thing."

Molly stormed back into the hotel like a summer squall. It shouldn't matter that he was angry or that he had lashed out at her. He was nothing to her, save a means to an end. Why, then, did his words sting so?

"Don't everybody look at me like that!" she snapped at the gathered throng. "He's going out to get drunk and I wish I could do the same thing."

The collective gasp was loud enough to be heard in Philadelphia.

"Now, now," said the sheriff's wife, patting Molly's shoulder as Molly hurried past the woman. "All new wives feel the same way."

Molly started to say she had no intention of being anybody's wife, much less the wife of that horrible Englishman, but a quelling look from Fritzie gave her pause. What wouldn't they think if they knew she had engineered the whole charade in order to lay claim to her inheritance?

"You'd be comin' with me," said Fritzie, bundling Molly up the staircase toward her room. "We need to talk."

Molly breathed a sigh of relief when they reached the third floor landing.

"A stroke of brilliance, Fritzie," she said, kissing the older woman on the cheek. "If I had to stand there and listen to that cow natter on about the wonders of marriage, I would go mad."

Fritzie said nothing. Opening the door to the rooms she shared with Will, Fritzie gave Molly a push through the doorway.

"Fritzie!" Molly's voice went high with surprise. "What on earth has gotten into you?"

Fritzie locked the door behind them and pocketed the key, an action that didn't bode well for Molly. "And I would be askin' you the same thing, missy."

Molly lowered her eyelids and tried to look contrite. "Mrs. Walters just made me mad, that's all. I was unnerved . . . upset. . . ."

"Gleeful," said Fritzie, pacing the room. "I saw that wicked gleam in your eye, and don't you think I didn't."

"I—I don't know what you're talking about."

"'Tis your doing, the whole thing."

Molly forced a weak laugh. "I think you need your sleep, Fritzie. You're beginning to imagine things."

"No need to imagine when the truth is right in front of me. You set a trap for him, didn't you, missy? The oldest trap in the world."

"I told you what happened. It was all a dreadful mistake."

"The only mistake is in lyin' to me."

Molly thrust out her chin in defiance. "And what if I did have a plan—would that be so terrible? I can't lose the Pem, Fritzie, I simply can't."

Fritzie sank onto the edge of the bed. "Your inheritance," she said as understanding dawned. "The fortune from your sainted mother."

"Yes," said Molly, dropping to her knees and grabbing Fritzie's hands in hers. "I had to, don't you see? This was my only chance to save the Pem."

Fritzie's eyes filled with tears. "And is the Pem so important that you would be bartering away your virtue?"

"My virtue!" Molly's laughter was genuine. "He's not interested in my virtue. All he's interested in is ending this marriage as quickly as possible."

"And what is it you want, missy?" Fritzie's expression softened, and Molly knew they were moving into dangerous territory.

"My money." She narrowed her eyes and glared at Fritzie. "What else is there?"

"And that is what I am askin' you. What more is goin' on here, my girl?"

"Nothing." She wished she sounded more convincing but that was the best she could do.

"I see the way you look at him. I may be old but I'm not so old that I'd be forgettin' the look in a woman's eye when she's met the man she wants."

"Good God in heaven!" Molly exploded, stumbling to her feet and backing away from Fritzie as if she had the plague. "Don't say things like that!" *Too close,* that treacherous inner voice whispered. *She's cutting too close to the bone.* "I needed a husband and he was the only prospect in sight."

Fritzie sighed and quickly listed five other bachelors of their acquaintance who would have fit the bill. "Surely you could have tricked any one of them more easily than you tricked the Englishman."

"That's not true," Molly protested weakly. "Besides, the Eng—" She stopped, her breath caught sharply in her throat. "Besides, the Englishman holds claim to the Pem. That's the only way for the whole thing to work out the way I have it planned. Is that such a terrible thing?" Molly whispered, meeting her eyes. "I love all of you. I want to protect you." She moved back near Fritzie and placed a hand on the older woman's shoulder. "I would do anything to secure the future for us."

"Except face the truth."

"That's not fair."

"The truth ofttimes seems that way."

"You sound like a Sunday school sermon, Fritzie. I thought you, of all people, would understand what I had to do."

"And I *do* understand, Molly. But I'd be thinkin' it's you who can't see her own face in the lookin' glass, for the fog that's surroundin' you."

"Now you're the one talking in riddles."

"Am I? Wantin' him isn't a crime, my girl, and I'd be bettin' my best Sunday hat that he is more than a little bit taken with your pretty face."

Molly's heart leaped, despite herself. "Really? What do you mean by that? Has he said something?"

"It's not somethin' I can be explainin' to you the way I'd explain a recipe for angel food cake. It's some-thin'—" She placed her hand over her heart. "It's just somethin' you know deep inside. I watch...I listen...when you've lived long enough to know the signs.''

"Well, no matter," said Molly with a sigh. "If he had any feelings at all for me, I'm certain this shotgun marriage will have destroyed them." She forced herself to put aside the memory of his kiss, the feel of his body against hers, the warmth of his skin. "It doesn't matter what he thinks of me," she declared, more to herself than to Fritzie. "I shall be at the bank when it opens and before the lunch hour the Pem will belong to me."

Fritzie looked at her closely. "He's your husband now. Your money belongs to him."

"What did you say?"

"You're a married woman now. What you have belongs to your husband."

"Not my inheritance."

"Everything you have is his, Molly."

"Then everything *he* has is *mine*."

It was Fritzie's turn to laugh. "I'm afraid it wouldn't be workin' that way, lovey. What a man has, a man keeps." She narrowed her eyes. "Includin' you, my girl, if he's so inclined."

"Why does any woman ever marry?" asked Molly, more alarmed than she was willing to acknowledge. "It sounds like indentured servitude."

"There are many reasons for marriage," said Fritzie with a small smile. "Many of the best have to do with love."

"Well, that's certainly not the case with us," said Molly briskly. "I have no doubt he wishes to end this marriage as swiftly as I do."

Men like Nicholas St. George had no use for matrimony. You had only to look at him to know that home and family meant little to him. Fritzie herself had told her how the Englishman had spent years in Australia, and Molly had overheard him chatting with Arthur about the sights he'd seen in Tahiti and other exotic places with names she couldn't pronounce, much less remember. The thought of him settling down with a wife and children was downright laughable.

Almost as laughable as the thought of Molly settling down with him.

She wanted to see the world, not be some man's unpaid servant. Once the Pem was as it should be, with everyone she loved all safe and secure, she intended to take the next train to New York City and from there—well, the world was her oyster and one day she would have the chance to seek out every hidden pearl.

That day, however, was somewhere in the future. Right now she had more important things on her mind: claiming her inheritance and ending her marriage.

In that very order.

Nicholas didn't know which he wanted to do first: get roaring drunk or kill somebody.

Preferably that damnable brat with the red hair and terrible temper. *His wife.* His jaws clenched until he marveled that his teeth didn't shatter beneath the pressure. Molly was a definite possibility. He wouldn't mind wrapping his hands around her slender throat and—

Why even think about it? He had no doubt they'd have him dancing on air from a rope before he had a chance to defend himself.

How the hell had he come to find himself staring at the business end of a pistol while that hellcat Molly Hughes cried her eyes out, gaining everyone's sympathy? A man comes back to what he believes to be his own hotel room, strips off his clothes and climbs into bed, and before he has a chance to lay his head against the pillow, his life is turned upside down.

He stormed up the boardwalk, hunting for some place where he could purchase a bottle of brandy but to no avail. All of Cape Charlotte's legitimate nightspots were locked tight as a miser's purse strings, and he wasn't in the mood for an interlude with one of the prostitutes at the houses tucked away not far from the boardwalk.

Not that he had anything against women who made their living off their finest assets. He'd learned about the art of lovemaking at the hands of a beautiful lady of the night and enjoyed many an evening with her sisters-in-spirit. But tonight he wasn't in the market for a tumble, no matter how appealing the partner.

It wasn't some perverse sense of fidelity to Molly that dissuaded him, he told himself. Tonight was his wedding night and he had to figure out a way to make certain this ridiculous situation didn't somehow turn into a marriage.

He could always bang on the front door of the first solicitor's office he found and demand help, but he doubted if even the most ambitious attorney welcomed business at six o'clock on a Sunday morning. He would wait, but he wouldn't be happy about it. As far as Nicholas was concerned, the sooner he started filing the papers necessary for the dissolution of this sham of a marriage, the happier he would be.

By eight o'clock, he had cooled down sufficiently to realize that Molly wasn't any happier about the situation than he was. There had been no mistaking the look of sheer terror on her pretty face as the puzzled judge asked her to repeat the marriage vows. She didn't want to be married to him any more than he wanted to be married to her—although why her obvious distaste should get under his skin was beyond his comprehension.

For a moment he had wondered if she was more like Jonathan Hughes than he'd imagined, but now he saw the situation for what it really was: a horrible mistake.

She was younger than he was and less sophisticated. Despite her orphaned status, she had grown up surrounded by love and that single fact had contributed more to the woman she was than any combination of family traits ever could. The last thing she needed in her life was a cynical husband who didn't believe in anything he couldn't control.

By nine he found a small café opposite the bank and quickly consumed a pot and a half of strong American coffee. Energy flowed through his veins. With a little luck this whole unsavory business could be taken care of by the noon hour and he could be on the afternoon train to New York as a free man.

"More cream, sir?" The dark-haired waitress popped up at his elbow.

He shook his head and withdrew money from his pocket. "If you'd take what I owe and a little more for yourself, I'd be grateful."

She withdrew two bills. "Nothing for me, sir. It was a pleasure."

He knew that look. The girl was ripe for a tumble.

"I get off at one o'clock," she said with a toss of her mane of hair. "It's a beautiful day, all sunny and—"

"I'm married."

Her eyes widened. "Married?"

He nodded. "Married."

"Good ones usually are," she said with an eloquent shrug. She reached over and withdrew a third bill from his hand, then tucked it into the bodice of her gown. "I'll take that extra one, after all."

He watched her as she walked away, her saucy hips swaying with the movement. The words, "I'm married," had tumbled from his lips. If Molly had been more worldly, he might not be in such a rush to put an end to this situation, but even though she deserved it, he couldn't do that to her. He didn't believe in love for himself, but he wasn't heartless enough to deny that it was possible for somebody else.

It occurred to him that, at least in the eyes of the law, she was now his responsibility. Strange that the notion didn't push him toward anger. Now that he had some distance from the chaos of a few hours ago, he could plainly see that she had been compromised in the eyes of her townspeople. Even though her friends had seen to it that her honor was spared by this hasty wedding, he knew that a failed marriage would leave a blot against her name.

There had to be some way he could compensate her for what she had lost in stature.

The Pem.

The idea appeared full-blown before him. He was glad he hadn't signed over the hotel to the realtor's care. He would give her the Pem. He would also sell off a portion of the grounds to the adjoining Abercrombie and give the money to Molly for use in renovating the hotel. She'd probably tell him exactly what he could do with his money, but he wouldn't take no for an answer.

He pushed back his chair and left the café, stepping outside into the fierce sunshine of a morning in July. Sunshine like this didn't exist in England. He'd forgotten the almost pagan pleasure to be found in basking in the sunshine, letting it burn away sorrow and hatred and the feeling that the best part of life would always be just beyond his reach.

The same as Molly Hughes.

At that moment, Molly was across the street with Mr. Carruthers, president of the Cape Charlotte Bank. It had taken a combination of tears, persistence and downright begging to persuade him to open the office for her, but James Carruthers had known Molly all her life and, like so many citizens of Cape Charlotte, he simply couldn't refuse her. He did, however, make certain he had his secretary, Alva Jennings, present.

"What do you mean I can't claim my inheritance?" she said, pacing the room like a caged tiger. "I'm married."

Mr. Carruthers, a jovial sort as a rule, leaned back in his chair with a pained look upon his face. "I know you're married, Molly." He waved the signed certificate in the air between them. "I have the proof. That isn't the issue."

"Then what is?" Molly leaned across his desk and looked him square in the eye. "I'm married. I want my inheritance."

"And you shall have it," he reassured her with the caution most men exercised around a volatile woman. "That is not in doubt. We simply need your husband's signature."

"But this has nothing to do with my husband, Mr. Carruthers. It's none of his business."

Carruthers arched a graying brow. "Your business *is* your husband's business, Molly. You're a married woman now."

"That's terribly unfair."

"Perhaps, but it is the way we do things."

Being married—even for a night—was much more complicated than she'd first thought. Nicholas St. George was almost a stranger to her. It simply wasn't fair that he had any say whatsoever in her affairs.

"If I bring him here, can I have my inheritance right away?"

"If not sooner," said Carruthers dryly. "You're certainly in a hurry, Molly."

So is the tax collector, she thought as she glanced toward the window just in time to see Nicholas exit the café across the street. He looked tired and beset, and she didn't have so much as an ounce of sympathy for him.

Mr. Carruthers followed her line of vision. "Isn't that the Englishman you married?"

Molly nodded, and before she could say a word Carruthers rapped loudly on the window, motioning for Nicholas to join them inside.

She continued to pace the room. One more complication keeping her from her money. She looked up as Nicholas appeared in the doorway. He wouldn't dare consider refusing to sign the document.

"Molly." He strode into the room, a puzzled expression on his face. "Is something wrong?"

Mr. Carruthers stepped into the breach and extended his hand toward her husband. "James Carruthers," he said with a nod. "I hear congratulations are in order."

Nicholas nodded back and shook the banker's hand. "What can I do for you?"

How dare he act as if she were invisible. Molly coughed loudly.

"I need your signature on a document," she offered before Carruthers could leap in and spill the beans.

The Englishman's eyes narrowed. "What kind of document?"

"A personal document," she said smoothly. She gestured toward the banker's desk. "It's over there."

"I make it a policy to read all documents before I sign them."

"And a wonderful policy that is," chimed in Mr. Carruthers. "I only wish more of our customers would—"

"You don't need to read it," said Molly, wishing the whole thing was over. "It has nothing to do with you." She took a deep breath, then continued, "My mother left me a few things when she died, to be collected upon my marriage."

Her husband arched a sardonic brow. "Has the ink on our marriage certificate had time to dry?"

"There's no reason for sarcasm."

He reached for the document on the desk and scanned it while Molly held her breath. *Sign it,* she urged silently, then breathed a sigh of relief when he did exactly that.

Mr. Carruthers, who had been watching the entire interlude with rapt attention, took the document and met Molly's eyes. "Everything seems to be in order now," he said, returning the marriage certificate to her. "If you'll wait a few minutes, I'll fetch your belongings."

Carruthers disappeared, leaving the newlyweds alone.

"Thank you," said Molly briskly. "I don't want to keep you if you have an appointment elsewhere."

"I don't mind," he said, sounding almost pleasant. "I was on my way to find a solicitor."

"Kenneth Bradley has an office near the King George. Fritzie engaged him after Will's accident and—"

"I don't foresee any problems dissolving this marriage," he said matter-of-factly. "Should be cut-and-dried."

There was a long, uncomfortable silence, then they both said, "I'd like to talk to you," at the same time, followed immediately by their first mutual laugh.

Molly's heartbeat accelerated. There was something different about him, something more open, more accessible. He looked terribly handsome when he smiled. His brilliant blue eyes crinkled at the outer corners in a most appealing way. How wonderful it would be to have a husband who looked at you that way...to have a real marriage, not one in name only...to share laughter with the man you loved.

"After you," said Nicholas, leaning against the windowsill. "You wanted to talk about something?"

"Y-yes," Molly began, wishing Carruthers would return with her bounty. "I would like to discuss a business proposition."

His smile widened, exposing his strong white teeth. There was something dangerous about that smile—and deliciously exciting. "I'm always willing to discuss business propositions."

She took a steadying breath, cleared her throat, then straightened her shoulders. "I should like to purchase the Pemberton Arms from you."

She had to hand it to him. His expression didn't change. "What do you intend to use for money?" he asked.

She ignored the question. "May I ask what price you're asking for it?"

He told her. It was far less than she had expected. Her spirits soared.

"The place is a shambles," he said bluntly. "I spoke to a realtor named Dunellen and he said the Pem needs major structural repairs if it is to survive." He quoted another figure, one less comforting than the last but still she didn't blink.

"I understand," she said.

"What are you up to, Molly? You cannot even manage to pay your taxes."

"That is none of your concern, Mr. St. George."

Again that crinkly-eyed smile. "Under the circumstances you might wish to call me Nicholas."

She nodded, struggling to seem cool and adult. "Nicholas." She liked saying his name. It had a strong, satisfying sound. "I can meet your price."

He was about to say something when there was a tap at the door and Mr. Carruthers marched in, lugging a shiny mahogany box of considerable dimensions.

"Now I'll need you to sign this receipt," he said in a voice that brooked no argument. Molly did so. "Have you the key to this?"

Molly nodded, withdrawing a ring of keys from the pocket of her skirt. "Yes." The box was even bigger than she'd remembered. She forgot everything but the answer to her prayers as Carruthers handed her the heavy box. Her palms grew damp with anticipation and she wished she'd brought a handkerchief with her.

Nicholas watched with undisguised curiosity. He was glad he'd made up his mind to return the hotel to her. She looked like a child on Christmas morning, so great was her excitement. A heavy feeling settled itself across his chest, the unfamiliar tugging of recognition and compassion. So this was how she'd planned to purchase the Pemberton Arms—with her paltry inheritance from her mother. He could just imagine what sorry treasures rested inside: an old watch with a broken crystal; a signet ring with the family seal; a yellowed packet of letters tied with a faded blue ribbon. Sentimental value carried little

weight in the real world. But then Molly was too young—
and too optimistic—to realize that.

Mr. Carruthers waited patiently while Molly fumbled
with the ring of keys, searching for the one that fit the
box. "What a surprise this wedding is," remarked Mrs.
Jennings, the man's secretary, as Molly tried key after
key. She met Nicholas's eyes and offered a broad wink.
"And here I thought she'd have to wait until she turned
twenty-one to collect her mama's inheritance."

Nicholas hadn't been paying a great deal of attention
to Mrs. Jennings and more than likely her words
wouldn't have registered on him any more than the dry
information in the legal documents had. However,
Molly's sudden intake of breath and the angry stain on
her high cheekbones brought him up short. "Would you
mind repeating that, Mrs. Jennings?"

"Oh, look!" Molly's voice sounded unnaturally
cheery. "I think I have it unlocked."

Nicholas said nothing but Mrs. Jennings rambled on.
"Who would have figured little Molly would get married so young? Whirlwind romance, I hear," she said,
lowering her voice as if she were telling them something
they didn't already know. "How exciting!"

Molly looked so miserably uncomfortable that Nicholas felt sorry for her. Certainly he didn't believe she'd
manipulated him into marriage. This shotgun wedding
had obviously been as big a surprise to her as it was to
him. Besides, it wasn't as if there was anything in that
wooden box that was worth getting married to inherit.

She lifted the lid.

Mrs. Jennings gasped.

And Nicholas finally realized the truth.

Chapter Nine

Jonathan Hughes would have been proud of his niece.

There was a king's ransom in jewels in that scarred wooden box Molly called her "inheritance." Diamond necklaces. Rings encrusted with blood-red rubies. Emeralds the size of pigeon eggs.

"Will you look at that," breathed Mrs. Jennings. "Who would have imagined...."

Bloody right, thought Nicholas, openly staring at the precious gems tumbling through his wife's eager hands. Not in a million years would he have imagined that that hellion with the threadbare dresses was an heiress.

The pleasure she was taking in running her fingers through emeralds and diamonds bordered on the obscene. He glanced at the small clock on the banker's desk. Quarter past nine. She must have been there when the front doors were unlocked, her traitorous heart pounding with anticipation.

Last night Sheriff Walters had pointed a gun at Nicholas's heart, but it had been sweet little orphaned Maureen Alice Hughes who had provided the ammunition.

"You didn't waste any time collecting your bounty, Mrs. St. George."

Molly jumped at his words, sending three big fat diamond rings slipping between her fingers and skittering across the room. It wasn't so much what he said—although the words themselves had a certain ominous sound—it was the dark inflection he gave them.

Mrs. Jennings, eyes wide with curiosity, retrieved the rings and replaced them in the box with obvious reluctance.

"Thank you," said Molly, doing her best to pretend the Englishman wasn't breathing down her neck. "If there's nothing more to do, I believe I'll be going home." She snapped shut the lid and locked it with a flourish. Bidding Mrs. Jennings good-morning, she swept from the bank with her inheritance clutched tight against her chest and Nicholas on her heels.

She had scarcely rounded the corner and started for the boardwalk when Nicholas grabbed her by the arms and propelled her toward an alley between two boarding-houses.

"How dare you!" she breathed. He pinned her to the wall by placing his hands alongside her head, effectively blocking her exit.

"You had it all planned, didn't you?" His voice was low, menacing. "The whole thing last night was orchestrated."

Still clutching the wooden box, she sagged against the brick wall, relieved the truth was out at last. "Only my part in it," she said, wishing she didn't sound quite so intimidated by his size and proximity. "No one else knew anything about it."

"You inspire great loyalty, don't you, Mrs. St. George?"

"Yes, I do," she snapped. "My friends love me as much as I love them." *Take that, Mr. Know-It-All.*

"You'll be disappointed to learn that your beloved husband isn't equally enthralled with you."

"I never expected you to be." The look on his face made her almost sorry she'd had to deceive him that way. "Believe me, this was in your best interests, as well."

He laughed in her face.

"Really," she said, pressing her point. "You wanted to sell the Pem, didn't you?" He nodded, although a trifle warily, as she triumphantly raised the wooden box in the narrow space between them. "Now I can buy it!"

"The price has gone up considerably."

"Fine," she said, wondering exactly how many diamonds this was going to cost her. "Whatever you want."

"There are certain...conditions," he continued, fixing his dark glance upon her.

Her heart thundered in her ears. "Such as?"

"You can keep the Pem."

She felt as if the air had been sucked from her lungs. "What?"

"I said, you can keep the Pem."

"For no money?"

"For no money." He nodded toward the wooden box clutched against her chest. "Use that to bring it back from the dead."

She didn't know whether to laugh or cry, so great was her relief. "I can't believe you would do something so wonderful," she breathed, voice tremulous with emotion. "You have no idea how much this means to me...to everyone!" Her eyes filled with grateful tears. "After what I—after the misunderstanding last night...the wedding." She paused, struggling with feelings of gratitude mingled with remorse for thinking ill of him. "I feel as if you deserve something for the trouble I've—"

Something about the look in his eyes stopped her cold.

"As I said," he continued, "there's a condition to my generosity."

"Anything," said Molly, trying to overlook the sense of unease washing over her. "Whatever you want."

"You, Molly," he said. "I want you."

Her knees went weak and she feared she would crumble to the ground. So that kiss shared beneath the boardwalk had been born of desire, not anger. Who would have imagined?

"Nicholas," she began, a fluttering of delight beginning in the pit of her belly. "I didn't know."

"You can have the Pemberton," he went on as if she hadn't said a word, "and you can keep your blasted money to fix it up. You, however, belong to me."

Delight shifted abruptly toward annoyance. "Belong? You make it sound as if I'm a stick of furniture."

"You're my wife," he said, dark blue eyes flashing dangerously. "You'll do as I say."

"I thought we agreed that we both wanted this marriage to be dissolved." Was he deliberately trying to confuse the issue or was she missing some important point? One moment she'd believed he was attracted to her; now he made it sound as if she were nothing more than a possession.

"I did want the marriage annulled," said the stranger who was her husband. "At least, I did until I found out what you were about."

He moved closer, pinning her more tightly against the brick wall, so close that she could catch the smell of his skin and feel the heat from his body.

"I don't know what you're talking about," she said, more bluster than bravery. "You're not making a bit of sense."

"You're a clever girl," he went on, his teeth gleaming white in the shadows. "Just not clever enough. You played a dangerous game. Now you're going to pay for it."

Her eyes widened. "Are you telling me you wish us to remain married?"

"I need a wife," he said coldly, the way another man might say he needed a new horse. "I have avoided wedlock until now, but you managed to show me the error of my ways. I'm not the most civilized of men. I need a woman who knows how to handle servants and run a large house the way it should be run. You, it seems, possess those skills in abundance."

Her voice was a whisper. "In England?"

He nodded. "Merriton Hall, on the outskirts of London."

"I've never been past Philadelphia."

"A situation that is soon to change."

"I don't want to go. My home is here."

"Your home is with your husband."

"But you're a stranger."

"You should have thought of that yesterday when you tricked me into marriage."

"Only a monster would ask such a thing."

His laugh held a broad wash of bitterness, and that bitterness reached Molly in a way his cold anger had not. Again she felt shame at her actions. She had tried so hard to convince herself that the end truly justified the means, but the look in his eyes told her otherwise.

"A monster would keep the Pem and your damn inheritance, then throw you and yours onto the street without a cent to your names." He pressed her against the brick wall with the weight of his body. Jagged edges of mortar dug into her flesh through the thin cotton dress, but she knew better than to protest. "And a monster would take more than your money, Molly... he would take the one thing a man expects from his bride."

Damn her traitorous body. The implication in his words made her burn despite the circumstances.

"I'm sorry," she said, meaning it. "I was desperate. Marriage was the only way I could think of to save the Pem."

"And you got what you wanted from it." He leaned forward, those dark blue eyes intent upon her, as if he knew everything she thought, everything she felt. "Now it's my turn."

Abruptly he stepped back, dropping his hands to his sides. Nothing held her there in the alleyway except the force of his presence.

"Come with me to England and the Pem is yours to do with as you wish."

She met his eyes, allowing her guard to drop. "And the alternative?"

"You lose everything you hold dear." The Pem. Her inheritance. Her self-respect.

"It seems I haven't much of a choice."

"Spoken like a loving wife."

She thought of her father and of the way he had described his marriage to her mother, of the love and devotion and joy he had found with her. She'd always believed she would know that joy herself, married to a man who loved her and cared about her, a man she could respect and adore all the days of her life.

She looked at Nicholas. *Her husband.* There had been a wedding last night, but never in her wildest dreams had she imagined there would be a marriage.

But there was no turning back from the path she had set for herself. She had always wanted to see the world;

who would have imagined it would happen quite this way? For weeks she had had the feeling that she was on the verge of adulthood, that the carefree girlhood she had enjoyed was fading fast into memory. Last night she had said goodbye to Molly Hughes.

Now it was time to face life as Mrs. Nicholas St. George.

The next few hours passed in a frenzied blur of activity. There were so many details to attend to that Molly found it easy to stay one jump ahead of the emotions that threatened to overwhelm her. This time she took Mr. Carruthers away from Sunday brunch with his family, and together they returned to his office where she spoke to him about selling off some of the jewels in order to begin renovations on the Pem. Carruthers was an honest man and a trusted banker and Molly knew he would do his utmost to help steer the Pem back into safer waters.

"What about this necklace?" he asked, fingering a beautiful choker of filigreed gold that boasted a breathtaking diamond in the center. "This piece alone could turn the Pem into the showplace of Cape Charlotte."

Molly shook her head. "That was my great-grandmother's," she said, slipping the necklace back into its velvet pouch. "She gave it to my grandmother and my grandmother gave it to my mother and one day I hope to pass it on to my own daughter."

Carruthers smiled at her. "I hope that new husband of yours knows what a treasure he's got."

Molly swallowed past a sudden lump in her throat. "I'm sure he knows exactly what he's got, Mr. Carruthers."

Telling Fritzie proved to be the hardest thing of all.

"I knew this would end badly," said Fritzie, shaking

her head as Molly laid out her plans for the future of the Pemberton Arms. "Play with fire and you're bound to be burned."

"It isn't as bad as all that," said Molly, checking the facts and figures she'd scribbled on a lined yellow pad. "It's a small price to pay for our future."

Fritzie rose from her rocking chair and walked to where Molly sat, bent over the kitchen table. "Marriages shouldn't be born of tricks."

"I know," said Molly softly. "But it's too late for that."

Fritzie stroked Molly's hair with her work-worn hands. Her voice deepened with sorrow. "'Tis our fault, all of it. Placin' our troubles on your young shoulders as if there was somethin' you could do to change things."

Molly looked up and clasped Fritzie's hands in hers. "But there *was* something I could do to change things. I married Nicholas. I collected my inheritance." She smiled through sentimental tears. "You'll never want for anything again, Fritzie."

"A full larder and a cracklin' fireplace are no substitute for your sweet face at the breakfast table, missy."

"I won't be gone forever," she said, trying to sound more certain than she felt. "Sooner or later his anger will cool and we'll come to a parting of the ways." She forced a laugh. "For all I know he'll have changed his mind before the train leaves the station."

"Is that regret I'm hearin' in your voice?" Fritzie placed a finger beneath Molly's chin and tilted her face up. "Let me see your eyes, girl."

"Fritzie, please. I—"

"You want to go with him, don't you?"

"Are you mad?" Molly's voice cracked on the last word. "I'd rather walk barefoot on hot sand."

"You can't be foolin' me. I've known you since you were in diapers."

"If he disappeared tomorrow, I'd never give him a second thought."

"This is Fritzie you'd be speakin' to, not some old fool. Do you love him?"

"Of course not."

"But you want him, don't you?"

Molly glanced away. "I—I don't know what you mean."

"I wouldn't be believin' that, missy, not the way you look at him."

"So what if I think he's handsome? That doesn't mean I have...feelings for him."

"Many's a love story begun in anger," said Fritzie with a sage nod of her graying head, "'though you may be too young to know that love and hate are two sides of the same penny coin."

"He kissed me," she whispered, a fierce heat suffusing her body. "Oh, Fritzie, I never knew...."

"So that's the way it is with you, then." Fritzie enveloped her in a motherly hug. "Did the world seem to disappear when he held you?"

"Oh, yes!" She closed her eyes, remembering. "I felt hot and cold and dizzy, all at the same time."

"Same as when my Will kissed me under the apple tree when I was seventeen."

"But that's not love, is it, Fritzie?"

"No, it's not love," said Fritzie carefully, "but it's part of it. Some might say the very best part."

"There has to be more to love than...kissing," Molly continued. She and Nicholas had kissed and certainly they were far from being in love.

"Men and women aren't meant to live together," said Fritzie with a shake of her head. "Two different animals, plain and simple. It's the kissin' that makes the impossible possible."

Molly started to laugh despite herself. "I never heard such a silly thing in my life."

"It might be silly, but it's true. Lord knows, my Will and I have had our troubles through the years. Life hasn't always been kind to either one of us, but when we climb into our bed each night and hold each other, somehow none of the rest matters."

Molly remembered the sweet sounds of laughter floating from Will and Fritzie's room the other night, the glances they exchanged when they thought no one was looking, the way they had weathered the storms of life when another couple might have crashed against the rocks.

"But isn't that just the physical side of marriage?" Molly asked, trying to unravel the puzzle. "There must be more to it than that."

"And there is," said Fritzie, "but it only comes with the knowin' of each other."

"Or maybe it won't come at all," said Molly bleakly.

"Marriage is a gamble same as a game of cards. Many a generous suitor has turned out to be a miserly husband with empty pockets." Fritzie placed a kiss on Molly's forehead. "If you follow your heart, you'll find a way to make this work."

"What would you do, Fritzie?" she implored the woman who had been a mother to her for as long as she could remember. "He says he needs a wife to take care of his house, like a fancy housemaid. Tell me what to do."

Fritzie's eyes welled with tears. "The time for that is over, missy," she said, her voice thick with emotion.

"You're a married woman now and must make your own decisions."

In the end it was Molly's sense of honor that decided the issue. Honor might have seemed a strange notion, considering the circumstances, but Molly had set the wheels of fate into motion and was prepared to take the consequences of her actions. She had considered throwing herself upon the Englishman's mercy and begging for a change of heart, but begging had never been her style. Of course, neither had deception been her style before last night.

She'd also considered packing her bags and running away to Baltimore or Philadelphia until he gave up and went back to England without her, but that was the coward's way out. Molly might have been many things, but a coward wasn't among them, and so when the moment came to depart, she was resolute in her determination to make the best of it.

"The coach is here," said Nicholas as Old Jake waited in front of the Pem to take them to the railway station for the train up to New York City.

"I'll be with you in a moment."

He nodded then left her alone in the lobby with Fritzie. She had already bade a tearful goodbye to the others, promising them that she would write as often as she could and return to Cape Charlotte as soon as possible.

"'Tis a grand adventure you're embarkin' on, missy," said Fritzie as she smoothed back Molly's unruly hair.

"I can't believe that before the night is over I'll be in New York City."

"'Tisn't the adventure I mean, my girl."

A delicious shiver ran up Molly's spine at Fritzie's words. "This is a marriage in name only," she reminded the older woman. If there had, indeed, been a spark between them, tricking him into a marriage for her convenience had doused the flames quite effectively.

"Follow your heart," Fritzie said again, dabbing at her red-rimmed eyes with a cambric handkerchief. "If you do that, it will all work out for the best."

Molly swallowed hard. "Mr. Carruthers promised me he'll keep his eye on the renovations, but—"

"Don't you worry yourself about a thing. Your Fritzie will make sure all goes as it should."

"The coach," called Nicholas. "We'll miss our train if you don't hurry."

"I love you," Molly said to Fritzie, hugging her one last time. "I promise you I won't stay away any longer than I have to."

Nicholas appeared in the doorway, his muscular frame backlit by the sun. The first time she'd seen him, Molly had been certain he was the most glorious man in the world. She'd never imagined that he would be the first man to kiss her—or that she would wear his wedding ring before the week was out.

"I'll come back," she said, over the wild pounding of her heart. "I promise you that before long everything will be the way it used to be."

Fritzie's eyes misted over with tears. "Go to your husband," she said, giving Molly a push toward the door. "You belong with him now."

Chapter Ten

His wife looked terribly young and eager as they
changed trains in Philadelphia en route to New York. Her
green eyes were wide with excitement and he had the
feeling she would have liked to somehow memorize each
and every detail of the trip north. Her enthusiasm
amazed him. Most women he knew feigned indifference
to their surroundings; his wife gloried in them. It was
only a train trip, after all, and a not terribly exciting one
at that, but Molly acted as if she were on the Grand Tour
of Europe.

From the very first, he had noticed the passion she
brought to all of her endeavors, from saving the Pemberton Arms to the kiss they had shared beneath the
boardwalk.

If life could be envisioned as a garden, then, mindless
of the thorns, Molly was determined to pluck the biggest
roses for her own bouquet.

He knew this had to be difficult for her. She was young
and far from worldly. Leaving the people she called
family had to be a wrenching experience. But this was no
shrinking violet, his wife. He'd watched her as she walked
down the porch steps of the Pemberton Arms with her

head held high and he'd felt that same grudging admiration for her spirit.

Admiration, however, was the last thing he wanted to feel. She was cunning and manipulative both, tricking him into a wedding to serve her own purposes—a true relative of Jonathan Hughes.

Still, there was something so compelling about his young wife that he found himself drawn to her warmth despite his better judgment.

It was four o'clock in the afternoon when they boarded the train that would take them the rest of the way to New York. Nicholas led her to the club car where they would enjoy the journey. This train was much more luxurious than the rattletrap that had taken them from Cape Charlotte and, as such, it was also more crowded.

"Oh, will you look at these cushy seats?" Molly breathed, to everyone's amusement but his own. "We haven't seats as comfortable as these back home."

The other passengers, society types all, chuckled indulgently while Nicholas clenched his teeth. He wasn't oblivious to the questioning glances cast their way by many of the men and women. He and Molly made a ridiculously mismatched couple with her threadbare gown and scuffed shoes and his shiny gold cuff links and polished boots. The onlookers must be wondering how it was that he allowed his wife to travel in rags while he wore only the finest. First thing tomorrow morning he would see that she was gowned as befit her position as his wife.

The train rumbled away from the platform, and before Philadelphia disappeared behind them, Molly was on her feet and strolling through the club car, inspecting the velvet seat cushions and gilt armrests with unabashed curiosity. She also managed to learn the name of every passenger in the car. It wouldn't have occurred to Nicholas to care. He wondered how it was she had managed to retain that almost childlike interest in the world at large. He remembered himself at eighteen, angry and bitter. Alone in the world with nothing but his wits to save him.

And yet she was alone, too, he thought as she accepted a cup of tea from a steward. She'd never known her mother, and her father had been gone nearly ten years. He detected no bitterness about her situation, no anger that her Uncle Jonathan hadn't seen fit to so much as write her a letter. She'd been poor as a church mouse, without position or hope for the future, and yet she had made the best of her life, gathering about her the people she loved, and wringing happiness from every second.

He watched intently as she chatted with a young doctor who was on his way to set up a practice in Buffalo. They'd met him on the platform in Philadelphia and Molly and he had instantly struck up a friendship. Nicholas couldn't fathom what it was about the plainspoken, bespectacled man that charmed his wife, but she treated him as if he were her dearest chum. The physician was pointing to some sight outside the window while Molly's delighted laugh rattled inside Nicholas's head, making it hard for him to remember why he shouldn't care.

The ever-changing landscape fascinated Molly as the train crossed the farmlands of New Jersey and headed toward New York. Tired as she was, she found it impossible to sleep, even though her husband had long since drifted off.

It was dusk when they arrived in New York. Nicholas had shifted position a number of times, only to come to rest with his head mere inches from her shoulder. His eyes were closed and his breathing was even and she couldn't help but note that he had loosened his tie and undone the top buttons of his shirt.

The train slowed as it entered the station a few minutes later, and Nicholas roused himself. A slight frown puckered between his dark brows and a dimple she'd never before noticed appeared, then disappeared, in his left cheek. A strange feeling of fullness settled in her chest in the vicinity of her heart, and she had to remind herself to breathe, so deep was her concentration.

He was slightly rumpled from his nap. A lock of thick chestnut hair tumbled across his forehead and she longed to brush it back with her fingers. The shadow of a beard stubbled his angular cheekbones and firm jaw. Somehow it only managed to enhance his masculine good looks. He looked at her, his gaze open and unguarded, and her hopes soared, only to be dashed as he realized where he was and what he was about and the wall of reserve snapped quickly into place.

"Gather up your things," he ordered as he rose to his feet and rebuttoned his jacket. "A coach will be meeting us to take us to the hotel."

She nodded and retrieved her drawstring bag from the floor near her feet. Their valises had been stowed by a smiling porter when they boarded the train, and she knew they would somehow magically reappear at exactly the right moment. That was how it was for rich people, she mused, as the fancy ladies and gentlemen smoothed their rumpled garments and prepared to leave the train. It didn't matter how heavy the valises were or how many of them you had; when you were rich there was always someone else to carry them.

Molly smiled to herself as they made their way toward the door of the club car. At least she wouldn't be straining the back of some underpaid, overworked porter. Everything she owned fit in her scuffed canvas valise and with room to spare. She couldn't help being reminded of Arthur and all the friends she had left behind.

"We'll dine at the hotel," said Nicholas as they climbed into the coach that had, indeed, been waiting for them in front of the station. He cast her a sidelong glance but she couldn't read his expression in the gathering darkness. "It's been a long day. We should retire early."

That simple statement caused her to forget all about the wonders of Manhattan as the driver urged his twin bays through a maze of people and omnibuses and hansom cabs. She hadn't once considered what would happen when they were finally alone. They were legally married, after all, and she hadn't a coterie of friends to rush in and defend her honor if he decided to claim his marital rights. The problem tormented her, for in truth she wasn't certain how vigorously she would defend her own honor. Fritzie's words of earlier that day had found their mark. Molly had never been good at fooling herself, any more than she'd been good at fooling Fritzie, and the plain truth was the memory of her husband's kisses beneath the boardwalk still lingered.

As did her longing for him. She wasn't happy with that revelation or proud of her weakness, but that was the truth of the matter. "Know thy enemy," the old saying went. Molly had never imagined her enemy would be her own traitorous heart.

She was silent until the coach came to a halt in front of a six-story, white marble building that seemed to take up an entire block. Tall columns guarded the portico and Molly was reminded of a picture she'd once seen of a palace fit for a king.

"Fifth Avenue Hotel," said the driver of the coach. "Finest place in town."

"We're staying here?" she asked, turning to Nicholas.

"Yes," he said, a small smile playing at the corners of his mouth. "I thought you might pick up a few ideas for the Pemberton Arms."

It didn't occur to Molly that he might be sniping at her. She was too awestruck to do anything but gape at the enormous structure. "This is magnificent," she said as he helped her from the coach. "I've never seen anything so beautiful in my life." Shyly she touched his forearm. "Thank you for bringing me here. I'm certain to come away with a thousand ideas for the Pem."

Her words were so simple and direct that Nicholas instantly regretted his comment. She had the most alarming ability to bring him up short. Each time he believed he understood what she was about, she managed to say or do something that touched his heart, despite his resolve to distance himself from her. He hadn't thought much about the hotel when he'd stayed there last week. Looking at it through Molly's eyes, he saw how magnificent a structure it truly was.

He offered his arm and, after a moment, she took it and together they walked into the lobby of the hotel. She gasped softly as they stepped onto a runner more beautiful than the Pemberton's finest carpet.

Not ten feet into the expanse of marble and gilt she stopped abruptly, her cheeks as red as the drapes that covered the windows. Her eyes strayed toward a knot of well-dressed men standing near the entrance.

"Is something wrong?"

"Not a thing," she said, head held high.

For the first time he noticed the muffled laughter from the swells. It took gargantuan effort on his part to keep from striding over to the buffoons and helping them to part company with their teeth. That would only serve to embarrass her more.

"Ignore them," he said briskly. "Tomorrow you'll purchase a new wardrobe."

"My inheritance... I turned it back over to Mr. Carruthers. I can't afford—"

"You're my wife," he said, ignoring the primal sense of possession inherent in that word. He would feel as much for a horse or a new coach. "Your wardrobe is my responsibility, not yours."

She said nothing. He had the feeling she wanted to protest, but there was little to be gained by airing their disagreement in the lobby. She wasn't greedy, he would grant her that. Most of the women of his acquaintance would have leaped at the chance to be married to a man with a title and an estate. While not in league with the very rich, Nicholas certainly had more money than Molly had ever dreamed of.

Yet she hadn't tricked him into marriage for his money; she had tricked him into marriage for her own.

An interesting difference, that. He wondered why he hadn't realized it before.

The porter deposited their bags in the center hall of the suite and, after pocketing a coin from Nicholas, bade them good-night. There was something terribly final about the sound of that heavy mahogany door swinging shut, as if Molly's last chance for escape had vanished with the porter. Perhaps if she hadn't been so overwhelmed with wonder at the miracle of riding up to the fifth floor in an actual Otis elevator paneled in cherry wood and mahogany and edged with shiny brass, she might have thought to ask for a room of her own. But it seemed that everywhere she turned in that establishment, there was something even more wondrous to steal her breath away.

She stood near the valises, shifting her weight from her right foot to her left. Nicholas had disappeared somewhere in the cavernous suite. How shabby her canvas bag looked resting next to her husband's elegant leather suitcases, rather like the way she looked at his side. It wasn't as if she cared a fig about leather valises or fancy clothes; it was simply that she hated the way people had looked at her, as if she were somehow inferior to them. It reminded her of how the Pavilion's maître d' had made her feel the first afternoon she confronted Nicholas about the fate of the Pem.

"You're exhausted." Nicholas appeared at her side.

"I'm fine," she managed, aware that the room was spinning slightly even as she spoke.

He swept her up into his arms despite her feeble protests. "You need to sleep," he said, marching toward a room to the right of the sitting room.

"Not tired," she murmured, feeling reality slipping away from her.

His chuckle rumbled against her ear and she giggled softly.

Gently he placed her on a mattress softer than a down-filled comforter, and before she could protest he had her shoes off and the waistband of her dress unbuttoned. His fingers brushed against her skin and she realized that if he wanted to undress her totally, there would be no way on earth she could stop him. Somewhere in the part of her brain that hadn't succumbed to fatigue, she knew this was dangerous, but the part of her brain that was pure sensation urged her to let go.

"Dinner," she said, trying to sit up while she fought in vain to keep her eyes from closing.

"Sleep," he said. She imagined he pressed a kiss against her forehead before he stood. "Dinner will wait."

Dinner was the last thing on Nicholas's mind as he stood over the bed and watched Molly sleep. She slept the way she did everything else, giving herself up to the arms of Morpheus with utter abandon. She embraced the pillow to her ripe breasts, burying her face deep in its soft contours. Her lush cascade of auburn hair tumbled across her face and shoulders, a vibrant counterpoint to the eggshell satin of the coverlet.

Sighing, she curved her body around the pillow, her skirts rising over her ankles, exposing the firm muscles of her calves. She was delicately made, all fragile bones and gentle curves, but there was a strength about her that was visible even as she slept. She seemed peaceful and content, if that were possible given the situation, and he marveled again at the combination of family heritage and experience that had fashioned this unusual woman he now claimed as his wife.

Obviously she'd never known fear or danger in her young life, and it made him wonder—of the two of them, who had truly known privilege?

Time passed, and when it became clear that she would sleep through the night, he returned to the sitting room. He poured himself a stiff whiskey, then lifted the house telephone to order dinner sent up to the suite. He had seen only a handful of telephones in his life and actually used the instruments but twice. There was something off-putting about holding a machine to your ear and yelling into it. But Americans seemed quite enamored of the contraption, and he had to admit the telephone had the potential to make communication between people amazingly easy.

"Your finest steak," he bellowed into the strange mouthpiece. "A green salad. A bottle of wine. Chocolate cake." He paused. "And a bouquet of red roses."

He looked about the sitting room, his gaze landing briefly on the chairs, the escritoire in the corner, the many-paned windows with the elaborate draperies. He tried to imagine how it would look to Molly, through eyes fresh and eager, but he couldn't. To him it was only a room. Nothing more.

He carried his tumbler of whiskey over to the window and looked out at the young and vibrant city spread beneath him. Now there was something he could appreciate. There was none of the staid darkness of London, the rigid adherence to convention and tradition. Who you were and where you came from carried little weight in this city. Here a man wasn't burdened with endless generations of expectations to live up to—or reputations to live down. He could feel the energy of the city as if it were a living, breathing entity. He hadn't felt that way since returning to England.

Except in Cape Charlotte.

What a laughable thought that Cape Charlotte had anything in common with this bustling metropolis, but there it was. Maybe it was some characteristic of the American spirit in general that he was reacting to, some boundless source of energy and high spirits that reached him in a way few things in his life ever had.

But no matter. He turned from the window and downed the rest of his whiskey. His destiny awaited him in England, at Merriton Hall among the remnants of his father's shattered dreams and his mother's treachery and a boy's deep and boundless loneliness.

Until he vanquished those memories, there could be no future for him at all.

"Ma'am?"

A woman's voice, soft and vaguely Irish-sounding, floated over Molly.

"Ma'am, I've drawn your bath."

Molly's eyes fluttered open and she sat up in bed, heart pounding wildly. For a moment she couldn't remember where she was or how she had gotten there, and it took a full second or two for the whole sequence of events of the past few days to come back to her.

"I—I must have fallen asleep," she said, smoothing her hair and tugging her skirts back down about her ankles. "What time is it?"

The maid crossed the room and pulled open the draperies. Bright sunshine spilled across the bed and Molly shielded her eyes against its glare.

"Eight o'clock in the morning," said the maid cheerfully. "Your husband has requested your presence at breakfast in forty-five minutes."

Quickly Molly cast a glance at the other side of the bed. It was instantly obvious that Nicholas had spent the night elsewhere. She swung her legs from the bed and stood.

"Thank you for drawing the bath," she said with a pleasant smile.

"You're welcome."

The maid stood there, still smiling at Molly.

Molly edged toward the private bath. "I shall be taking my bath now."

The maid edged toward the private bath as well. "Let me help you with your clothes."

"That's not necessary."

"It's my job, ma'am."

Molly hesitated. Less than forty-eight hours ago it had been her job, as well, to see to the comfort of guests. "I am used to taking care of my own needs," she said honestly. "I'm afraid I'm not accustomed to luxury such as this."

The maid's smile widened and she urged Molly toward the sanctuary of the bath. "Then just you leave it all up to Bridget, ma'am. You'd be surprised how quick a girl can become accustomed to the best!"

Bridget was right.

The deep marble bathtub was the most beautiful thing Molly had ever seen. She would have stayed in the hot, fragrant water all day if she'd been able, but Bridget tapped on the door to remind her that Mr. St. George was expecting his wife's presence at breakfast. The maid wrapped Molly's dripping body in warm Turkish towels, then sat her down on a boudoir chair while she arranged her hair in an elegant upsweep. Her mint-green dress with the maize-colored cummerbund appeared, miraculously mended and meticulously ironed. At least she would look presentable, if not stylish.

All in all, the young woman who looked back at Molly from the cheval glass in her bedroom was a far cry from the bedraggled creature of the night before.

Head high, she waltzed into the drawing room to find a table set with china and silver and crystal goblets filled with orange juice. In the center of the table was a stunning arrangement of the most beautiful roses she had ever seen. What a marvelous hotel, to supply a bouquet of roses as an accompaniment to eggs and toast!

Nicholas was scanning the newspaper when she entered. He looked up at the sound of her skirts rustling against her legs and quickly rose to his feet.

"Molly." He couldn't hide his surprise. "You—you look rested."

"You don't," she said, then instantly regretted her impulsive tongue. She bent down to sniff at the roses and regain her composure. "I mean, you look tired. I'm sorry I was so thoughtless as to take the only bedroom."

"You didn't," he said, pulling out her chair for her. "This is a two-bedroom suite."

"Oh." She busied herself with placing the snowy-white linen napkin on her lap. Obviously he hadn't entertained the notion of seduction or he would never have asked for a second bedroom. She wasn't certain if she was relieved or disappointed. Reaching for her goblet of orange juice, she met his eyes. "Didn't you sleep well?"

"Not particularly."

There was little she could think of to say in response. "Do you often have trouble sleeping?"

"Yes."

Again the conversation lagged. She tried again. "I hope I didn't keep you from dinner last night."

"I was served here in the drawing room."

"How nice." She sipped her juice. It was sweet and cold and put her immediately in a more cheerful frame of mind. She had wondered if he might have gone out to find more pleasant female company elsewhere. The fact that he hadn't added to her sense of well-being. If only he would talk to her! There were so many things she wanted to know about her new husband, but as yet she hadn't had the opportunity to ask them. She placed her elbows on the table, rested her chin in her hands, then fixed him with her most direct look. "Why did you want me to breakfast with you if you're not going to talk?"

"I've found polite conversation to be a waste of time."

"I thought rich people were experts at it."

"I'm not."

"I'm surprised," she said. "I had believed you were expert at everything."

From another woman that remark might have been blatantly seductive. From his wife it was just typically blunt.

"Sorry to disappoint you," he said, lifting the silver domes from their dishes. "Even I have my limitations."

Her laughter was low and extremely feminine. It was a nice sound to hear first thing in the morning.

"I'm glad to know you're not perfect," she said in a breezy tone of voice. "Now I don't feel quite so out of place."

It was his turn to laugh. "Why is it I don't believe you've ever felt out of place in your entire life, Molly?" He remembered the scarlet stain on her cheeks last night when those bastards had laughed at her threadbare costume. She had felt out of place last night and that fact hurt him, although he wouldn't admit it, not even to himself.

"I've made an appointment for you at Stern Brothers this morning with a Mademoiselle Ines," he continued, not waiting for her to answer. "I want you to outfit yourself with everything you'll be needing for the trip to England."

He watched as her strong white teeth bit into a crunchy piece of toast.

"I have no idea what I'll be needing," she said between bites. "I've never had more than three presentable dresses at one time in my life." She said it in such an offhand way that he knew she wasn't looking for his pity, but simply stating a fact.

"It's a six-day trip, if that is any help."

"Six dresses, then, I suppose." She shrugged her slender shoulders. "Although I doubt if anyone will notice if I wear a gown more than once."

"Six dresses at the very least," he said.

"That seems extravagant."

"You're my wife now," he said gruffly. "I don't intend to be ashamed of the way you're dressed."

"No, of course not," she snapped, pushing back her chair and rising to her feet. "I should hate to have the illustrious Mr. St. George humiliated by my mended gowns. You might have considered that before you brought me to this palace."

She stormed off to her bedroom, slamming the door shut behind her. He wanted to go after her and say it wasn't only his own stature he was thinking about, but hers as well. The laughter last night had hurt her and he would see to it that such a thing never happened again. But he couldn't tell her that. Telling her would expose a part of himself that he didn't understand. A tender part of himself that could only open up his heart and inevitably lead to pain.

Better in the long run to let her believe he was a heartless bastard. At least then she wouldn't be disappointed later on when he proved it to be so.

Chapter Eleven

Molly's dark mood lifted the moment she walked through the large walnut doors of Stern Brothers on Twenty-third Street and found herself standing in a vast rotunda worthy of the nation's Capitol Building. The coachman who had transported her from the hotel had instructed her to go up the elaborate main staircase to the second floor, then ask for Mademoiselle Ines. The store smelled like French perfume and money, and Molly tilted her head at the tinkling of bells emanating from various points in the building.

Even mended and pressed, she knew her mint-green dress appeared woefully shabby in such an exalted emporium, but she straightened her shoulders and held her head high as Fritzie had taught her to do as a child. "Silks and satins don't make a lady," Fritzie had said on more than one occasion. Molly smiled to herself and wondered if even ladies sometimes wore cotton gowns. Well, today the store would see cotton. She'd always found it easy to make friends and she wasn't about to allow herself to be intimidated by a fancy store.

As it turned out, she hadn't a thing to worry about. Mademoiselle Ines was a woman of boundless enthusiasm, who immediately saw past Molly's well-worn wardrobe and went into raptures about her slender figure and full breasts. Nicholas had already sent over Molly's pale blue dress to indicate Molly's size, and Ines was thrilled that her finest sample gowns fit Molly almost perfectly.

"Just here," said Ines, tugging at the bodice. "You are more—how do you say?—voluptuous than my models, but we can fix. Absolutely! You shall have a wardrobe fit for a queen before you sail from the harbor tomorrow morning."

Molly had never realized such hard work went into being a well-dressed woman. Mademoiselle Ines ushered her into a private fitting room where Molly was stripped down to her chemise and mended stockings.

"Pah!" said Ines, ordering her to remove the cotton garments and toss them away. "A sin to hide such beautiful legs in such dreadful hose."

The fine silk hose Ines handed her seemed almost too exquisite to wear, but Molly carefully rolled them up over her ankles and calves, marveling at the delicate strength of the fabric. Silk hosiery was most uncommon. She had never actually seen a pair in her entire life, much less known the pure bliss of wearing them.

And that wasn't all. Her utilitarian undergarments were replaced by exquisitely hand-embroidered items that seemed too beautiful to hide beneath layers of clothing. But then what clothing it was! Molly oohed and aahed over Directoire coats and gowns with waterfall backs, sighing in wonder at the vibrant silks and the pompadour sateen. She was certain the richest woman in the world couldn't possibly own dresses more beautiful than the ones being chosen for her.

An assistant served Ines and Molly a charming lunch of watercress sandwiches and fresh peaches in the outer chamber of the dressing room, and Molly felt positively elegant as, enveloped in a silk dressing gown embroidered with pink roses, she reclined on a chaise longue and sipped jasmine tea.

She soon discovered the gowns weren't the only wonders to be found at Stern Brothers. The afternoon brought a parade of hats; among them, cunning bonnets with curling ribbons and flat toques that stylish ladies wore at a rakish angle. Once she'd found the perfect headwear, she chose a chatelaine pouch, two pairs of long evening gloves and three short pairs for daytime. Ines reminded her that she needed jeweled combs for her hair, an ostrich feather fan and a simple cloak for walking windy decks as she crossed the Atlantic. There were dresses for walking, dresses for visiting, dresses for sitting and standing and thinking—or so it seemed to Molly. Ines had pressed a riding gown upon her. "I don't ride," Molly said, but Ines assured her that in England all women of position rode and soon Molly would, as well. Molly had a healthy fear of horses and doubted she would ever avail herself of the riding gown, but Ines was so insistent that she allowed herself to be convinced.

"Perhaps I should decline the dressing gowns and the ivory evening dress," she said as one of Ines's assistants began to dress her hair into a style befitting her brand-new wardrobe. "I feel as if I have spent too much."

"Ah, but you have a most generous husband, *madame*." Ines smiled at her in the mirror. "He left those details to my discretion and I would never let you down."

"I feel like Cinderella," Molly said, watching in amazement as her unruly red hair willingly obeyed the hairdresser's every command.

"You are luckier than Cinderella," said Ines with a knowing wink. "Your coach will not turn back into a pumpkin at midnight."

Maybe not, thought Molly, but then neither would Prince Charming pledge his undying love and devotion when he discovered that the glass slipper fit the humble maiden who had tricked him into marriage.

Nicholas arrived at Stern Brothers shortly before five o'clock to fetch Molly. He'd been warned it would be a long day, but he was surprised to discover his wife was still in the dressing room.

"We have a dinner engagement at six," he told Mademoiselle Ines. "Will she be ready?"

"Oui, m'sieur," said Ines with a nod of her graying head. "I am certain once you see *madame,* you will agree it has been well worth the wait."

He paced the length of the waiting room impatiently for a few minutes and was about to barge into the dressing room and demand his wife join him *now,* when the curtain was pulled back and Molly appeared.

Or did she?

He stared at the vision in ivory silk and satin. Could this beautiful woman be the hellcat he'd married less than two days ago? One of the stops he'd made today was at a jewelry store, where he'd purchased a simple wedding ring for her to wear. He could see now how inadequate it was. If this had been a true marriage, he would have showered her with a blaze of diamonds.

"She's beautiful, is she not?" asked Ines, beaming.

Nicholas could only nod. She was magnificent: regal and sensual and extremely feminine all at once. Yet her youthful zest and natural optimism had not been obscured by her sophisticated garb.

"You've worked wonders," he said to Ines and her assistant. "Thank you."

Molly stood there, resplendent in her evening wear, and waited for some acknowledgment. None came. She had thought her heart would burst when she saw the look of surprise on his face when he first saw her; when the surprise was supplanted by delight, her spirits had soared. But now he acted as if she were invisible and only Mademoiselle Ines and her magic were important.

And that's what you get for letting your imagination run away with you, she thought ruefully as Nicholas and Ines made plans for the delivery of her wardrobe tomorrow morning to the dock. He needed a wife he could be proud of, not some ragamuffin fit only to scrub floors. Every single beautiful item purchased for her today had been more to feed his reputation than to clothe her body.

This was far from a love match. She would be a fool if she allowed herself free rein to follow that train of thought. Her ridiculous romantic imagination was running away with her. Nicholas wasn't the man of her dreams; he *couldn't* be. Just because he looked like a young woman's dream beau was no reason to confuse fantasy with reality. For as long as she could remember, she'd heard stories of foolish parlor maids who allowed themselves to believe their gentlemen friends wanted love, not just a frolic between the sheets. She had known the risks when she climbed into the Englishman's empty bed two nights ago, and this feeling of sadness was the price she had to pay.

Delmonico's Restaurant was situated on the corner of Fifth Avenue and Twenty-sixth Street, near Madison Square. A beautiful four-story building, it boasted narrow striped awnings at the windows and broader awnings across the entranceway to keep the elements away from fashionable coifs.

When given the choice of a private cabinet, a dining apartment or the regular saloon, Nicholas chose the latter. They needed the distraction of other people, and the saloon was crowded with glittering examples of New York high society.

He soon noticed to his surprise that all eyes were upon Molly. The women were obviously speculating about her wardrobe; the men, about her availability. Nicholas had planned to give her the wedding ring at the hotel, but he found himself pushing the small black box across the table before they'd seen a menu.

"This isn't necessary," she said, pushing the box back toward him. "The clothes are more than enough."

"It *is* necessary," he said, his voice gruff. More so than he would have figured.

With little fanfare she opened the box and stared down at the gold band. He experienced an oddly unexpected moment of elation as she removed the ring from its bed of black velvet. Her expression never wavered and he found himself shifting uncomfortably in his chair, wishing he had chosen a ring encrusted with diamonds and emeralds. Something as beautiful as she was.

"Thank you," she said quietly, slipping the ring onto the proper finger. She held out her hand to admire it, then obviously catching herself, placed both her hands on her lap.

"If you don't care for it, I would be happy to allow you to choose another when we arrive in London."

"This is fine," said his wife. "I don't want another."

He wasn't certain if she was being sentimental, practical or sarcastic—and he didn't ask.

Strange how something as simple as a gold wedding band could command a woman's undivided attention. Molly kept stealing covert glances at the shiny ring, amazed to see it gracing her hand. She'd never given a thought to a ring. The fact that her reluctant husband obviously had, gave her pause. Surely there could be no romantic meaning to the gesture, given the circumstances under which they'd taken their vows, but still...

There was something so powerfully moving about the sight of that circle of gold embracing her finger that Molly found herself once again falling prey to her ever-optimistic imagination. It wasn't that she believed Nicholas would suddenly fall in love with her and declare his undying devotion, but deep in her heart there was the flicker of hope that they might, at least, become friends.

People liked her. They had since she was a little girl. She was friendly and outgoing and loyal, even if her temper was something to behold. Tricking Nicholas into marriage had been a terrible thing, but she refused to believe he would burden himself with her on a permanent basis if there wasn't something about her that he liked.

Sighing, she touched the shiny gold ring and hoped she'd figure out what that something was before they ended up killing each other.

The menu at Delmonico's was Continental, a far cry from the hearty fare served at the Pemberton Arms. It occurred to Nicholas that Molly might not be able to tell the difference between a finger bowl and a soup plate, and he knew a moment of anxiety when the waiter deposited the first course, a delicate and translucent consommé, in front of them with a flourish.

"You're using the wrong spoon," said Molly sweetly as he lifted the soup to his mouth. "That's for the sorbet."

He gulped the soup, refusing to acknowledge that it was hotter than the devil. "I know which spoon to use."

"Apparently not," continued his wife. She leaned over and pointed to a short spoon with a round bowl. "*That* is a soupspoon," she said with assurance. She tapped the shaft of the one he was using. "And *this* is for sorbet."

"I find it difficult to believe the Pemberton Arms has ever found itself in need of sorbet spoons," he said dryly, laying down his spoon beside the plate.

"I wasn't always poor, Nicholas."

She said his name easily, letting it flow from her lips as if she had been saying it for years. He liked the way it sounded in her defiantly American voice—and hated himself for noticing.

"When I was a little girl, we had a full flatware service for one hundred," she said as she demurely raised her own spoon to her lips. "Papa made certain I could identify each and every piece before I was five years old."

He watched as the bowl of the spoon disappeared between her full lips and was dismayed by the unexpectedly physical reaction he had to that simple act. He thanked God for candlelight and full tablecloths. She took another spoonful of soup and again he watched the gleaming silver slide between those ruby-red lips. His discomfort increased tenfold. He'd never seen a woman invest the simple act of eating with so much erotic grace. For a moment he found himself envying the spoon....

He addressed his attention to his own bowl of soup, picking up the spoon she had designated, rather than the one he had been using.

She didn't miss a thing. Across the table, her eyes glittered with delight. "I believe you'll find it much more efficient," she said in a tone of mock innocence. "That other spoon couldn't feed a hummingbird."

She was right, but he didn't say so. "And what else did you learn about tableware?"

"I won't embarrass you by drinking from the finger bowl, if that was a concern of yours."

"The thought hadn't occurred to me."

"Oh, I'll just bet," she said with the laugh of a woman who knew she looked particularly fetching. "That's probably why you didn't sleep last night, worrying about my lack of social graces."

"You're wrong," he said, meeting her eyes. "Dead wrong." He'd tossed and turned last night for one reason only: the fierce and unexpected rush of desire that had blazed through him at the sight of her, vulnerable and lovely, asleep on the bed.

The glittering ambience of Delmonico's suddenly disappeared, and Molly found herself back in the shadows of the Cape Charlotte boardwalk with Nicholas's arms around her and his mouth on hers. There was no explaining the sensation of being caressed, just as there was no explaining the way her temperature rose as he looked at her across the table.

She willed away the memory of the boardwalk and brought herself back to the delicious dinner spread before them.

"I'd be more than happy to explain the difference between a salad fork and a dinner fork," she said, summoning up a smile.

"That won't be necessary."

"I can't blame you for thinking I might not know my way around a fancy dinner table."

A waiter appeared at the table, bearing their dinner.

"Rare, as it should be," Molly pronounced after the waiter withdrew once again. "Not one hotel in Cape Charlotte prepares a proper chateaubriand." She chuckled wryly. "At least, that's what I've been told."

"And I suppose one day the Pemberton Arms will?"

"Absolutely," said Molly, spearing a tender slice with her fork. "Fritzie works wonders with brisket. Can you imagine what miracles she could perform with a tenderloin?"

Nicholas refilled their wineglasses, his gaze intent upon her. "Do you ever think of anything besides the Pem?"

"It's what I know," she said simply. "It's what I'm good at." *It's all that I have.*

"And what about you?" He found himself possessed of a sudden, intense need to discover more about his wife. "Have you dreams of your own?"

An expression more wistful than sad passed across her lovely face. "To make the Pem the finest hotel on the Cape."

"Nothing else?"

She smiled briefly. "Nothing I wish to tell you."

"No dreams of a husband and a family?"

She continued to smile at him, but offered nothing in the way of revelations.

He didn't press the issue. They were strangers after all, despite the marriage certificate, and he had no right to her secrets. It struck him as laughable that Judge Lane's words had given him the right to her body, but not to her thoughts. Not that he cared. It was curiosity that made him wonder about her, nothing more.

Molly chatted on about wines, waxing eloquent about the perfect wine cellar that she hoped to stock one day.

"You have it all planned, don't you?" he asked. "From the color paint on the shingles to the last glass of wine. I'm impressed. The Pem has no choice but to be successful."

His words seemed to catch her off guard. "Do you really think so?"

"I have no doubt, Molly. It seems you always get exactly what you want."

An uncomfortable silence descended over the table, reminding them both of the odd circumstances that had brought them together.

Molly rarely hesitated when it came to expressing her opinions, yet she had found it exceedingly difficult to bare her innermost dreams to her husband. As it was, she had talked only about her plans for the Pem, not her far-off dreams for a husband and children. How foolish her dreams appeared when contrasted with the marriage tráp she had sprung on Nicholas.

"Is your dinner not to your liking?"

She looked over at Nicholas. "It's delicious."

"You've barely touched it."

"I will." She smiled brightly and gestured toward the other diners laughing and drinking champagne around them. "There's so much else to enjoy here that I forgot about the food."

The expression on Nicholas's face told her that he didn't believe her for a moment, but neither did he pursue the topic. For that she was grateful. She wanted to tell him that she had never seen so beautiful a city in her entire life...or so handsome a man. The words, however, would not come. She had expected to feel frightened and homesick, so far away from Cape Charlotte, but instead she was filled with a sense of excitement that would not be denied.

Fritzie had said she would know the right man when she met him. The time was wrong, the situation was certainly wrong, but there was no doubt in Molly's mind that there was no place else on earth she would rather be at that moment than exactly where she was.

They finished their main course in a companionable silence. Efficient busboys whisked away the soiled dishes and silver before the diners realized what they were about.

"Isn't that wonderful?" Molly breathed as snowy-white linen napkins and shiny cutlery appeared on the table. "It doesn't cost them anything, save soap and water, and the difference is quite remarkable."

He looked at her and started to laugh. *He's laughing with me,* thought Molly in pleased surprise, *not at me.*

"More plans for the Pemberton Arms?"

"Oh, yes! I must make a list and sent it to Fritzie as soon as possible."

"There is hotel stationery in the escritoire," he said companionably. "You might wish to post it in the morning before we leave."

"I shall," she said, nodding her head. "At the Pem, you have to hang on to your knives and forks for dear life or you'll end up eating with your fingers!"

What a wicked and wonderful grin he had. "I noticed."

"According to Fritzie, it didn't diminish your appetite one whit."

"My appetites are healthy, Molly."

Instantly Molly felt as if she were standing in front of a roaring fireplace. She thanked God for the appearance of their waiter, who presented Nicholas with an enormous parchment dessert menu, then discreetly stepped away from the table.

"May I see?" asked Molly, eager to peruse the elegant calligraphy used to describe the items. She had a lovely hand herself; perhaps she could put it to use on menus for the Pemberton Arms.

"It's in French."

"I speak a little French."

He arched a brow. "Your father?"

"My father." She arched a brow in return. "Why is it I think you're surprised I know how to read at all? Papa believed firmly in education. I'm well versed in Latin, as well, and am a veritable whiz at bookkeeping." She shrugged casually. "Not that there was much money to keep track of. When Papa died, we were dependent upon my uncle for help."

"I can't imagine he gave it willingly."

"Of course he did. The stipend arrived on the first of the month, regular as clockwork, every month for almost ten years." She sighed. "I should have known something had happened to him when the money stopped coming."

Nicholas found it hard to equate this paragon of virtue with the coldhearted monster he knew Jonathan Hughes to have been. "Did he ever come to Cape Charlotte?"

She shook her head, trailing a finger down the list of fancy desserts. "Fritzie said maybe he didn't care to travel abroad, but I always wondered if there was more to it than that."

There was much more to it than the girl would ever realize. He could tell her a thing about the bastard and how it was he had come to die alone, but to what avail? He would hate for the poison that had ruined his youth to taint Molly in any way.

You're getting soft, man, caution warned him. This girl was as sharp and cunning as they came. Hughes blood flowed hot in her veins. Nicholas prided himself on his ability to avoid entanglements, and yet he had walked into this one with the eagerness of a lamb being led to the slaughter.

They ordered *mousse au chocolat* and two demi-tasses. Nicholas asked if Molly minded if he lit up an afterdinner cigar, and she said no. "Papa used to smoke Havanas," she said, her eyes growing misty at the memory. "To this day, the smell of them makes me think he's going to pop around the corner and say, 'Miss me, Molly girl?'"

The thought of that kind soul being kin to his step-father boggled Nicholas's mind. "What about your mother?" he asked, clipping off the end of his cigar, then reaching for his matches. "What was she like?"

"She died when I was a baby. I know she was beautiful because I have their wedding picture and a miniature of her, but it's hard to conjure up a real person from a piece of paper."

"Fritzie told me you take after her."

"Only my coloring," said his wife with a rueful shake of her head. "My temper is my own."

"Your father was an even-tempered man?"

At that Molly laughed out loud. "Papa wouldn't so much as step on a spider. He was the sweetest, kindest soul I ever knew."

"A kind man might have left his child better provided for," he pointed out. "More secure." A cruel observation, but one night at the Pemberton Arms had proved to him the precarious nature of Molly's existence.

"My father had the business sense of a goose," she said, not ducking the question the way another woman might have done, "but he knew how to love and be loved. I would say that was as much security as any child could ask for."

"Love didn't help you keep the roof repaired."

"No, but love made the hole in the roof seem less important."

Her words sounded pretty and he would have liked to believe them, but they were just words, after all, nothing tangible or real. The concept of love had long since vanished from his life, replaced by anger and ambition. Maybe she could believe that love filled empty bellies and mended broken hearts, but he could not.

"Now you know everything there is to know about me," she said, those beautiful green eyes of hers intent upon him. "But I know nothing about you."

"There is nothing to know."

"Of course there is!" She was alight with curiosity. "Do you have any brothers or sisters? What will your friends think of me? I know your house is near London, but I cannot imagine the first thing about how it looks." She leaned forward and touched his forearm. The flickering candlelight was reflected in the soft yellow gold of her wedding band, drawing both of their gazes. "Won't you tell me?"

It was a simple request. Despite everything, she had a right to know where he was taking her, what kind of life she would be leading. But the last thing he wanted to talk about tonight was England in general, and Merriton Hall in particular. What could he say? *I have no one, Molly. An empty house that's crumbling from the ground up and haunted with memories I couldn't escape, even by running halfway around the world.* There were no aunts and uncles to greet their arrival. No nieces and nephews to dance about, begging for a sweet. He was the last of a dying family, and it was Molly's misfortune to have tricked herself into becoming a part of it.

A kinder man would end her punishment now. He'd proved his power over her life by tearing her away from the home and family she loved so well. He could see she was honorable, in her own way, and willing to do penance for her treachery. It wasn't too late to arrange for her train ticket back to Cape Charlotte. She had money now and a thousand ideas on how to spend it. There was nothing she needed from him except her freedom.

Nicholas asked the carriage driver to take the long way back to their hotel. "This is my wife's first visit to New York," he said by way of explanation. "I'd like her to bring some memories home with her."

"Sure thing," said the driver, doffing his cap. "Just sit back and leave it to Murphy."

A thoughtful gesture, and one that touched Molly's vulnerable heart. Little did Nicholas know that the wonders of Manhattan Island came in a poor second to the secret delight she took in watching her husband devour the sights and sounds of the bustling city. He seemed so sophisticated and worldly to her that she was surprised at his open fascination with New York. *How many times have you taken a coach down Fifth Avenue?* she wondered. *And how many women have sat beside you like this?* She thought of the question about his family that he had left unanswered.

All too soon they reached the hotel. Nicholas helped her from the carriage, gripping her by the waist and swinging her to the ground as if she were made of spun sugar. She waited while he paid the driver, aware of the group of three gentlemen who stood near the curb, watching her. One actually had the audacity to wink at her! She knew a moment of intense pride when Nicholas approached her and offered his arm.

"Thank you," she said, linking her arm with his, as they glided past the group of men. She hoped they noticed the wedding band on her left hand.

Inside, the lobby was abuzz with smiling couples in evening dress.

"I hear music," said Nicholas. "Chopin?"

"Strauss," said Molly. "They always play Strauss at the Pavilion." It was part of her favorite daydream—the glittering Pavilion, the lush music, the handsome man of her dreams. Faint laughter rode the music, adding to the delicate illusion of walking in a dream. "There's most likely a ballroom somewhere," she continued. "I've read all about New York society parties and how grand they are."

"That's right. You can read, too." He led her toward the elevator. "You're a woman of many accomplishments."

She glanced up at him, ready to do battle, and found instead that he was looking at her with the strangest expression on his face. Amusement, tenderness, a touch of curiosity were all at work.

She laughed and tapped him lightly on the arm with the ostrich feather fan Mademoiselle Ines said was so vitally important to the well-dressed woman. Now she understood why: it was to flirt with! Who would have imagined?

He seemed as surprised as she was by her gesture and before she knew what he was about, he spun her into his arms right there in the lobby in front of all to see, and together they moved to the music.

It was the stuff of dreams. Again she had the strange and heady sensation of destiny holding her in the palm of its hand.

The music stopped. The elevator rumbled. The doors opened. The moment, as fragile as a bubble of soap, vanished.

They stopped dancing and he ushered her into the Otis elevator. The operator, a pleasant-faced man with a wide smile, cranked shut the doors. Molly and Nicholas stood primly erect, eyes forward. Only their elbows touched. She longed to peek at him, to see if he had felt a fraction of the magic she had known as they'd waltzed in the lobby.

If they'd met under different circumstances, Nicholas might have been able to see past her flaws and recognize what a genuinely nice person she was, but how on earth did you prove your generosity of spirit to the man you had tricked into wedlock at the point of a gun?

She stifled a sigh. There was absolutely no point thinking about it. She had made her choice, and thanks to that choice the Pem was on the road back to its former glory. Fritzie and Stella and Arthur—not a one of them would ever again know a moment's worry.

It was worth it, all of it, she tried to convince herself as the elevator man shimmied the car into position at the sixth floor. The operator doffed his cap. "Good evening to you, folks."

Nicholas nodded, then helped Molly from the mechanical marvel. They said little as they approached the door to their suite. Nicholas extracted the brass room key from his pocket and opened the door.

"How quiet it is in here," Molly remarked as she draped her silky shawl over the back of a Queen Anne chair. She smiled up at Nicholas. "The orchestra sounded wonderful."

He nodded. "We sail tomorrow at nine a.m.," he said abruptly. "You should retire early."

She met his eyes across the room. The twinkle in his eyes that had captivated her over dinner was extinguished, replaced by a carefully guarded expression that made her feel somehow sad. She wanted to tell him that tonight had been the most exciting day of her life, that she felt like Cinderella, transformed by her beautiful gown and the candlelight and lush music—

And the splendor of her husband.

But she couldn't say any of that to him. The words were lodged deep within her chest and she found it impossible to give voice to them.

"Good night, Nicholas," she said instead.

He waited a long time before answering, so long that she wondered if he was going to acknowledge her at all. When she was about to turn and walk away, he closed the distance between them with a few quick strides.

His expression never wavered. Molly wanted to step back and regain her distance, but she held her ground. Her pulse quickened and she swallowed against a rising tide of anticipation.

"We sail at nine," he said, a half smile on his face.

"You already told me that," she said. "Good night."

Closing the bedroom door behind her, she leaned against the wall, one hand pressed against her chest as if she could calm the pounding of her heart. What a foolish child she was, thinking he wanted to kiss her. She must have looked like a love-struck schoolgirl, gazing up at him with her lips parted in expectation.

She had played God with people's lives, and this was her punishment: to be married to a man who would never love her as she wanted to be loved.

"Oh, Nicholas," she whispered. "What on earth have I done to us both?"

Chapter Twelve

Neither Nicholas nor Molly slept well that night.

There was something unnatural about a newly married couple sleeping in separate rooms and, despite the unusual circumstances surrounding their union, both of them felt the tension in the suite.

Molly sat up in her luxuriously appointed bed and drew her knees up close to her chest, wrapping her arms about them. She had spent every other night of her life alone in bed, and yet somehow tonight it felt terribly wrong. She yearned for something she couldn't quite define, a vague ache inside her heart that she knew only the stranger who was her husband could ease.

As for Nicholas, he spent the night pacing the length of the sitting room, struggling with the urge to stride into her bedroom and claim his rights as her husband. The memory of how she had felt in his arms as they danced was sweet torture. What he should do was venture outside and find himself a woman as willing as she was pragmatic to relieve himself of the fire building inside him. But each time he headed for the door, the thought of his beautiful—and innocent—wife stopped him in his tracks, and he grew angrier as time passed.

Both met dawn's light with relief.

There was comfort to be found in the ritual of preparing to face the day and by the time they greeted each other in the shared sitting room, Molly and Nicholas had both managed to bank their emotions.

"Our bags have been sent on to the dock," said Nicholas without preamble as Molly entered the room. "Unless you wish a full breakfast, we should be off."

Molly's stomach was tied up in sailor's knots, and she declined all but a cup of tea. He stood there watching her while she added both sugar and cream, and she heard the sound of his booted foot tapping impatiently. He certainly was difficult in the mornings, prickly as nettles. Absently she noted that his tie was perfectly knotted, his suit coat buttoned, everything in its place. It must put enormous stress on him to be completely dressed, she thought, remembering his various states of dishabille while in Cape Charlotte. She considered making a comment to that effect but decided against it.

He seemed distant and businesslike as he led her to the elevator. They waited in silence for the car to arrive. They rode in silence to the lobby. Molly wondered if they would sail all the way across the Atlantic Ocean in silence, as well.

The silence was broken two hours later as Molly stood in the doorway of their cabin on the HMS *Albert*. Eyes wide, she spun around to Nicholas.

"There's only one bed!"

"It was all that was available," he said, face impassive. "Every cabin on the ship is occupied."

"But—"

"Don't worry about your honor," he said, his tone sharp. "I'll sleep in the sitting room."

She turned to look at the sofa. It was small and hard as a rock and no more than he deserved, considering his bad mood. "Have we a private bath?"

He pointed to a sliding door to the left of the porthole. "Through there."

A wave of heat made Molly feel as if the walls of the cabin were closing in on her. Dear God, was she supposed to bathe with him right there in the cabin, not ten feet away from where she sat naked in a tub of water? She felt light-headed at the thought.

"My room at the Pem was bigger than this," she declared, pushing aside some very interesting thoughts of being ten feet away from *him* while he sat naked in a tub of water.

A muscle in his jaw worked furiously. "You should have considered that before you climbed into my bed."

Don't argue with him, Molly, she warned herself. Six days in such cramped quarters would strain the relationship of any two people. For a couple married in name only, it might prove to be disastrous. She breathed deeply to calm herself. "I meant nothing by that statement, Nicholas. I was surprised, that's all."

He nodded as a stream of porters arrived with the trunks that held Molly's new wardrobe. "As you can see, we have no room for those," Nicholas said with the air of one to the manner born. "We'll need storage space."

The head porter started to object, but there was something about the look of suppressed rage on Nicholas's face that brought him up short, the same as it had Molly.

"As you wish, sir." The porter motioned for his underlings to follow suit.

"Now what am I to do for clothes?" Molly asked as she watched her wardrobe disappear.

"Speak with the room steward and arrange something. You're resourceful. I'm sure you can find a solution."

She gestured toward his valises piled up near the couch. "Why didn't you send your luggage away?"

He laughed out loud, but there was an edge of danger in the sound. "All of my belongings could fit in one of your trunks."

"Fair's fair," she said, temper flaring. "I didn't ask you to dress me up like an organ-grinder's monkey. The fancy clothes were your idea."

"I apologize for not wanting my wife to be mistaken for a scullery maid."

"You certainly do spend a great deal of time worrying about how I'll appear to others," she observed. "Last night it was the cutlery, this morning it's my attire. Perhaps you should have thought of that before you kidnapped me."

He tugged at his tie, then sent it flying across the room, followed by his suit coat. Alarm sprang to life inside Molly as he dropped his gentlemanly veneer with his garments and reverted to the more rough-hewn man she'd glimpsed at the Pem. Instinctively she recognized that this was a man capable of physical violence if pushed to his limits. Why that intrigued rather than frightened her was a mystery, one that should have disturbed her a great deal more than it did, considering the fact that she was alone with him on a ship headed for the middle of the Atlantic Ocean.

But there was something so exciting about the way he looked when he was angry, all bristling male outrage, that made her feel trembly and powerful at the same time.

He stormed over to the tiny bar set up near the couch and reached for the whiskey.

"You do drink a great deal of that stuff, don't you?" she asked, thinking of the near-empty bottle she'd spied on the credenza in their hotel suite when she awoke that morning. "Do you really think it wise?"

He approached her, his large hand wrapped menacingly around the neck of the bottle. "You are provoking me, Molly," he said, his voice wickedly deep. "Do you really think it wise, given the situation?"

At least he was talking to her. Even anger was better than bone-chilling silence. "Drinking is bad for the pancreas," she said, parroting a piece of information she'd learned from Fritzie.

"And abstinence is bad for the soul," he shot back, taking a thirsty gulp of the liquor straight from the bottle.

"You would do well to exercise some self-control," she continued. "Fritzie's husband had partaken of the grape just before he had the carriage accident where he injured his leg."

Her husband gave her a baleful look from over the mouth of the whiskey bottle. "If he had a wife like you, it's a wonder he didn't throw himself under the wheels."

"Why, you hateful—"

He stepped as close to her as he could without becoming part of her. "Think before you speak," he warned in that low and deadly voice. "Your next words might be your last."

"Oh, you'd like that, wouldn't you!" She refused to step back so much as an inch. "Me dead and in my grave and you with your greedy hands on my inheritance!"

He looked at her as if he didn't know whether to laugh or toss her out the porthole into the drink.

"You are the most irritatingly illogical brat. I don't give a bloody damn about your money."

"A likely story."

"I wasn't the one with the loaded pistol."

"Be that as it may, you were all set to get our marriage annulled until you saw my inheritance. I saw your face when I opened the box—you had dollar bills for eyes."

"I don't want your inheritance," he said. "I want y—" He stopped midword.

She looked at him curiously. "What?"

"Nothing."

"You started to say something. You want—what?"

Abruptly he wheeled toward the door. "I'll be on deck," he said and before she had the chance to pursue the topic, he was gone.

By the time Molly had sought out the room steward and arranged for her wardrobe to be made available to her, the HMS *Albert* was well under way. After a simple luncheon, which her husband chose not to attend, she strolled up to the deck and found herself gazing back at the country she was leaving behind. Manhattan Island was scarcely a blot on the horizon, and she had to blink away tears more than once as she said goodbye to the land of her birth.

She'd always craved excitement and dreamed of the day when she would travel and see the world, yet for an instant she knew utter panic as she realized that now there could be no turning back. She couldn't hop aboard a train and return to Cape Charlotte and the safety of her old life if she decided her new marriage was too dreadful to endure. There would be an ocean between herself and the country she loved and, for better or worse, Nicholas was her only security.

What a sobering thought.

A sharp sea breeze buffeted her as she leaned against the railing and she drew her shawl more tightly about her shoulders. Right about now Fritzie would be complaining that her feet hurt as she started the daily chore of picking salad greens from the backyard garden for the evening meal. She wondered if Mr. Carruthers had sent a carpenter and crew to the Pem as promised, to begin the preliminary work necessary to restore the building to its former glory.

Of course, there was no sense worrying about it. There wasn't a thing she could do out there in the middle of the ocean. Besides, Carruthers was as trustworthy as they came, and Fritzie possessed the tenacity of a terrier. Together they could be trusted to make sure Molly's hard-won money was put to proper use.

If only there was something they could do with the tangle the rest of her life had become.

"I'm afraid I don't know where my husband is," said Molly for the fifth time between the appetizer and the entrée at dinner that evening.

"Jumped overboard, eh?" asked an elderly Englishman with an enormous ear trumpet. "Don't you worry, my dear. I'd be most gratified to partner you in bridge later on."

Molly smiled her thanks and continued eating. There was absolutely no point in explaining to Sir Archibald Paquette that she didn't know the first thing about bridge. English people certainly did play a lot of that game, she mused as conversation ebbed and flowed around her. Everyone, it seemed, was lining up partners to help pass the time on the long voyage. She would have to remember to put that in her letter to Fritzie.

"Now, Archie, don't tease our Mrs. St. George that way," said his wife with a shake of her magnificently coiffed gray head. "She's newly married and I'm certain she and her husband have more important things to do with their time than play cards with fossils like us."

Again Molly was at a loss for words. If she agreed with Lady Catherine, she would not only be calling those two lovely old people fossils, she would be spreading romantic nonsense about herself and Nicholas that could only come back to haunt her. Unfortunately, if she denied it, she would most likely blush and no one would believe her. The bawdy teasing would only continue right through dessert.

She'd never realized that being newly married made one such a tempting target for unsolicited comments. Was this why her husband had chosen to absent himself from the proceedings? She sliced into her roast chicken with a vengeance. She'd certainly give him a piece of her mind tonight when he finally made his way back to their cabin. If he thought she was going to endure six days of heavy-handed humor, he was dead wrong. She'd promised to honor and obey, but she'd never once said anything about dining alone.

There must have been something of desperation in her eyes because Mrs. Tompkins, wife of a London publisher, came to the rescue. "Tell me, Molly—you don't mind if I call you Molly, do you? You remind me so much of my own dear girl back home—tell me, is this your first crossing?"

Bless you, Mrs. Tompkins. I'll fill a library with your husband's books! "It certainly is, and I must say I don't understand what all the fuss is about. So far the sea's been as calm as a baby's cradle."

Mrs. Tompkins winked at her from across the table as the other passengers eagerly launched into their own "worst crossing" stories. To hear them tell it, no one since Columbus had sailed the Atlantic without spending a good deal of time clinging to life preservers and praying for salvation. Instinct told her that most of these good people had probably spent most of their shipboard time in the past happily sipping brandy and playing bridge, but there was something eminently satisfying about trading tales of horror.

Dessert came and went, and still the topic seemed inexhaustible. Molly had entertained them all with her story about her thirteenth birthday when she had mistaken spiked punch for lemonade and was found hours later asleep in a rowboat in the middle of Garson's Bay, some three miles from Cape Charlotte.

It pleased her no end to note that the British were no different from Americans. They all seemed quite taken with her, from prune-faced Lady Catherine to the rotund Anglican priest with the pointed nose and sober laugh. Fritzie had told her that the best thing she could do in a new situation was to be true to herself, and she had done exactly that. She hadn't pretended to be anyone but Molly Hughes...St. George, and that had seemed to be good enough for all of them.

If only her husband felt the same way.

There was some debate as to whether the ladies would retire to the main salon and leave the gentlemen to their cigars and brandy, but conversation was flowing like the champagne had with dinner and so they all adjourned together to the salon.

Mrs. Tompkins linked her arm with Molly's. "You're doing wonderfully, my dear," she said sotto voce as they made their way from the dining room with the others. "No one realized you were nervous."

Molly breathed a sigh of relief. "But you did," she said. "How was that?"

"When you've raised six daughters, as I have, it becomes second nature."

"Six daughters!"

"Astounding, isn't it?" asked Mrs. Tompkins with a laugh. "And there my Reggie and I were, ten years married and content with our books and our rose gardens, why my dyspepsia turned out to be our beautiful Eve."

"Oh my!" Molly could think of absolutely nothing more profound to say. She found it difficult to imagine being ten years married; the notion of being the mother of six girls was more than she could fathom.

"You mustn't look so amazed," said Mrs. Tompkins, patting her arm in a gesture not unlike Fritzie's. "Motherhood turned out to be quite a natural thing for me. In truth I am much better tending daughters than I was tending roses." She gave Molly a sharp and knowing look. "Are you . . . ?" She delicately let her words end in a question.

Molly's reaction was anything but delicate. Her entire body jerked as if she had been struck by lightning. "No!" She struggled to bring her voice back down into its normal register. "I—we've only been married since Saturday." She paused. It had been well after midnight by the time Judge Lane had arrived. "Sunday," she said to the poor woman's puzzlement. "I meant to say Sunday."

"My own sister Mabel found herself with child before the honeymoon was over."

Molly bit her lip. Wouldn't Mrs. Tompkins and all the other well-meaning passengers be surprised to learn that the ship's resident newlyweds had yet to share a pillow? And, if Nicholas's absence tonight was any indication, it might be ten years before they did—if ever.

They entered the main salon, a beautiful room furnished in soft blues and ivories with comfortable, well-upholstered chairs and divans scattered about. Three tables were set up in the far corner and the bridge players hurried to pair off and begin the night's bidding.

"I don't play bridge," Molly said to Mrs. Tompkins.

"Neither do I," confessed the older woman. "Dreadful game." She took a seat on a divan and motioned for Molly to join her. A steward, impeccably clad in a white uniform with shiny brass buttons, appeared at their sides as if by magic and offered them a pot of tea. Mrs. Tompkins waited until he'd disappeared, then leaned toward Molly. "You mustn't worry, my dear. I saw him in the gaming room. Your husband and mine are hard at work playing a game of chance with two rather dour-looking Scotsmen, who are glowering as if they believe the border wars are still being waged."

Molly laughed out loud, feeling some of her tension dissipating. "I had begun to wonder," she admitted hesitantly. "Nicholas—we had a bit of a misunderstanding earlier and he..."

Mrs. Tompkins raised a plump hand. "Say no more, Molly. Arguments are part of the fabric of the union. It will pass, I promise you."

Molly wasn't entirely certain of that. Mrs. Tompkins believed Molly and Nicholas had a normal marriage, the kind this good woman so obviously enjoyed. She yearned to tell the matron that arguments were the entire fabric of their union, but there was simply no point to it.

Instead, she poured them each a cup of strong tea, then settled down for an evening of conversation. If her husband went looking for her in the cabin, let him see how it felt to be abandoned. It would serve him right.

Toward midnight it occurred to Nicholas that he could not spend the next 144 hours of the voyage locked in combat with a deck of playing cards and three aging gentlemen. Not that he wasn't willing to give it a try, but for some reason his companions seemed anxious to rejoin their respective wives in their respective cabins.

"Tomorrow, gentlemen," he said as they donned their coats and started for the promenade. "Same time."

The two Scotsmen grunted something that Nicholas took to be an assent, then Reggie Tompkins clapped him on the back. "You're a ruthless player, St. George, and an honest one. I like that in a man."

Nicholas smiled. "I return the compliment."

"I'd best be returning to the stateroom. Mona claims she cannot fall asleep until I'm next to her. You understand how it is."

Nicholas didn't understand at all, but he nodded anyway. "Go to your wife, Reggie. We'll begin again tomorrow."

With a handshake, he and Reggie parted company for the night. The deck was deserted, except for a deckhand—no older than Nicholas had been when he first fled England on a cargo ship—who scurried past with a string mop and a wooden bucket. "G'd evenin', guv'nor," said the boy. "Bleedin' windy out here, wouldn't you say?"

Nicholas nodded. "That it is." He watched as the boy mopped his way around the corner. He'd been that boy once. Fifteen years ago he'd slept in the belly of the ship on a pallet of threadbare blankets and lofty dreams.

He had money now and position, but the same bone-deep loneliness that had been his constant companion as an adolescent was with him still. He had done such a fine job of constructing walls around his heart that even now, with Jonathan Hughes no longer a factor in his life, he hadn't the foggiest notion how to lower his defenses.

And so it was that he faced the moment he'd been avoiding all day. That damn stateroom wasn't large enough to house a flea, much less two adults. Molly had been right about that. He just hadn't wanted to hear it. His own hot temper had sent him storming from the cabin without so much as an attempt to rectify matters. He'd done his level best to avoid her all afternoon and evening, in the vain hope that she'd be sleeping peacefully when he returned and he could bypass the inevitable confrontation.

He heard the deckhand talking with a shipmate. "...right nice young lass all by herself," Nicholas heard him say. "And a new bride, too..." The last thing he needed was to become part of the ship's grapevine of gossip. He and Molly had more than enough to worry about without that added pressure.

Turning, he headed toward their stateroom and the narrow couch that would serve as his honeymoon bed.

Molly had said good-night to Mrs. Tompkins and the others a little after ten o'clock and retired to her stateroom. Actually it was *their* stateroom, but since her husband had not seen fit to put in an appearance since early this morning, she considered the oversight quite understandable. A steward had turned down the coverlet and fluffed the down-filled pillows. A small lamp with a pale blue shade burned on the nightstand, lending a soft glow to the room. The steward had even draped her new jade-

green silk wrapper across the foot of the double bed and
left a humidor of expensive cigars and a bottle of brandy
in their small sitting room for Nicholas.

It was obvious, however, that her husband was not
going to make an appearance.

Not that she cared. The less she saw of him on this
voyage, the better. If he intended to be moody and ill-
tempered, he could sleep in a deck chair from here to
England.

One thing she could do while he was otherwise occupied was take a long, leisurely bath. She brightened at the
thought of luxuriating in a tub of warm, fragrant water
while the cares of the day disappeared. This morning she
had been worried about privacy; it no longer seemed as
if that would be a problem.

The first thing Nicholas saw when he entered the
stateroom he shared with Molly was the humidor of cigars and the decanter of brandy on the butler's table. For
a moment he wondered if his wife had seen fit to provide
him with those luxuries, but sanity quickly prevailed. He
reminded himself to thank the cabin steward next chance
he had.

He quickly divested himself of his jacket and shirt,
then kicked off his boots. The hard and narrow couch
smiled up at him, and he shot it a withering look. He
wondered if the room steward also supplied extra bed
linens for bridegrooms who slept alone.

One quick glance about the sitting room answered that
question. Maybe there was an extra pillow or something
hidden away in an armoire in the bedroom. Of course,
that would mean entering his wife's sanctuary, but he was
willing to risk her wrath in order to get a good night's
sleep. Besides, there was always the chance that she was

fast asleep herself and they could avoid communication entirely.

He pulled back the sliding door that divided the drawing room from the bedroom and stepped inside. A lamp burned on the nightstand and it didn't take him more than a second to see that she was not in the room.

Her clothes were, however. Everywhere. Two satin slippers were overturned near the chaise longue. Her butter-yellow gown was tossed haphazardly over the footboard. An assortment of frilly, lacy items of indeterminate nature was scattered all about.

And the scent of her perfume, sweet with a hint of spice, seemed to fill the air. He lifted one silk stocking from the bed and let it slide between his fingers. Delicate as a spider's web, soft as a summer breeze . . . still warm from her body.

He realized suddenly that the bed was empty. The covers had been turned down but it was obvious she had yet to retire. Tilting his head, he caught the sound of singing from behind the door leading to the bath. He couldn't make out the words, but the tune was most agreeable.

Molly was in there. The image of her, naked and rosy from her bath, filled his mind as her perfume filled the air. He saw the way her hair would look, damp and thick and piled loosely atop her head. A few tendrils would drift across her shoulders, begging a man's hand to smooth them back. Her skin would be moist and warm, scented and—

Get what you came in here for and leave, ordered the rational side of his mind, and it was a testament to his strength of will that he even considered leaving the room. The pull he felt was as strong as the tides. It had been from the very beginning. He heard her footsteps approaching the door. His pulse quickened, short fierce bursts of heat and desire.

He stood there motionless. Waiting. Anticipating. Wanting her.

The door to the bathroom opened. She stood framed in the doorway, the light from the bedroom turning her wild tumble of hair into living fire about her beautiful face. She wore a wrapper of jade-green silk, belted at the waist. The valley between her breasts was rich and inviting.

For Molly it was as if she had reached the end of a long journey and the reason for it all was only a heartbeat away. She met his eyes and reason vanished in a sudden burst of flame. He crushed the silk stocking between his fingers, then tossed it to the ground. Her sigh floated across the scented air to where he stood, and it told him everything he needed to know.

He was next to her before she drew her next breath.

"This isn't love," he said, lifting her into his arms.

"I know," she whispered, burying her face against his neck.

"It's only lust."

She nodded, her hair drifting across his chest and arms.

"Do you understand this, Molly?" His voice was a low growl. "This isn't about love."

"It isn't about love," she repeated, the words sounding softer, sweeter as she said them.

The bed shimmered in the gentle glow of the gas lamp. Soft and inviting, the beginning and the end and all that there could ever be....

"In another minute there can be no turning back."

She looked up at him, her great green eyes wide with longing. "Oh, do be quiet, Nicholas," she said, "and just kiss me."

Chapter Thirteen

A fierce hunger sprang to life inside Nicholas at her words. He wanted to take her right then, with no preliminaries, no sweet words of encouragement, only the primal mating of blood and desire.

But she was young and untried and she deserved so much more. Ducking his head, he covered her mouth with his in a fevered burst of love bites that served only to inflame his senses even higher. She sighed, a sound low in her throat, and he knew he would pay any price to hear that sound again and again.

"Hold tight," he said as he knelt against the mattress, then gently lowered her to the bed. Her silk robe exposed the endless line of her legs, and he traced that line with his eyes...soon he would trace it with his hands...his mouth....

Her eyes were wide, the color as deep and green as the silk of her wrapper. She was that rare combination of seduction and innocence that he had spent his lifetime avoiding. As he bent forward to reach for the sash on her robe, he understood that he had been right. She was as dangerous as she was beautiful and tonight she would belong to him.

Molly's sudden intake of breath sounded painfully loud in the quiet cabin. With one swift movement he undid the sash on her robe, and she stifled the urge to pull the two sides of the wrapper together over her breasts.

"Don't," he said, as if reading her mind. "Let me see you, Molly."

"The light," she whispered.

"It stays on."

"I don't think I—"

"That's right," he said, drawing his index finger down the column of her throat and into the space between her breasts. "Don't think. I don't want you to think of anything but this."

He curved his hand until her breast was lightly cupped in his palm and she gasped as he ran the pad of his thumb across her nipple. She felt his touch in every part of her body...even in that most secret, intimate part.

Her nipple hardened against his hand. She was ripe and tempting, and he longed to taste her. Ducking his head, he brought his mouth to the base of her throat where her pulse fluttered visibly. She was softer than the petal of the most beautiful rose and as sweet. He wanted to possess her and adore her, claim her body and touch her soul.

Molly came alive each place he touched. When his warm mouth grazed her throat, she became the pulse beat beneath his lips. His lips against the curve of her breast made all else seem insignificant. When he touched the tip of his tongue to her budding nipple, an electric current of sensation radiated outward and she wondered if ecstasy and madness always walked hand in hand.

"I don't know what to do," she whispered, "what's expected of me...." The warmth was inside her skin and racing through her blood, toward that spot at the top of her thighs that seemed the center of all things wonderful that were yet to be. His gaze swept her torso and lingered on the curve of her hip.

He lifted her hand to his mouth, turning it palm up, then pressing a hot, moist kiss to the point where the lines of fortune intersected. She shivered involuntarily, then watched, mesmerized, as he kissed each finger in turn. He drew her middle finger slowly between his lips, grazing the flesh with his teeth. She moved restlessly against the sheets as he slowly drew her finger deeper into his hot mouth. A rhythm began to build inside her body, a dark and ancient call that she had never before heard but understood in every fiber of her being.

The sight of his wife, feverish with desire, moved Nicholas as nothing else in his life had ever done. There was something deeply erotic about the instinctive rise and fall of her splendid hips, made even more so by the knowledge that it was all brand-new to her. No other man had ever seen her face flushed with longing. The sound she made deep in her throat as he moved his hand up the smooth skin of her leg belonged to him alone.

Lying next to her, he kissed her mouth as his fingers toyed with the wet curls at the apex of her thighs. With his tongue he sought the nectar of her mouth even as he gently stroked the silken folds of her womanhood. She whimpered softly as he pulled away for a moment to strip off his remaining clothes. The look on her lovely face as he came to her, naked and aroused, heated his blood.

"Ohh." Molly found herself frankly staring at the hidden wonders of the male body. The notion that he . . . that it was possible . . . that they could ever—

He returned to the bed and quickly relieved her of her satin robe. A sea breeze ruffled the curtains at the porthole, but it did nothing to cool her heated skin. She lay still before him, proudly naked, glorying in the look of unabashed wonder on his handsome face, filled with a combination of terror and exultation.

Bending low, he pressed a kiss to the curve of her belly, and she wondered how it was she didn't incinerate in a burst of white heat. She placed a hand on his shoulders.

"Nicholas?"

"Trust me, Molly," he whispered against her skin. "I'll stop if you want me to."

And then he did the most amazing thing, kissing the tender flesh of her inner thighs, drawing his lips around the tiny, throbbing bud that suddenly was the core of her very being.

Vivid bursts of color and sound exploded behind her eyes as her head fell back against the pillow. Surely no one had ever done such a thing before. Something so wickedly glorious had to be wrong. She was certain most people had never even imagined such a wondrous thing was even possible.

She felt as if she were sailing through the sky on a cloud, looking down upon the poor benighted souls in this world who would never know such bliss. Just when she thought there couldn't possibly be anything to match the feeling of his mouth and tongue against her, he kissed his way up to her belly, to her breasts, the underside of her jaw, then brought his mouth to hers.

She drew back at first, surprised by the new sensations.

"Sweet Molly," he murmured against her mouth. "Hot and sweet and—"

She gasped and his tongue swept across her lips, then entered her mouth. His muscular body covered hers, pressing her down into the soft mattress, yet somehow he managed to keep from crushing her with his weight. His chest was broad and hard and she knew she would remember the first electrifying feel of her breasts brushing against him until her dying day.

The smell and feel and sound of her was fast taking Nicholas past the breaking point. Only one thing, a primal mating between them, could release the fierce tension building inside. Shifting position, he eased his knee between her legs, spreading her thighs to receive him. She stiffened in his arms then grew still, and he placed his hand against her mound, entangling his fingers in the hot, damp curls. She moaned and her hips rose from the bed to move against his hand in an ever-increasing tempo.

She couldn't possibly know what she was doing to him. Her wet heat. The deeply erotic smell of her.

"Touch me," he said, his voice scarcely recognizable even to himself. "Put your hand on me, Molly."

His words set off tiny explosions inside Molly. His words came to her as if from far away, almost as if she had imagined them. But there was nothing imaginary about the effect they had upon her. She was shameless in her desire, straining toward something she didn't understand, yet willing to do anything to reach it.

Gingerly she placed her hand on his chest, savoring the savage beating of his heart beneath her fingertips. Inch by tantalizing inch, her hand trailed down toward his navel. His reaction to her touch made her feel as if she had been granted powers beyond imagination. His breathing grew labored. His muscles literally trembled as she drew her fingers over his flat belly and toward his manhood.

She inhaled sharply, then brought her hand to rest against him. He was velvet and steel, and when she wrapped her fingers around his shaft his groan was one of such exquisite torment that she looked at him in question.

He covered her hand with his and showed her how to please him, long rhythmic strokes that fanned the flames to white-hot intensity.

And then in an instant she was on her back, open and needy, with her husband poised between her legs to breach the last barrier that separated her from knowing the secrets of womanhood.

"Will it hurt?" she whispered.

He bent low and pressed a kiss to her lips. "Only for an instant."

She nodded, swallowing hard against the surge of fear. The pain was there, fierce and hot as the blood that flowed, and then just as suddenly it was gone, replaced by the most miraculous wave of sensation that Molly had ever known. He filled her; he overpowered her; he took her with him on a journey beyond the stars.

And when it was over and she found herself in his arms, with his body still joined with hers, she knew the deepest happiness of her life. She was his wife now in every sense of the word.

He held her as if he never wanted to let her go. Time passed and still they lay there together. Molly napped with her head against his chest. When she awoke Nicholas was looking at her, an odd expression upon his handsome face.

She ducked her head, pressing her face against the hard muscle of his shoulder. "Why are you looking at me like that?" The intensity of his gaze frightened her. It was as if he were memorizing the contours of her face against the day she would be gone.

"I must look a sight," she said, reaching up to smooth her tangled hair.

"You look beautiful," he said, capturing her hand and kissing her palm. "Even more beautiful than before."

"That's not possible! How can you say such a foolish thing?"

He answered her with a lazy kiss. "Has anybody ever told you that you ask too many questions?"

She chuckled. "Everybody. When Fritzie told me how it was between men and women, I asked so many questions that I feared the poor woman would die of embarrassment before I was done."

He smoothed her hair from her cheek as she curled against his side. "Many women are uncomfortable with the physical aspects of marriage."

"Not Fritzie! Talking about it was one thing, but certainly she and Will..." She allowed her voice to trail off. "You understand what I mean."

He grinned in the darkness, bewitched by his unpredictable young wife. "So Fritzie and her husband enjoy what happens between the sheets. Good for them."

Molly poked him in the ribs. "Don't you dare say a word to them about it! I shouldn't be speaking of such things with you."

"I'm your husband, Molly. Who better?" The fact that they were lying naked in each other's arms hadn't occurred to his beautiful bride.

"There was always a special bond between them," Molly continued after a moment's pause. "Something that was private and for them alone. I knew it had to do with the bedroom, but I wasn't entirely certain what it was."

"I thought Fritzie told you about lovemaking."

"Oh, of course, she did," said Molly, "but I certainly didn't believe anyone in their right mind would do such a thing."

He cupped her breast in his hand. "Have you had a change of heart?"

"Perhaps," she said in a prim, schoolgirlish tone of voice, "but you may try to convince me more so, if you wish."

He rolled her over onto her back and positioned himself between her legs. "Convinced?" he asked.

Her back arched. "Not yet."

He pressed against her femininity. "Are you beginning to see my point?"

"I'm not certain."

He lowered himself onto her, burying his manhood in her welcoming sheath.

"Ahh, yes," said Molly on a sigh. "I see exactly what you mean...."

"They know," said Molly the next morning as they made their way into the crowded dining saloon for breakfast.

"They don't know," said Nicholas, the corners of his mouth twitching in a half smile.

"Of course they know. See the way they're looking at us. I'm certain they know exactly what we...that we..."

"We're newlyweds," he said after they took their places at the table. "It's to be expected."

Molly's cheeks blossomed with color, and he resisted the urge to pull her into his lap and kiss her thoroughly.

"Perhaps," she said hesitantly, "but must they smile at us like that, as if they had been peeking into our cabin?"

Nicholas reached for her hand and laced his fingers with hers. "Look at Reggie and Mona," he said, gesturing casually toward the Tompkinses, "now imagine them in their nightshirts." He lowered his voice and whispered something so outrageously bawdy that Molly burst into laughter despite her shock.

"Nicholas!" she protested, eyes wide with amazement.

"It isn't as if we didn't do exactly that last night," he pointed out.

"Yes, but I simply can't even think about anyone else doing so." She covered her face with her hands while she battled with some very undignified giggles. Peering through her fingers, she noticed the wicked twinkle in his eyes and her heart soared. "Even Lord Bruxton and Lady Agnes?"

"Swinging from the chandelier in full regalia," said Nicholas with a straight face.

The waiter greeted them with a smile and deposited a pot of tea and a tray of freshly baked scones before them. The sideboard groaned beneath a full array of meats, fish and eggs, and passengers were invited to help themselves to whatever they desired for their morning meal. Nicholas immediately set out to consider the offerings. Molly demurred, finding the tea was enough.

Life was so odd, she mused as she watched him fill his platter with kippers and scrambled eggs and thick slabs of Virginia ham. She'd spent so much of her life daydreaming about the time when she could feast on fancy foods, and now that the opportunity was before her, she discovered food to be the last thing on her mind. In truth she could feast on the sight of her husband, so tall and strong and handsome, and never sate her hunger—a hunger she hadn't realized existed until last night.

He took his seat opposite her. He was a paradox: a man of large passions, yet tempered by a wall of reserve she sensed that she had yet to breach. She wondered if she ever would.

"You should eat," he said, frowning at her.

"You sound like Fritzie. She always said I was too skinny."

"You're perfect," he said. "I want you to stay that way."

"Are you flattering me?" She wouldn't have figured him for the type.

"I don't flatter anybody. I'm telling the truth as I see it." He glanced away toward the far end of the room, then back again at her. "To me, you're perfect."

Molly, on the verge of swooning with delight, was saved only by the approach of Mona and Reggie Tompkins. Nicholas rose to greet them.

"I must say, you both look decidedly happy this morning," boomed Reggie. "The sea air must agree with you."

Molly blushed beet red, and for a moment she thought her husband turned a trifle pink as well. He, however, recovered much more quickly than she did.

"Join us," he said, motioning for the steward to fetch extra chairs.

"Yes," said Molly, regaining her composure. "Please do."

Mona Tompkins was a woman of great perspicacity, and Molly realized the older woman had already figured out that they wanted to share this breakfast alone. Reggie was about to settle himself down for a long chat when Mona slipped her arm through her husband's.

"You promised me a stroll on the promenade," Mona said, "and I shan't let you deprive me of your company." With a mock scowl she turned toward Nicholas. "I hear that you and my husband gave the Frasier brothers quite a time at cards last night."

"Yes," said Reggie, his teeth broad and white beneath his walrus mustache, "that we did. And I'm trusting Nicholas will join me again today in an encore."

"Not today," said Nicholas, his eyes meeting Molly's.

"No," said Molly, wondering if you could drown in a man's blue eyes. "Not today."

Reggie and Mona bade them good-morning, then departed for their constitutional.

"I hope we weren't rude," she said, fussing with her cup of tea.

"They understand," said Nicholas. "They know how it is."

Indeed, as the day wore on it seemed to Molly as if everyone on board ship knew exactly how it was between them. Everyone from the captain to the lowliest deckhand had a smile and a kind word for them as she and Nicholas reclined on the striped deck chairs or strolled, arm in arm, about the deck. They said little to each other. Words seemed unnecessary. Molly felt as if everything she was thinking, all the tumultuous emotions she was experiencing, were all there in her eyes, visible for him to see.

Molly had never been very good at hiding her feelings. She had about her that soft, dewy look that made plain women pretty and turned beautiful women into angels. In her case, that look rendered her celestial.

Everything Nicholas had ever feared about the magic of being the first lover in a woman's life was happening right now, in front of his very eyes, and he didn't seem able to summon up the will to stop it. It would be so easy to pull away from her, to take Reggie up on his offer to spend the day at the card table with the Frasiers. A sharp word. An air of distraction. Her heart was a blossoming flower; a quick frost would put an end to its bloom.

He should stop it now. He had the power. She had given it to him last night when she opened her arms and welcomed him inside her innocent body. Her response hadn't surprised him; her feelings had been there in her eyes. It was his own loss of control that scared hell out of him. When it came to the game of love, he had always been in command. His heart had stayed clear of the bedroom, solitary and invulnerable until last night. Last night his heart had been there with him in the room, beating loud and strong, reminding him that sometimes making love could be the most dangerous thing a man could ever do.

Not that Molly had any idea. She'd been unaware how close she was to seeing over the walls he'd erected about himself and discovering the man hidden inside. Last night was the first time she'd offered a man the gift of her lovely young body; and it was the first time he'd come close to offering a woman his heart.

He hadn't, of course. He knew better. He knew where it would lead and how he would feel when she found someone else. And she would. Nothing in life was permanent, especially not happiness.

But they were in the middle of nowhere right now, a vast and timeless ocean where for a little while he could be anything he wanted to be.

Even happy.

The next few days passed quickly for Molly. She felt as if she'd spent all of the years until this moment only half-alive, unaware of the wonders the world had to offer. Colors seemed sharper to her eyes: the translucent blue of the sky, the warm gold of her wedding ring as it shimmered in the candlelight of the dinner table. She loved the roar of the ocean as it pounded against the ship at night.

Safe in the haven of her husband's strong arms, she would breathe deeply of the intoxicating scent of his skin and know a moment of happiness so pure and wondrous that she wished she could stop time.

And he felt the same way. She knew in her heart that he must, for the tenderness and passion he showed her could mean only one thing: that he, too, was falling in love. Surely it was impossible for any two people to know the joy she and Nicholas shared each night unless it sprang from something deeper and more lasting than physical pleasure.

On the fourth night of their journey the captain hosted a gala reception in the ship's main ballroom. Molly was beside herself with excitement. Mona Tompkins had sailed on the *Albert* many times and she said the receptions were second to none.

Molly spent the late afternoon working on her toilette. She took a long, leisurely bath, scenting the water with the perfumed bath salts the cabin steward had found for her. All the foolish, feminine things she had never understood before suddenly took on meaning. She washed her long hair and rinsed it thoroughly, then spent ages combing out the tangles and coaxing it dry. Mona had promised to send her lady's maid to help Molly with her coiffure, and by the time the friendly woman was finished, Molly scarcely recognized herself in the mirror.

"Oh, Fritzie," she said, twirling before the glass in delight. "How I wish you could see me now!" Wouldn't her friends at the Pem hoot with surprise at the sight of their beloved Molly all decked out in silks and satins.

She'd chosen a pale pink satin gown with a tight-fitting bodice and waist. The décolletage emphasized her full breasts while the low back lent a graceful counterpoint to the more modest bustle currently in fashion. According to Mona Tompkins, a lady kept on her kidskin gloves even while dancing. It seemed terribly silly to Molly, but Mona said no well-bred woman would ever do otherwise, though she was hard put to explain why.

"Nicholas!" Molly called out to him as she gathered up her white elbow-length gloves. "I need your help."

He appeared in the doorway, resplendent in his formal attire. He made a show of checking the time on his gold pocket watch. "I doubt if we have time for that, Molly."

"Oh, you!" She tapped him lightly with her soft kid gloves, then turned her back to him. "The last three buttons. Try as I might, I simply couldn't manage to work them through the loops."

Nicholas was all thumbs as he struggled to ease the tiny pearl buttons through the minuscule loops. Finally he managed to fasten the last one, and he breathed an exaggerated sigh of relief.

Molly spun around to face him, then planted a quick kiss to the underside of his jaw. "We should go," she said, fairly dancing with excitement. "Mona said they would meet us at the foot of the promenade."

"Are you certain you wish to attend this soiree?" he asked, keeping his tone carefully light. "I had thought we could have the steward serve us dinner in our stateroom."

The expression of disappointment on her face made him regret his attempt at humor.

He pulled her into his arms and kissed her thoroughly. "Of course we'll go to the captain's party."

She looked up at him. "I might be persuaded to leave the party early—for a good reason."

He whispered a reason into her ear and she laughed low.

"You're a wicked man, Mr. St. George."

"I know." He placed her arm through his. "Now let's get that blasted reception over with so we can move on to more enjoyable ways to spend an evening."

As she'd promised, Mona Tompkins and her husband, Reggie, were awaiting them at the start of the promenade.

"You're late," said Mona with a twinkle in her eye.

"I had wanted to come rap on your door," said Reggie with an equally wicked twinkle, "but Mona reminded me that young couples relish their privacy."

"You're incorrigible," said Molly with a shake of her head, "teasing us the way you do."

"Come, my dear," said Reggie, taking her away from Nicholas. "It is terribly unfashionable to be seen entering a reception with one's own spouse."

She laughed and accepted his arm. "The ways of the rich continue to amaze me."

"My dear," said Reggie, "you have yet to discover just how amazing Britain's wealthy can be. Once the Marquess of Aylsford actually—"

"Not that story, Reginald!" Mona broke in quickly. "Molly is much too young to hear of such things."

Molly, of course, was suddenly and intensely curious, but she knew such curiosity would seem most unladylike so she smiled instead as her husband offered his arm to Mona. Together the four of them entered the ballroom.

"The Pavilion couldn't be any more beautiful than this," Molly said to Nicholas later as they attempted a waltz on the crowded and tiny dance floor. "When I was a little girl, I used to dream of how it would be to wear a beautiful gown and dance with the man of my—" She stopped abruptly. "Oh, will you look at the Tompkinses! I had no idea Reggie was such a marvelous dancer."

How close she had come to telling him he was the man of her dreams. She supposed under more normal circumstances a wife would gladly tell her husband that he was everything wonderful she had ever imagined in a man, but despite the physical intimacy they shared, Molly was aware that not once had they ever put their feelings into words.

If only she had the courage to break the silence and tell him how wonderful he was . . . how important he had become to her in such a short length of time. But how on earth did you say that to the man you had tricked into marriage in order to further your own cause? She had to remember why she was here with him and not allow her foolishly romantic imagination to turn it into something it could never be.

Learn to appreciate what is. Fritzie's words sounded as clear to Molly as if the kind woman were standing right next to her. The past lived on in memory. The future lay ahead, unknowable. She had only the here and now. Had any woman ever been so lucky?

"Molly. Nicholas. You must meet Sir Nigel and Lady Arabella. I believe your Merriton Hall is but a stone's throw from Burnside Manor."

"Oh, do let's join them," said Molly. "It's so exciting to meet our neighbors."

Nicholas seemed unduly reticent. "There's plenty of time for neighbors, Molly. The time will come when you'll wish we hadn't as many of them."

"But it's so wonderful to have friends there before we even arrive," she persisted, trying to will away the sense of unease beginning to take hold. "What a wonderful way to begin our life at Merriton."

Nicholas stopped dancing. "As you wish, Molly." He led her toward the two couples waiting for them across the ballroom.

The other afternoon over tea Mona Tompkins had tried to explain the various ranks of British nobility, but Molly had had a dreadful time trying to comprehend the difference between a duke, an earl, and a lowly baron. For some reason there were but twenty-seven dukes in the world at any one time, but an infinite number of barons and "sirs." Sometimes you used their first name with the title, sometimes the last, and on a number of inexplicable occasions it seemed to Molly that both first and last names were tossed aside in favor of a name that made no sense at all.

Maybe Nicholas was right, she thought as they approached the aristocratic-looking elderly couple who stood with the affable Tompkinses. There was plenty of time to meet the neighbors. Perhaps after she had studied the intricacies of the peerage, she would be ready to actually put herself to the test. For the first time in her life, she fully appreciated the simplicity of the American way of life. *Good morning, Molly... How are you, Mr. James... Is Fritzie going to market today?* Even President Cleveland would one day go back to being plain old Grover.

But she had no time for such silly musings. Mona, with almost parental pride, was performing the introductions and before Molly could gather her wits about her, she was plunged headlong into the mainstream of British society. She could only pray she remembered how to swim.

She had what was called the "common touch." Queen Victoria didn't have it, nor did her eldest daughter. Albert Edward, the Prince of Wales, definitely had it and the people loved him for it. Even half a world away in Australia, Bertie commanded the affection of his subjects.

And it appeared to Nicholas that his young American bride had that same magical quality that drew the unlikeliest of people to her side. Sir Nigel and Lady Arabella looked to be perfect examples of crusty English society, but in a matter of minutes, Molly had them eating from her definitively American hand. She neither fawned nor gushed. She was just herself, the same friendly and good-natured girl who greeted the shopkeeper as if he were a king—and would no doubt treat a king as if he were a friend.

"Charming," said Sir Nigel as he drew Nicholas aside over a glass of champagne. "Utterly charming. Where on earth did you find such an enchanting creature?"

He had to laugh at the question.

"Is something funny, my good man? I scarcely think my question is untoward."

"Of course it's not, Sir Nigel," Nicholas said smoothly, aware of Molly's curious glance. "The truth is, we met at a seaside hotel."

"In the States?"

"Delaware," said Nicholas. "Beautiful place." He ignored Molly's barely repressed giggle. What would the good man think if he knew the truth, that Molly and Nicholas had been married at gunpoint in the lobby of the ugliest establishment in the Western hemisphere. He opted to steer the conversation along a safer path. "I'm not familiar with Burnside Manor. Where is it?"

"Southwest of Merriton."

He nodded, as memories returned. "Georgian mansion?" he asked. "Ivy-covered walls...a kennel of hounds?"

"A perfect description of Burnside," said Lord Nigel agreeably. "Only now we have three kennels of the finest hounds to be found anywhere in the British Isles." The old man's pale blue eyes softened. "Promised one to your father when he was a lad. Never did see to it that he got his pup." He frowned thoughtfully. "I'd like to rectify that oversight."

"You wish to give us a hound?"

"Our finest bitch is due to whelp any day. As soon as the pups are weaned, you are welcome to the pick of the litter."

Molly, who had been eavesdropping shamelessly, went into raptures at the prospect of a puppy. Nicholas knew when he had been bested and offered his thanks to Sir Nigel.

"You knew my husband's father?" she asked, eyes wide with innocent curiosity.

"A good, kind man," said Sir Nigel. "Shame what happened. Bad business, that. No good ever comes of such things."

Every muscle in his body grew taut with alarm. Molly looked from Sir Nigel to Nicholas, but he didn't meet her eyes. The memories were too raw and ugly; as it was, they would be waiting for him when the HMS *Albert* docked in Southampton in a very few days. He refused to allow them to ruin this interlude. From behind him he caught the strains of another waltz blossoming from the small shipboard orchestra. "Strauss, isn't it?" he asked, turning toward Molly. "I believe my wife owes me a dance."

With a bow toward the assembled company, he swept her into his arms and they were off.

Waltzing with her husband was wonderful, as always, but not even that pleasure could help Molly shake the feeling of unease that had settled over her. She couldn't quite put her finger on the problem, but she knew that the atmosphere had changed with her question to Sir Nigel. Certainly it was normal for a new bride to be curious about her husband's family. She wanted to know everything she possibly could about his people: the color of his mother's hair, his father's sense of humor, uncles and aunts and grandparents. Every last detail about the people and places and events that had made him the man he was.

This was the perfect opportunity to inquire again about his past, to discover what kind of boy he had been, but she'd seen his reaction to Sir Nigel's innocent comments and she hesitated. Everything was so wonderful between them right now, so magical and romantic, that calling down a black cloud to dim the luster of the night seemed foolish.

There would be other opportunities to unravel the fabric of his life. After all, she would have a lifetime to do so.

Chapter Fourteen

The HMS *Albert* was within a day of Southampton, and Nicholas knew the end of their idyll was at hand. He wished Molly hadn't insisted upon joining Mona Tompkins and Lady Arabella for high tea. He glanced toward the bed in the middle of the room. There were a number of other ways he could think of with which to pass the time.

The past six days aboard ship had been the most extraordinary in Nicholas's life. He couldn't remember a time when he had felt more at peace within himself—or more happy.

Happiness was an alien concept to him. Perhaps there had been times in his early childhood when he'd known the simple, unadulterated joy of a new set of tin soldiers or an extra sweet at Christmastime, but he couldn't remember them. He had so little faith in the concept of happiness that whenever it occurred he patched over it like a bad spot on the roof.

So when it occurred to him that this joyous feeling he experienced each morning when he awoke to find Molly asleep in his arms was, indeed, happiness, his first instinct was to run. He wasn't a fool. He knew where feelings like these could lead a man. Love was a faithless emotion, one you couldn't count on. He knew better than to count on anything but himself. Still, there was something so disarming about his wife, so appealing, that he had to remind himself that she, too, had been capable of deception to get her own way.

But it had been done out of love. A man would do anything to save his family, anything at all. Why should it have been any different for her? Her loyalties ran deep as the ocean that held them in its embrace. Once Molly loved, she loved with the fierce and utter devotion that was the stuff of legend.

He wasn't fool enough to think what she felt for him was anything but the first blush of sexuality. He'd always known the danger of being the first man in a woman's life. Love and sex had a way of getting tangled, complicating what should be a simple enough sating of physical hunger. Oh, she probably believed it was love at the moment, but he knew the day would come when she realized that there was more to a marriage than sexual compatibility—or should be.

In a way he wished he could offer her the things that she needed, but he recognized his shortcomings. Already he was coming to regret tearing her away from everything she held dear. She was the type of woman who needed a real home with friends and family traipsing in and out and a pack of hounds trailing mud through the entrance foyer.

And babies.

The notion brought him up short.

He'd never had dreams of a son to carry on his name...or of a daughter as beautiful as his wife. He hadn't much of a legacy to pass on, only old scores to settle—and, after that was accomplished, he hadn't a clue.

Memories of the intimacies they'd shared burned against his eyelids. Caution hadn't once entered into the picture.

"Damn it to hell!" He pounded his fist into the wall, bruising his knuckles. Why hadn't he considered the obvious consequence of lovemaking? The world was a dark and painful place—his corner of the world, in particular—and he had no intention of bringing an innocent child into turmoil.

Children needed security to grow strong. The cradle of their parents' love. They weren't fancy clothes to be discarded when fashion changed. He knew that. He understood it. And there was no way in hell he could imagine being able to offer any of those assurances to a child.

Besides, Molly wasn't much more than a child herself. She didn't know bloody hell about the world. She had lost both of her parents before her tenth birthday, but still the ugly side of life seemed to have passed over her without leaving its shadow behind. When the end came for them, as he knew it one day must, she would be better off leaving unencumbered by a child.

Tomorrow he would see to it that he took matters under control. Today he would simply be more inventive.

Mona Tompkins handed Molly a calling card, then sat back in her chair. "Now tell me what you see."

Molly fingered the heavy parchment. "The upper right-hand corner is turned down," she said, looking across the tea table at her friend. "What on earth does that mean?"

"Quite simple," said Mona. "The caller popped by to pay her respect to the lady of the house."

"And that is not the least of it," said Lady Arabella. "There are first calls, party calls, farewell calls—there is no end to the number of calls an enterprising young wife can make." She smiled knowingly. "But the one thing you must never do is make the first call."

"Why not?"

"Because it simply isn't done, my dear."

"How silly," said Molly with a toss of her head.

"Newcomers are viewed with suspicion," said Mona Tompkins, cutting through the layers of gauzy protocol. "Arabella is right. You must wait until you are called upon by those in a . . . loftier position in society."

Molly's American temperament bristled. "But what if no one comes to call?" she protested, adding extra sugar to her tea. "It seems foolish to sit alone day after day waiting for visitors. I would rather put on my best outfit and pay a call on my neighbors and introduce myself."

Lady Arabella seemed to find that statement immensely funny. "My dear, I shan't think you'll have to wait long for callers. Certainly not with Merriton's history."

"Merriton's history. Do you mean kings and queens and that sort of thing?" How exciting to think royalty might have lived in her home.

"No, dear. The history I'm speaking of is considerably more recent than that. Heaven knows, Merriton hosted some of the most marvelous balls imaginable—at least, before the *scandale*."

Again Molly felt the brush of shadows across her heart. "This is all quite new to me," she said carefully, wishing Nicholas had seen fit to tell her something of his background. "Perhaps you can refresh my memory."

"There was that business with his mother and Jo—"

"Clumsy me!" Mona Tompkins leaped to her feet as warm tea splashed across the table and onto her lap. She brushed at her skirts. "I cannot imagine what possessed me to overturn my teacup that way."

"Frightful mess." Lady Arabella rose to her feet. "As it is, I must be returning to the stateroom. I shall make sure to send a steward to assist."

Neither Molly nor Mrs. Tompkins said a word until Lady Arabella disappeared from sight.

"You deliberately overturned your teacup," said Molly.

"Was I that frightfully obvious?" Mona asked with a rueful shake of her head.

"What was she about to say?"

"Silly old cow," said Mona. "Terrible lot of nonsense."

"It's something about my husband, is it not?"

"Molly." The older woman placed a hand upon Molly's hand. "Perhaps you should speak to your husband about Merriton. It isn't my place to tell you."

"You're making me very nervous," said Molly, eyes wide. "Are there ghosts walking the halls, rattling their chains and howling like the devil?"

"No ghosts," said Mona. "Just gossip better left laid to rest."

"Nicholas hasn't a score of wives buried beneath a gazebo, has he?"

Mona burst into laughter and Molly felt the shadow begin to pass.

"No score of wives, either," said Mona. "Speak with him about it, Molly. I'm sure he'll tell you all you need to know about your new home."

Molly returned to their stateroom, determined to do exactly that, only to discover her husband awaiting her with other things on his mind.

Before she had the chance to catch her breath, she found herself divested of her clothing and swept into his arms.

"Good heavens!" she exclaimed. "You are certainly in an amorous mood this afternoon."

"Our last afternoon at sea." He placed her on the bed, then quickly shed his clothes.

She recalled that first afternoon in Cape Charlotte when she had surprised him in his room and gloried in the splendor of his form.

"You're smiling," he said as he joined her on the bed.

"I know."

"Care to tell me why?"

"Your clothes," she said, pressing her lips to the underside of his jaw. "You cannot seem to keep them on your body. It was one of the first things I noticed about you. I never knew a man could be beautiful."

She could tell from the pleased expression on his face that her words had touched him, but he said nothing. Instead he began a slow and thorough exploration of her body that soon drove everything but pleasure from her mind. He made love to her in ways that were as inventive as they were exciting, and she was amazed to discover how many variations there could be upon a theme.

Afterward she drew a bath and they soaked together in the tub. She felt boneless and disgracefully lazy, lying back in his arms as the warm, scented water lapped about her breasts and throat.

"I wish we could sail around the world," she murmured, her head resting against his chest.

"So do I, Molly." He cupped her breasts with his hands, and the slippery sensation sent waves of delight through her body. Would she never grow accustomed to the pleasures of the flesh?

"Italy," she said with a dreamy sigh. "The Eternal City...the Colosseum...it would be so wonderful to discover them all with you."

"Tahiti," said her husband. "The smell of flowers everywhere...sparkling turquoise sea warmer than this tub...beautiful native women—"

"Nicholas!" She sat bolt upright, splashing water over the rim of the tub and onto the floor. "What do you mean, 'beautiful native women'?"

He pulled her back against his chest. "You have nothing to worry about, Molly. In my eyes, your beauty has no equal."

She didn't care to think about all those beautiful, unclothed native women. Especially not with her husband, who had his own difficulties when it came to remaining clothed.

"Australia," she said. They wore clothes in Australia. "Didn't you tell Fritzie that you spent time in Australia? I'd love for you to show me the country."

"That part of my life is over," he said. She wondered if she detected more than a hint of regret in his voice. "England is home now. For both of us."

"Home can be anywhere you want it to be."

"England," he repeated. "I've waited a long time to claim what is mine."

That notion was one that Molly could understand. Yet, when he spoke of England, he sounded vaguely unhappy. She'd asked him to describe Merriton and the surrounding countryside, but all he had done was sketch a black-and-white verbal sketch of a land she wasn't entirely sure she could learn to love. If only he sounded more enthusiastic about Merriton, she might be able to summon up her usual optimism. But the more he talked, the more certain she became that Lady Arabella's comments were rooted in fact.

She wasn't certain how she knew it, but Molly somehow understood that Nicholas wasn't returning to Merriton Hall because he loved the familial estate. He was returning to settle an old score.

Every house had a history, she told herself. Certainly the Pemberton Arms had been the site of many a memorable occurrence. Why, her own wedding to Nicholas would be talked about for years to come! Tomorrow she would see Merriton Hall with her very own eyes. There would be time enough then to discover its secrets. And when she did, she had the feeling she would discover the key to her husband's heart, as well.

"I shall be your first caller," declared Lady Arabella as she bade farewell to Molly and Nicholas at dockside in Southampton the next morning. "I am most anxious to see Merriton again."

Lord Nigel kissed Molly's hand. "Remember, my dear, pick of the litter. I'll see to it you have the finest hound for miles around."

"Thank you, sir. I look forward to it."

Nicholas was rigidly polite, offering no more in the way of friendship than was strictly necessary.

"I had hoped to be your first caller," said Mona Tompkins, giving Molly a warm hug, "but it seems I shall have to move quickly if I am to best that female garden snake."

Molly giggled at the thought of Lady Arabella slithering through the grass in search of a juicy mouse. "You are welcome anytime," she said sincerely to both Mona and her husband, Reggie. Nicholas echoed her sentiments with a great deal more cordiality than he'd expressed toward Lord Nigel and Lady Arabella.

The Tompkinses planned to spend a few days with their married daughter and her family at their house a few miles outside Southampton. Molly and Nicholas said goodbye, then climbed aboard their rented coach. The train for London left in three-quarters of an hour and before long Molly would be at her new home.

She and Nicholas talked little on the trip. Sleep had been elusive for both of them the night before, and so they dozed companionably as the train rattled on its tracks. Molly woke up just as they approached the outskirts of London.

"Nicholas." She shook him. "Look at the sky. What on earth is wrong?" A thick, gray cloud of what seemed like smoke hovered over everything, obscuring her view. In the distance she thought she could see the outline of houses and buildings, but it was difficult to be certain through the haze.

"Welcome to the age of industrialization," he said dryly. "This is actually quite a nice afternoon—at least, for London."

Molly felt a fierce and sudden longing for the blue skies and sunny beaches of Cape Charlotte. She had read about factory towns in Pennsylvania and Massachusetts that suffered from this problem, but she'd never imagined she would live in such a place. "It isn't always like this, is it?"

"Sometimes it's worse," he said. "After all, England is known for its rain."

Molly sank into her seat, depressed beyond measure. What a horrid place. Cities had never held much appeal for her, but New York had been surprisingly exciting. She'd certainly expected London to be equally thrilling.

If only Mona had told her what to expect. All of that talk of calling cards and servants and the proper gloves to wear while dancing, and no one had ever seen fit to tell her that the sun never shone.

She peered out the window again, wishing she had a handkerchief to wipe away the grit from the glass. There was the possibility, of course, that the sun *was* shining, but it was difficult to tell through the dirt and the haze.

"A city for mushrooms," she muttered as the train rumbled on toward the station. She brightened as a thought occurred to her. "Merriton Hall isn't in London, is it?"

Nicholas, his expression distant, glanced at her. "No, it isn't. We're on the outskirts."

That will make all the difference, she thought, summoning up her old optimism. *It must!*

The sky was less thick with soot than in London proper, but still the gray fog hung low over the buildings and trees, making Molly feel as if the air were being sucked from her lungs.

"Over the next ridge," said Nicholas to the driver of the carriage. He turned to Molly. "We're almost there."

Again she noted his almost eerie detachment, as if his surroundings were of little import. *This is your home, Nicholas,* she thought, watching his face. *This is where you were born, where your people lived and died. Why do you look as if this is the last place on earth you want to be?*

How splendid the Pem had seemed to her when she came home after spending a night in Philadelphia with Fritzie. She had raced up the porch steps and burst into the lobby, wishing she could wrap her arms about the

house and hug it tight. Why, when she returned to Cape
Charlotte for a visit, she might do exactly that!

But there was no excitement about her husband. No
sense of homecoming or sentiment. If anything, the
closer they came to Merriton Hall, the more distant he
grew. It made her feel uneasy and more than a bit frightened. Merriton Hall was his home and if he disliked it so,
what hope was there for her?

The driver eased the coach up a curved drive, then
halted the horses. Molly, eager for a glimpse of the house,
peered out the window and nearly fell from the coach in
surprise. Merriton was a rectangular building of brick
and stone with an enormous mahogany door right in the
center. Scores of leaded windows looked down at Molly,
and she imagined scores of curious servants peering out
at her from behind the curtains. Two enormous wings
projected at right angles from either side of the main
structure, forming what could have been a very imposing front courtyard—at least it could have been if the
grounds had seen a gardener's touch in the past twenty
years or so. It seemed to Molly that the weeds were halfway to the second story and climbing fast.

"You could fit four Pems inside there and have room
for the King George Hotel!" she exclaimed, as she waited
for Nicholas to exit the carriage then assist her to the
ground. "This must be bigger than the White House."

"I wouldn't know." Nicholas grabbed her by the waist
and swung her to the ground. "I have never seen the
White House."

Neither had Molly, but she was certain only a president or a king could possible live in a bigger house.

"Come," said Nicholas, offering his arm. "We'll go
in."

She hesitated. "Our trunks and valises," she began. "What about—" She stopped in midsentence as servants in livery streamed from the house.

"I hired staff just before I went to the States," he said. "Apparently they are eager to make an impression on their employer."

Molly watched, stunned, as a butler of apparent stature bowed to her husband.

"Welcome home, sir," said the elegant man in the elegant uniform. "We trust your trip was a successful one."

"Quite successful," said Nicholas with a nod of his head. He turned to Molly, and for an instant she felt as if he were a stranger to her. "This is Jarvis, the head butler. Jarvis, I'd like to present the new Mrs. St. George."

"An honor, ma'am."

Molly gaped as the butler bowed to her. She looked to Nicholas for assistance but none was forthcoming.

"I'm glad to meet you, Mr. Jarvis," she said, extending her hand in greeting.

Jarvis looked at her as if she'd been caught spitting in church.

"Have I done something wrong?" she asked her husband, aware of the angry flush staining her throat and cheeks.

"We'll discuss it later." Taking her arm, he led her up the pathway toward the house.

Inside, a dozen or so servants awaited them in the front hallway, and Molly suffered the agony of further introductions. She didn't repeat her mistake of offering a hand in greeting, but even with the youngest housemaid, she felt a definite chill.

"They must suspect I was one of them," she remarked as Nicholas led her into a sparsely furnished drawing room off the hallway. She tried to make light of her embarrassment. "Have I the look of the kitchen about me?"

Her husband didn't rise to the bait. "They'll learn," he said in a measured tone of voice, "or they'll be replaced."

Again she had the feeling of uncertainty, as if the man she had come to know this past week had been a figment of her imagination. "Could they possibly think I'm one of those giddy American heiresses who caught herself a fancy English husband?"

He looked at her. "Where did you get such a foolish idea?"

"Lady Arabella told me all about them. Apparently it's quite the thing to do these days."

"Lady Arabella is a horse's ass."

"I agree," said Molly, trying hard not to appear shocked by his words, "but she certainly seems to know her way about English society." And she also seemed to know a great deal more about Molly's husband and new home than Molly did.

Nicholas poured them each a sherry from the bottle on the ebony bar, then motioned for her to take a seat near the window.

"Lady Arabella thrives on the affairs of others. You would do well to avoid her."

Molly glanced up from her sherry, frankly puzzled. "How is it you know so much about Lady Arabella? I thought you had spent but two months in England in the past fifteen years."

"I don't want that woman in this house."

Molly's temper flared, and she placed the glass of sherry down on the side table with a bang. "She intends to pay me a call. Would you prefer I hang a No Trespassing sign on the front door?"

"I would prefer you choose your acquaintances with more care."

"It isn't my acquaintance that Lady Arabella is interested in," she shot back. "It's this house."

She watched as his jawline hardened.

"What did she say about Merriton?"

"She said that I shouldn't have to worry about first calls because Merriton would be quite an attraction."

"Ignore her."

"How can I ignore her when I do not have any idea what she's talking about?" She rose to her feet and crossed the room to stand near him. "You are terribly secretive, Nicholas. Is there something I should know?"

"Nothing of importance."

The dark expression in his eyes made that hard to believe. "Why are we here?" She placed a tentative hand on his forearm. "You haven't smiled once since we docked in Southampton." And it wasn't simply the absence of a smile that worried her; it was the palpable air of tension that surrounded him. If only he seemed happier...

"This is where I belong," he said in a tone of voice so devoid of emotion that she wondered why he'd said anything at all. "I have waited a long time to reclaim what's mine." The expression in his eyes made her breath catch in her throat. "You should understand what that is like."

She did, but what she didn't understand was why it was so important to him—or why it seemed to afford him so little happiness.

"There's so much I want to know about you," she began, once again treading into uncharted territory. "If only you would tell me something about Merriton, or even my uncle, I would—"

"You know all you need to know." He downed his sherry and put the empty glass on the table next to her full one. "My past belongs to me, but I am willing to share the present with you."

"The present?" Her throat grew so tight with emotion that her words came with difficulty. "Most married couples dream about the future."

"I cannot offer you something I don't believe in, Molly."

"Everyone believes in the future." The future was what you planned for, worked for, prayed for. How could he not believe in it?

"I can't change," he said, moving to draw her into his arms. "This is the man you have married."

A feeling of sorrow washed over her, a feeling she knew she would not be able to banish easily. She'd always been able to sense the emotional climate of a house, the way someone else might gauge the weather. The Pem had been filled with joy, no matter what problems life tossed its way.

Merriton Hall, however, ached with sadness. She felt it creeping into her bones. He claimed he had no interest in the past, but she wasn't entirely certain about that. There was the sense of unfinished business about him, as if he had something to accomplish before he could allow himself to be happy.

Memories of the past and dreams for the future were an integral part of love, of life itself. If he denied himself those, then he was also denying her the chance to understand the man she'd married.

She leaned her head against his shoulder and closed her eyes. Then again, perhaps that was exactly what he wanted.

As Nicholas had feared, the ghosts were there waiting for him. Darkness lurked around every corner. Sadness hid behind closed doors. The sound of the gunshot blast that had ended his father's life lay just below the silence echoing through the empty corridors.

Damn Lady Arabella and her morbid curiosity. He wondered how much the woman had told Molly about Merriton and all that had happened here. Fifteen years had gone by since the whole thing happened. You would think a woman like that would have more important things to occupy her mind. Apparently scandals—especially ones that involved a faithless wife, a cunning lover and a desperate husband—lingered forever.

The day he'd fled England he'd vowed that he would never talk about his father's suicide, and thus far he had kept that vow. He intended to go on doing so, even if it meant erecting a wall between him and his wife.

In truth that wall was begun. Their magical idyll was over. She already suspected something was amiss. Lady Arabella had pointed her in the right direction, but Nicholas had no doubt that before long his wife would sense that Merriton Hall needed more than a roof that didn't leak and furniture to fill the empty corners. When she did he wouldn't blame her if she set sail for America and her old life in Cape Charlotte. He wouldn't try to stop her, no matter how much it hurt.

Happiness was fleeting, if it existed at all, but then hadn't he learned that a very long time ago in this very house?

Chapter Fifteen

Merriton Hall

Dear Fritzie,

I am at my new home and a sorrier place you have never seen. Nothing is as I had thought it would be. My heart aches for all the beautiful items that must be locked away in the attic, growing as dusty as the furniture in the parlor. English servants are certainly nothing like our homegrown variety. They seem more snobbish than the lords and ladies I met aboard HMS *Albert*. Jarvis, the head butler, makes Lady Arabella seem like one of us.

Yet, despite all their fancy ways, they don't seem to know how to do the simplest things. Your eyes would pop if you saw the grimy marble mantels and the warped wooden floors. The Oriental rugs look like they were used as horse blankets. The maids spend most of their time giggling in the hallways and the senior staff eats more than we do. Something should be done, but I feel as if I am invisible to them.

How it makes me laugh when I think of the complaints the Pem has suffered through the years, when this fancy English mansion is in far worse shape! London is dark and dreary, and even here, some few miles out of town, a gray haze seems to hang over everything. Even Nicholas seems different since our arrival. He—

Molly put down her pen and stared out at the English countryside beyond her bedroom window. It was dark outside and she could see little beyond the shapes of trees bending in the night breezes. She couldn't possibly tell Fritzie that she and her husband had not made love for two nights. Her cheeks burned just thinking about making so personal a revelation. Yet how she longed for someone to talk to. Maybe this was a normal part of being newly married.

She had no idea if newlyweds made love twice a day, once a night or every other week, and there was no one she could ask. It couldn't be that Nicholas no longer wanted her. She had seen the look in his eyes when she came to bed. She had no doubt that he desired her, but for some reason he had not followed through on that desire.

Perhaps he was tired. Returning to Merriton had obviously been trying for him. She had only to look at the furrows on his brow and the harsh line of his mouth to know this homecoming was anything but a happy one.

She had been so excited about seeing Merriton, but now the best she could do was try to ignore the dismal view, the strange sounds, the musty smell of the mattress and tell herself that one day the place would seem like home.

"Have you finished your letter to Fritzie?"

Molly turned her head to see her husband standing in the doorway. She smiled up at him as he approached. "I have barely begun. There is so much to tell her about."

"I can imagine."

She gestured toward the chest of drawers across the room. "I brought up a pot of tea and some cake."

"Dinner was an abomination, was it not?"

She didn't deny it. "I found myself thinking longingly of Fritzie's beef stew."

She watched as he stripped off his shirt, then extinguished the lamp on her desk. "You can finish the letter in the morning."

"I suppose so." She wasn't up to arguing over her letter to Fritzie. At least if she did not finish the letter now, she would have something of import with which to occupy herself tomorrow.

"I'm going into London in the morning," he said as they climbed into bed. "Will you be all right alone?"

"We've been here but two days and there is so much to attend to. I wish you would stay."

"I have business in town, Molly. As it is, it's been put off much longer than is practical."

"One more day?" she asked, hating the vulnerable sound of her voice. "Certainly one more day cannot make that much difference."

"It has already been weeks," he said. "I cannot put it off any longer. You understand, don't you?"

"Of course," she said, but she did not.

In truth, Nicholas hadn't expected her to understand. She thought he was avoiding her, keeping her an arm's length away—and he was. He wanted nothing more than to take her into his arms and hold her close, but he was painfully aware of where that would lead. He couldn't take that chance. In London he would take care of that simple matter, and tomorrow night he would once again know the pleasures of her body.

He extinguished the candle on the nightstand and for a very long time he lay awake, listening to the sound of his young wife's breathing in the dark and quiet room.

The hours hung heavy on Molly's hands. Nicholas was already gone when she awoke the next morning. She rang for a pot of tea, but by the time a surly maid delivered it, the brew was cold and her temper was hot. She vented her anger in her letter to Fritzie, and while it felt good to put all of her terrible thoughts down on paper, letter writing was no substitute for a true heart-to-heart.

But no sense wishing for the moon. She supposed she could describe her bedroom to Fritzie, but there was precious little in there worth the ink. To her surprise, the entire house was devoid of personal touches. She'd expected pictures and mementos, the sort of visual legacy she'd always imagined the English prided themselves on displaying. She'd asked one of the servants about this surprising lack, and the girl had said, "They have crates of them up in the attic, ma'am, but we heard noises and nobody wants to go up there."

So Molly amused herself by arranging her clothing in the wardrobe, grouping her new outfits according to activity. She sat in front of her dressing table mirror and experimented with elaborate coiffures that would have made her laugh not one month ago. She considered writing separate letters to Arthur and Stella, but decided that would be ridiculous since Fritzie would undoubtedly share each and every missive from Molly with the entire staff.

She glanced at the seven-day clock on the mantel. Noon was still an hour away. For the first time since her

arrival, she understood why upper-class Englishwomen
spent their days traipsing from mansion to mansion de-
livering silly calling cards to other upper-class Englishwomen with time on their hands.

She laughed mirthlessly as she pressed her forehead
against the window glass. Not that any of those blue-
blooded Englishwomen was beating a path to her door.
The only visitor to Merriton since her arrival had been a
tinker, come to sharpen the knives. Once again she was
struck by the foolishness of the rules for visiting. No one
came to call on her, and she was not allowed to call on her
social betters.

And how was she supposed to know who was her superior and who was her inferior? The very concept sick-
ened Molly. Oh, she wasn't fool enough to believe there
was no class system in America. She knew better than
that. But she also knew a thing or two about neighborli-
ness and the art of making friends, and she wasn't about
to sit still another minute and wait for someone else to
make the first move.

She pulled a beautiful sky-blue-and-white dress from
her closet and laid it across the bed. She wasn't entirely
certain if this was a walking dress, a visiting dress or an
at-home dress, but it would have to do. Spirits rising with
excitement, she chose the proper crinolines and hose, and
before she could lose her nerve she dressed and headed
downstairs.

"I am going visiting," she announced to Jarvis without preamble. "Please bring a trap to the front door."
There. She sounded like a proper English matron.

He arched a brow in the same superior way as the
maître d' at the Pavilion had. This time, however, she
refused to be cowed. "Madam wishes a driver?"

"That won't be necessary. I have driven a trap before."

"As you wish, madam." With a bow he headed back toward the kitchen and, moments later, she heard the sound of laughter and a loud, "Shh!"

Well, no matter. Let them think whatever they wanted to think. She wasn't some pampered lady capable of doing nothing more strenuous than buffing her nails.

Moments later a trap was brought round. The vehicle was scuffed and the wheels squeaked loudly, but it was her means of escape. She almost felt sorry for the horse; he looked rather surprised to be called upon. He also seemed undernourished, and she made a mental note to have Nicholas check on the stables to make certain whatever animals were in residence there were being properly cared for.

"Well, I hope you know where our neighbors are," she said to the horse as they started off. The odds were if she kept to the road that wound past Merriton, she would encounter another estate before too long.

There wasn't a soul to be seen anywhere. Birds flitted from tree to tree and a rabbit scampered across the road, much to Molly's delight. How on earth did the other wives manage the isolation? Day after day with no one but yourself for company. If only Nicholas hadn't decided to travel to London today. It would have been nice to discover the area with her husband by her side. She supposed children made a difference in a woman's life. Once a woman had a baby or two, certainly she hadn't time for things like loneliness or boredom.

Back home in Cape Charlotte the day was just beginning. Molly smiled to herself as she imagined Fritzie bustling down the rickety staircase as she called out, "No bacon today, but the best oatmeal in town!" There was always something to do at the Pem. If Molly wasn't changing bed linens or dusting or helping Fritzie in the kitchen, she was out in the crystalline sunshine as she hung laundry or tended to the marketing. And there was no such thing as being alone in Cape Charlotte. There was a friendly face and a jovial hello around every corner.

How much she had taken for granted. Sharp pangs of homesickness nipped at her heart. She missed her friends at the Pem sorely, Fritzie most of all. There were so many things she wanted to ask, so many confidences she wished to share with the woman who had been the only mother Molly had ever known. That, of course, was impossible now, but Molly took a measure of comfort in the fact that the Pem was on the way back to its former glory—and that there would be all the bacon and roasts of beef that her friends could ever desire.

Molly guided the trap through a nasty curve, congratulating herself on remembering how to handle the reins. Finally, after what seemed like an endless ride, she was rewarded by the sight of an impressive baronial mansion atop a gentle hill. The wheels of the trap creaked alarmingly as it bounced its way up the rutted drive, and for an instant she wondered if a wheel might pop off.

That would certainly be a unique way to meet the neighbors, she thought as she pulled back on the reins, then climbed down from her perch. As if by magic, the elaborately carved front door swung open as soon as her booted feet touched the ground, and a butler stepped out to help her from the trap. The butler was whip-thin and terribly tall, and he wore a uniform an admiral in the U.S. Navy might envy. The English certainly did go for pomp and circumstance.

"I'm here to see the lady of the house," said Molly, offering up her best smile. "My name is Molly St. George."

Nothing. Not a smile. Not a handshake. Not even the slightest flicker of acknowledgment.

"I'm from Merriton Hall," she said, wishing she didn't feel quite so nervous. From the look on his face he apparently thought her a well-dressed maid. "I'm—I'm the lady of the house."

The mask slipped back in place. "May I have your card, madam?"

"I'm afraid I don't have a card quite yet. I have only just arrived at Merriton Hall, and there is still a great deal to be done."

"I cannot approach Lady Belville without a card."

She widened her smile. "I'm certain you can make an exception for a new neighbor, can't you? I'll make certain Lady Belville receives my very first card."

"Lady Belville does not receive…strangers. You may, however, leave your card."

Molly swallowed down her frustration. "I don't have a card," she repeated. "If you tell her I am here to pay my respects, I'm certain she'll see me."

"Lady Belville prefers to make the first call," he said, obviously a man immune to friendliness. "I shall tell her you are in residence."

Short of punching the butler in the nose and marching into Lady Belville's home, there was nothing more Molly could do. Obviously these people took their protocol seriously—more seriously than the situation warranted, in her opinion. She knew when she had been put in her place and she beat a hasty retreat to the relative security of Merriton. Storming into the house, she headed upstairs to the bedroom she shared with Nicholas, eager to express her opinion of his countrymen.

Nicholas had yet to return from London. Frustrated and angry, she took off the pretty blue and white dress. Somehow one of her faded cotton gowns had escaped the dustbin, and she defiantly slipped it over her head and fastened the buttons. If she was going to be treated like a charwoman, then she might as well look like one.

She glanced about at the dusty and dirty bedroom and wrinkled her nose. She might have been poor when she lived at the Pem, but she'd never lived in squalor. Maybe the servants were too proud to scrub and polish but she wasn't. Rolling up her sleeves she got down to work.

The trip to London was shaping up to be successful on all counts. Nicholas's money was multiplying, as it should, and his plans to form a shipping company were at last moving forward. Now that he was back in England to stay, he intended to apply himself to that endeavor with the same intensity with which he had approached his pursuit of Australian gold.

He had to admit there was something arid and unsatisfying about the way his fortune was growing without him. "Your affairs are in perfect order," said the banker with a pleased smile. "You needn't have returned from the States so soon. Everything is under control." He found himself missing the years when each pound and shilling was the result of hard work. In a way he wished he could have stayed in the States, and not returned to England at all. But that was ridiculous. He'd waited years to reclaim his heritage.

From the bank he had gone to see his solicitor, only to find the man's reaction extremely disconcerting.

Franklin Morris had laughed loud and long upon hearing the identity of the new Mrs. St. George. "Dear boy, you have finally bested Jonathan Hughes once and for all. Taking his niece to wife undermined everything he attempted to do with that blackhearted bequest of his." According to Franklin, Nicholas had turned the malevolent intent of that inheritance upside down. "The last of the Hughes clan is now a St. George! I daresay this is the ultimate revenge."

Franklin reached for the whiskey while Nicholas attempted to banish the sense of unease his solicitor's words conjured up. "I'm afraid the story isn't quite as cut-and-dried as it would seem in the initial telling." It was Molly who had engineered the stunt that resulted in their marriage, but he had sought to spare Molly that embarrassment. Franklin was a fine solicitor but he enjoyed social gossip as much as he enjoyed his whiskey.

"To revenge," said Franklin, handing Nicholas his glass. "The foundation of many a fortune."

"Charming toast," said Nicholas. "Such heartfelt sentimentality."

Franklin took a swallow. "We're both men of the world, Nicholas. Marriage isn't about sentimentality—or at least a successful marriage isn't. Money, position and power—those are the reasons a man ties the noose about his neck." He laughed again and slapped Nicholas on the back. "But why am I lecturing you on that? It isn't as if you married for love, is it?"

"No," said Nicholas, after a moment. "I did not."

"Then you have everything a man could desire," Franklin continued. "I envy you, dear boy, having your revenge against Hughes in such a creative way. A lovely wife to take care of your home, warm your bed and turn the other way when you dally elsewhere. Congratulations.''

Franklin quaffed the rest of his whiskey, but Nicholas's glass remained untouched.

There was an old saying that warned about the danger of answered prayers, and it seemed to Nicholas that it was true. Franklin's words lingered with him on the drive back to Merriton. The ultimate revenge, his solicitor had said. Jonathan Hughes must be turning in his grave. For fifteen years Nicholas had looked forward to the moment when he would finally best his nemesis, and now that it had arrived, he found he could think of nothing but Molly.

He'd wanted to believe that Molly with her sunny disposition and impossibly optimistic heart would be able to cast light where none had been for so long, but he wasn't a man given to believing in the impossible. The shadows at Merriton were still there, as dark and long as they had been years ago. Time and distance had done nothing to change things. He doubted if even Molly could do that.

Sitting first in his banker's office and then in his solicitor's, he'd been distracted, his thoughts drifting back toward the week at sea with Molly, when there had been nothing in the world but magic. He doubted if it would be that simple for him ever again.

The risks he had taken were considerable. He and Molly had never spoken about children. Tonight they must. He had paid a visit to a chemist near Hyde Park and made a necessary purchase. His young bride might not understand that happiness was an illusion, but he did. He would hate for a child to bear the burden of their mistakes.

It was early evening when the driver brought the horses to a halt in front of Merriton. Nicholas strode into the house, shedding his topcoat and tie as soon as he crossed the threshold. He started to undo his shirt but the horrified look on the face of a young maid brought him up short. He'd laughed when Molly had said that he had a terrible time keeping his clothes on. Now he wondered if there might be something to her observation after all. He felt as if he were being suffocated by the layers of cotton and broadcloth and wool.

"Where is my wife?" he asked the startled maid.

"In her room, sir."

"Has dinner been served?"

The maid looked at him blankly. What a sorry lot he'd hired. He remembered the simple fare at the Pem with longing.

He tried again. "Has my wife already dined?"

She blinked and took a step backward. "Food was laid out on the sideboard, sir. I wouldn't know if she ate it or not."

"An attentive staff," he mumbled as he bounded up the stairs. Some changes would be made there and soon.

He stopped abruptly in the doorway to the suite of rooms he and Molly shared. Perhaps the changes would begin with his wife, who was down on her hands and knees, fanny in the air, wielding a scrub brush.

"What in bloody hell are you doing?"

"I'm cleaning," she said, giving him a slight smile. "Something that should have been done a long time ago."

She brushed her hair off her face and looked up at him. He noticed she was wearing the same faded blue cotton dress she had had on when they first met. An odd emotion tugged at his heart but he pushed it aside.

"That's why we have servants, Molly. That's their responsibility."

She rose to her feet. He noted a smudge of dirt on her nose and one on her chin. He'd never seen a woman look so delectably disheveled. "Maybe someone should tell them that," she said. "It seems to me they're being paid a great deal of money to sit in the kitchen and gossip."

"You're the lady of the house now," he pointed out. "You set the tone with the servants. I don't intend to see my wife cleaning floors like a maid."

She met his eyes. "I have to do something, Nicholas, or I shall go insane. You cannot imagine how lonely it is here."

"You should make friends. God knows we have more than our share of neighbors."

"I took the trap over to Lady Belville's today." She made a face. "For all the good that did me."

"She wasn't at home?"

"I have no idea," said Molly. "For all I know she was sitting in her bedroom window laughing at me as I drove away." She untied her apron and tossed it over the chair in the corner. "I never made it past her fancy butler."

He bristled. "You were refused?"

"I was refused. It seems without those blasted calling cards a woman does not even exist."

"I'm of the mind to ride over there and beat some manners into that son of a—"

"Don't," said Molly with surprising vehemence. "The last thing I wish is to have my company forced on my neighbors. If they don't wish to see me, then I don't wish to be seen."

She said her words with a simple dignity that took him by surprise. Again he wondered what it was about her upbringing that gave her such a strong sense of her value in the world. Only once had he seen that self-confidence of hers falter—the night she'd entered the Fifth Avenue

Hotel in her faded dress and heard cruel laughter at her expense. Nicholas had wanted to seek justice with his fists then, too.

He took the scrub brush from her, then placed it outside the door. "Why don't you have one of the servants run a bath for you while I see about having dinner brought up to our sitting room."

"Oh, Nicholas!" Her smile made him feel as if he'd captured the sun. "I dreaded the thought of sitting in that dismal dining room again."

So had he, although he didn't say so. "Ring for a maid," he said, his voice gruff. "I'll meet you in the sitting room later."

Dinner was a tasteless concoction of lamb and vegetables, served with a bowl of sandy salad greens and a dressing that consisted entirely of malt vinegar.

"I should love a simple plate of scrambled eggs and toast," said Molly, pushing away her dish.

"Sounds like manna from the gods," said Nicholas, tossing down his fork.

Molly sat up straighter in her chair. "We could go downstairs to the kitchen. I know my way around a stove."

"And permanently undermine our position with the staff?"

"Oh, who cares about them?" asked Molly with a toss of her head. "They certainly don't care about us or they'd be doing their jobs properly."

"This isn't America, Molly. You're a woman of position now. If they'd seen you scrubbing the floor, you would never again be able to command their respect."

"And that's a small price to pay for a clean bedroom," she tossed back at him. "Besides it isn't as if I have any other demands upon my time."

"I'll visit a service in London tomorrow and see about hiring a new staff."

"I daresay I'm the only one in this house who has ever scrubbed a floor or peeled potatoes."

He laughed out loud.

"Did I say something amusing?"

He pushed back his chair and opened his arms. "Come here, Molly."

"Not if you're laughing at me."

"You are unlike any woman I have ever known." She had more enthusiasm, more energy, more *life* than any ten people.

"Is that a compliment?"

He reached for her hand across the table. "What do you think?"

Smiling, she rose from the table and floated toward him on a cloud of delight. "I think it's a compliment."

"You're very perceptive."

"I know." She curled up on his lap, feeling happier than she had since they arrived in England a few days ago. The magic they'd shared aboard ship was within reach if only—

He stilled her thoughts with a series of light, feathery kisses to the curve of her jaw, the tip of her nose. She laughed softly, happy to be in his arms again. She'd felt so bereft these past few nights. How quickly she had grown accustomed to the intimacy of married life.

"Isn't it silly," she murmured, cuddling closer. "I'd almost convinced myself that you no longer wanted me."

He took her hand and placed it against him.

"You were wrong."

"Very." She caressed him, thrilling to the power a woman held over a man. Last night she'd lain awake, wondering if he would ever turn to her again. How foolish she'd been to worry. Everything was as wonderful as it had been before they arrived in England.

She shifted position on his lap, moving her hands up over his flat belly. His shirt was open and she pushed it out of the way, baring his chest to her hands and mouth.

"What on earth—" She touched his breast pocket. "What is this?"

He captured her hands in his. "In due time."

"Not another ring, Nicholas. I love my wedding band and have no need of other jewelry." The package was relatively small and flat. "Do I see a picture of Queen Victoria on the box?"

He looked decidedly uncomfortable. "You're making this difficult, Molly. I had hoped the circumstances would be different when we had this discussion."

She froze. "You sound terribly serious, Nicholas. Have I done something wrong?"

"You have done nothing at all," he said, kissing her hands. "It is what I allowed to happen that is in question."

"You're making me awfully nervous."

"The last thing I mean to do, Molly." He forced her to meet his eyes. Choosing his words with care, he said, "I am concerned that we do not hasten the start of a family."

"Well, that isn't up to us, is it?" Molly asked in a small voice. "That is up to nature."

"Nature can be controlled."

She rose from his lap, feeling as if she'd been slapped. "I apologize if I misunderstood your intentions. I thought—I mean I had believed. . . ." Her words trailed away in embarrassment. She had thrown herself into his arms with all the subtlety of one of the trollops who plied their trade in the shadow of the Cape Charlotte boardwalk.

He removed the small package from his pocket. Queen Victoria's stern face stared up at Molly as if she knew exactly what they were about. Molly watched, fascinated, as he tore off the paper covering and showed her something that looked like a round and deflated balloon.

"This prophylactic gives us the freedom to enjoy lovemaking without danger of pregnancy."

Molly's brows drew together in a frown. "I didn't know babies were dangerous."

"You must trust me when I say I'm right about this, Molly."

"That thing is horrid."

"It's necessary."

"What on earth do you do with it?" Everything she could imagine seemed either impossible or repulsive. He told her and she turned bright red. "You would use that?"

"Yes."

"Because you don't want a child."

"Because we aren't ready for a child yet."

The words were innocent enough, but she knew the greater truth behind them. All men wanted children, especially men of position. Nicholas cared enough about his position to return to England to reclaim his home. The truth was painfully clear to Molly. He didn't want a child *with her*. He didn't love her. He wanted her, yes, but she knew in her heart that was something entirely different. The difference between love and lust that he had told her about on their first night together.

It was so simple that she wondered why she hadn't realized it sooner.

She looked at him with eyes wide with pain and in that instant he saw the end of innocence.

As always, her emotions were right there for the world to see. He'd hurt her. He hadn't meant to, but there had been no avoiding it, given the situation and her inexperience.

One day you'll thank me. The day would come when she wanted a different life, maybe back in her beloved Cape Charlotte, with a man who would love her with his heart as well as his body and give her the family she needed.

But he couldn't be that man.

Chapter Sixteen

That night everything between Molly and Nicholas changed. In placing that physical barrier between them, he had also placed an emotional one, as well. A barrier Molly doubted she could ever break through. No longer could she pretend he loved her. His decision made that impossible for even an incurable optimist.

There was still pleasure to be found in his arms, but the deeper, more transcendent joy she'd known was gone, and she feared it would never return. She hated herself for seeking that pleasure when she knew how much more wonderful it could be.

In the next few weeks both settled into a routine. Nicholas spent a great deal of his time in London, doing whatever it was a man did to reclaim his position in a society he no longer understood or liked. Molly hired a new chef and head butler, and although the food at Merriton Hall improved, the atmosphere did not.

Fritzie sent a chatty, newsy letter filled with details about the renovation of the Pem. "You wouldn't be recognizing the place," wrote Fritzie. "In the blink of an eye, we're almost respectable!" As for Molly, her own letters grew shorter and more vague as the days went by. How could she tell Fritzie the truth? It would break the woman's heart to hear of the mess Molly's life had become.

There was a sadness about the house that disturbed her. Although there was nothing she could point to, she sensed a darkness within Merriton that went beyond dimly lit passageways and gloomy rooms. Once she tried to question Nicholas about the lack of family portraits and the like, but he turned a deaf ear and her curiosity continued to grow. She'd considered climbing up to the attic to search for such things, but the new head butler said the attic was in a terrible state of disrepair and would madam please wait a little longer.

Madam could think of no reason why not. She had nothing but time on her hands. Endless hours each and every day with absolutely no way to fill them. She envied Nicholas for whatever business endeavors required his presence in London almost every day. London was crowded and filthy, it was true, but the city was alive with people; more than anything she longed for the sounds of laughter and conversation. Unfortunately Nicholas didn't ask her to accompany him and Molly couldn't find the words to ask. Had she ever felt confident and easy with him, eager to give as good as she got, sure of herself and her place in the world? It seemed like another lifetime.

She envied women with babies and little children to care for. At least their days had a semblance of form. But there would be no babies for Molly in the foreseeable future. Her husband had made his views on that subject painfully clear. It occurred to her that she knew her husband's body infinitely better than she knew his heart, and there was no reason to believe the situation between them would ever be any different.

August slipped into September. Boredom sapped Molly's energy and she found herself spending endless

hours staring out at the drizzly gray skies and dreaming
about the crisp sea breezes of Cape Charlotte. Twice she
even caught herself dozing in the middle of the day,
something that unnerved her a great deal. She hadn't a
notion how to begin restoring Merriton. It seemed more
of a museum than a home. Cold, impersonal, somewhat
forbidding. The servants kept themselves strictly apart
from Molly, and she had the feeling they knew more
about her husband and home than she did.

Her calling cards were delivered from the London sta-
tioner where Nicholas had placed the order. One hundred crisp vellum cards carefully wrapped in tissue paper
and tied with a narrow red velvet ribbon and Molly could
think of no use for them, save marking her place in a
book. She had seen Lady Belville once as the woman's
coach rumbled past Merriton. Molly had been inspecting the rosebushes near the road and Lady Belville hadn't
bothered to acknowledge Molly's friendly wave.

That still didn't explain why none of their other
neighbors came to pay a call on the new residents of
Merriton Hall. Where was Lady Arabella, who had
vowed to be Molly's first visitor?

"Forget them," said Nicholas, looking strangely relieved. "Come Christmas we'll host a ball and they'll
swarm to us like bees to a hive." Molly tried discreetly to
question the staff in an attempt to find out if there was
some problem she should know about, but no answers
were forthcoming.

Toward the end of the first week in September Mona
Tompkins, resplendent in a red merino suit and jaunty
hat, appeared at Merriton.

"I am on my way to see my brother and his family and
I could not resist the urge to pay a call upon my favorite
young bride."

"Thank God for you!" Molly embraced the older woman eagerly. "You're our first visitor."

"And here I deliberately waited a fortnight to give you time to settle yourself in. I cannot believe I bested that dreadful Lady Arabella after all."

"You would think we had the plague," Molly said, ushering Mona into the drab sitting room. "Here I'd believed the world would beat a path to our door, and in truth, there hasn't been a soul."

Mona patted her arm in a motherly gesture that reminded Molly so much of Fritzie that a huge, painful lump formed in her throat.

"You poor thing," said Mona. "Everyone goes to the seaside in August. There isn't a soul in town."

"But it is now September."

"And they go to Scotland in September. Just wait, Molly. By this time next month you shall have more visitors than you know what to do with."

"Why is it I feel you don't believe that any more than I do?"

"Has it truly been that dreadful?"

"Oh, Mona—" To Molly's horror she burst into tears. All the fear and loneliness she had been battling for weeks rushed out in a torrent of words, most of which were blessedly incoherent.

"You're homesick! No wonder you look so dreadfully pale," said Mona as she handed Molly a handkerchief to wipe her eyes. She held Molly an arm's length away. "And you've lost weight. Haven't they been feeding you here?"

Molly blotted at her eyes. "I haven't much of an appetite of late. The cook was dreadful and we just engaged a new one...." She let her words drift away. "Nicholas said I mustn't go down to the kitchen and take over the cooking myself, but if I weren't so tired I just might." She knew the queasiness in her stomach was the result of being hungry and finding nothing appetizing with which to appease her hunger.

"How I wish I could have you for two weeks," said Mona, her maternal instincts coming to the fore. "I'd put the roses back in your cheeks."

"Food isn't the problem," said Molly in a quiet voice. "It's Nicholas. He doesn't . . . we don't—" She gestured toward the bedrooms on the second floor. "It's all so different than it was."

"Are you telling me that Nicholas doesn't wish to share your bed?" Mona looked horribly serious.

Molly sniffled, then blew her nose. "He—he shares my bed," she began, blushing furiously, "but he doesn't wish to have a child with me."

A smile broke through the older woman's somber expression. "Some men want more time with their wives, Molly. It isn't at all unusual . . . especially when the physical side of the marriage is most satisfactory."

"You're trying to make me feel better."

"Not at the expense of the truth, my dear. My Reggie says he wouldn't have missed our years alone together for anything."

"He regrets becoming a father?"

"Not at all. He loves our children with all his heart, but we are both glad we didn't have them sooner in our marriage."

"You don't understand," said Molly, burying her face in her hands. "It's different for us."

"Every couple feels that way. I assure you that there is nothing unusual about your situation."

"You wouldn't say that if you knew the whole story."

"My girls tell me I am a wonderful listener."

"We don't love each other, Mona. Our marriage was a terrible mistake."

Mona's expression darkened. "He forced you into marriage?"

"Not exactly." Molly swallowed hard. "I forced him."

"Now, dear, you don't have to say any more. He's your husband, after all, and I'm sure you'd rather I not have a bad opinion of him."

"You don't understand," said Molly. "I tricked him."

"You tricked him? You're not with child, Molly. How on earth could you trick him into marriage?"

"Oh, God." Molly hid her face in her hands. "It was all I could think of to do. The Pem...Fritzie...the tax collector was threatening to take everything...." How dreadful this all sounded. If only the earth would open wide and swallow her up. "I hid in his bed...the sheriff held a gun on Nicholas...before you knew it, we were married."

"You wanted his money to save your home?"

"Of course not! I wanted *my* money."

Mona sank back in her chair. "You are a most confusing young woman, Molly."

Molly sighed. There was no hope for it. She outlined the entire miserable story for Mona as clearly as she could. "I know it sounds terrible," she said, "but I never wanted anything more from Nicholas than a signed marriage certificate. If he hadn't seen my inheritance, the marriage would have been annulled and all of this would be forgotten."

"And you never wanted to fall in love."

Mona's words stole the breath from Molly's lungs. "I'm not in love, Mona."

"I have seen that look before in my own girls' eyes."

"You sound like Fritzie. I should know what's in my own heart."

"And I believe you do."

Tears threatened but she blinked them back. "He doesn't love me," she whispered. "He told me he doesn't believe in love."

"He might have his reasons." Mona's voice was soft and soothing. "Something in his past."

"I don't know anything at all about his past, except that his father died and his mother married my Uncle Jonathan."

Mona gasped, then covered it with a cough.

"What is it?" asked Molly. "Do you know something about Nicholas?"

"Very little," said Mona, her round cheeks devoid of color.

"You must tell me." Molly grabbed Mona's hand and held tight. "It would mean so much."

"His father," said Mona, obviously uncomfortable. "I believe his father was a suicide, but I don't know the particulars."

Molly listened, horrified, as the older woman told what little she knew of the story. Apparently Nicholas's father had turned a pistol upon himself right there at Merriton. Was it any wonder Nicholas had such mixed emotions when it came to his family estate—or to the notion of happiness?

"I cannot thank you enough." Molly enveloped her friend in an enormous bear hug. "What you've told me has made a world of difference!"

"I have told you so little," Mona demurred. "Only the facts as I know them to be."

"And I appreciate it more than you could possibly imagine. You are the only person I can trust to tell me the truth and not a load of foolish gossip."

Mona hugged her back. "Then, my dear girl, I am doubly happy that it was I who was your first caller and not our friend Lady Arabella."

Molly laughed and told Mona about her ill-fated call upon her other neighbor, the unfriendly Lady Belville.

"There is nothing worse than a butler plagued by delusions of grandeur," said Mona with a bemused shake of her head. "How odd we must seem to you Americans."

They settled down for a long chat about the differences between the two countries. Molly laughed a lot and learned even more. She was sure Mona could never understand how very much it meant to Molly to finally know the dark secret that weighed so heavily on her husband's heart.

"Do stop by on your way back to London," Molly insisted as she and Mona said goodbye. "I'm certain Nicholas would love to see you."

"Only if you promise to pay me a visit in London in return. There are so many wonderful things I would love to show you."

"I promise," said Molly. There had to be something more to London than fog and noise. "We need so many things here at Merriton. If you could introduce me to the shops, I would be grateful."

"It would be a pleasure," said Mona. "We'll talk about it on my return visit. I should reach Merriton two days from now."

Molly walked the older woman to her carriage, then stood at the end of the curving drive to wave goodbye. What a wonderful visit it had been. Finally she knew the reason for her husband's reluctance to believe that life could be filled with happiness. Her heart broke for the little boy who had lost his father.

Oh, Nicholas, she thought as she waved goodbye to her friend. *I'll make you believe in happiness again.* She'd work hard to erase the cloud of sorrow that hung over the house, the darkness that had taken possession of his soul.

She came to him that night with a passion and intensity that had been missing for weeks. She seemed to anticipate his every desire, her lips and hands moving with a sureness that made his blood run hot and fast. But it was more than that. Nicholas had the sense that Molly knew him better than he knew himself, that somehow his secrets had been laid bare and instead of driving her away, those secrets had bound her more closely to him.

Romantic nonsense, he thought later on as they lay together in the big double bed. Love and desire were two very separate emotions. It wasn't like him to make that mistake.

He tried to make light of the emotions her unexpected ardor had stirred to life inside him. "I suppose I should make a point to thank Mona Tompkins for her visit."

She lifted her head from his chest and looked at him. "Why would you say that?"

"Your mood. I haven't seen you this cheerful in a very long time."

"And what makes you think Mona is responsible for my mood?"

He kissed the tip of her nose. "Something is."

"Perhaps I just desired your company."

"If that is the reason, then I'm glad."

She curled up next to him once again with her head on his chest. "So am I."

"I could cancel my trip to Liverpool tomorrow."

"No," she said. "Don't do that."

"I hate to leave you alone here."

"I'll be fine."

He moved against her. "I won't be."

She tapped him lightly on the arm. "Behave yourself."

"Why don't you come with me? Liverpool is a bustling seaport, and I hear it has some of the finest emporiums in the country."

"Not this time, Nicholas. I would rather stay here at Merriton."

His laughter rumbled up from his chest. "You have had quite a change of heart, Molly."

"I know," she said. "It's time I stopped moping about and got down to work. If I am to be mistress of Merriton Hall, then it's my responsibility to see to it that it is restored to its former glory."

"First the Pem and now this. Do you never tire of lost causes?"

"No," she said in a soft voice. "I don't."

"Perhaps when I return, we could stay in town one evening and have dinner with the Tompkinses."

"I would love that. Mona invited me to stay with her any time." She trailed her finger across his chest. "I'm certain she would have no objection if I had a roommate."

"Mona invited you to stay with her?" They were newlyweds, after all. Why would Mona Tompkins think Molly needed a respite from married life? "That seems odd to me."

"She thought I looked unwell," said Molly in that direct way of hers. "She thinks I need fattening up."

Nicholas bristled at the implied criticism. "She can cease worrying. I'm sure the new chef will see to that."

"This house can be a wonderful place, Nicholas," she said, her voice soft as the night breezes. "All it needs is attention and love."

He said nothing, but for once his silence didn't make Molly feel as if she had ventured into dangerous territory. Thanks to Mona Tompkins, she finally understood why he felt as he did about this house, about their future. Merriton had known tragedy, it was true, but Molly was convinced she could bring sunlight inside and drive away the shadows of the past.

She would begin with the attic. After saying goodbye to Nicholas, Molly changed into her old dress, knotted her hair atop her head, then clambered up the rickety stairs to the attic. The servants were aghast. "You can't do that, ma'am," said the nerviest of the lot. "There's bats up there and the floor ain't safe."

"I'll be fine," said Molly as she pried open the door with her fingers. "Just tend to your duties and I'll see to mine." Success. The door creaked open on its hinges and she stepped into a veritable storm of dust. Weak sunlight trickled through the filthy windows, and it seemed to Molly that there was no air in the room. Most of the windows were painted shut, but she managed to inch open one at the far end of the room.

"This place hasn't seen the light of day in years," she said out loud, more to scare away rodents than to hear the sound of her own voice. Pieces of heavy mahogany furniture were piled one atop the other in the center of the room. Old mirrors, draped in faded sheets, rested against the walls. Stacks of boxes tied with cord were stacked everywhere she looked. It was anybody's guess where to start.

She tried to put herself in the place of the maids who had undoubtedly packed up the family's treasures for storage. Where would she put photographs and other mementos? She rooted through some boxes near the door but unearthed nothing more exciting than bed linens and old trousers. She perched on one of a set of twelve dining room chairs that were tucked under the eaves and admired the wood. It was dusty but she knew a little polish and some elbow grease would work wonders. She had great hopes for Merriton Hall, and she intended to infuse the staff with some of her own enthusiasm.

She spent an agreeable hour searching through a half dozen more boxes, one of which yielded an absolutely breathtaking peach satin dress that Molly was certain was a Worth original. She held it up to her body, smoothing the creases with her hand as she executed a waltz step. Could this have belonged to Nicholas's mother? She tried to imagine what his parents must have looked like, but they remained shadowy figures. Family revealed so much. Even a portrait of his parents would help her to understand more about her husband.

Continuing her search, she uncovered a tarnished silver tea service, a set of china with tiny handpainted roses along the border and a set of books bound in burgundy-colored leather. She'd noticed a library in the west wing. It was one of the few rooms in the entire house that had character and charm. She'd been especially taken with the floor-to-ceiling bookshelves that were filled with beautiful volumes all begging to be read.

Unmindful of the dirt, she sat down on the floor, tucking her legs beneath her, to inspect the bindings. Each book was imprinted with a golden Roman numeral from i to x, but no title or author. Dickens, perhaps, or maybe a set of Shakespeare's plays and poetry? Opening the first volume, she was astounded to see not a professionally printed page, but the smudged, rounded hand of a child.

Merriton Hall, 15 April 1842

Today I am ten years old. Granny says that great men keep diaries so that when they are famous they can remember all the great things that they did.

I don't know if I will ever be famous but she gave me these books and said I must write in them everyday.

I will have a party this afternoon. Jack and Emilie from Burnside Manor will be here, and the Affton twins. I shall have a butter cake and lemonade.

Signed,
Edward Nicholas St. George, age 10

Molly stared down at the page. Nicholas's father? She figured back to the year indicated as an odd tightness gripped her chest. It had to be. Eagerly she flipped the pages and read bits and pieces of a small boy's life. *. . . The headmaster dislikes me. He says I am lazy and given to daydreaming. He says he will take the rod to me if I do not pay attention. . . .* She read about the bone-chilling cold of a Scottish winter and the loneliness of a boy sent far away from home to learn to be an aristocrat. She didn't notice the heat in the attic or the dust or the dim sunlight, for the boy's simple words had transported her to another time and place.

The hours passed unnoticed. What a wonderful gift this would be for Nicholas—the chance to rediscover his father after so many years! She lingered over volume seven. Edward St. George, who had become a most proficient diarist, captured the splendor of falling in love for the time with deft, sure strokes of his pen. Her name was Cynthia Stanton, the daughter of the third Earl of Rossmoor, and he loved her as no man had ever loved before. Molly's heartstrings tugged in response. Who would have imagined her pragmatic husband to be the son of such a dyed-in-the-wool romantic?

It was a classic upper-crust courtship, a mélange of military balls, formal dinners and stolen moments in the very gazebo that she had noticed from the dining room window. She tried to imagine it as it had been then, before neglect and the elements had taken their toll, all painted white with crimson roses trailing up the sides and a lovestruck man and woman sitting side by side on the wooden bench as birds sang in the trees.

Molly skipped lunch, so engrossed was she by the wedding plans and the honeymoon trip to Venice and Rome. Despite Edward's glowing word pictures of his young bride's beauty, Cynthia remained somehow shadowy to Molly, although for the life of her she couldn't say why. Edward wrote little on the honeymoon, which was understandable, short descriptions of meals eaten and sights seen. Not that Molly had expected deathless prose about the wonders of the marriage bed, but she was surprised to sense a tinge of disillusionment behind Edward's entries.

Edward and Cynthia quickly settled into a routine at Merriton. They held a grand autumn ball, a fox hunt and a glittering, spectacular Christmas party that was the talk of the surrounding villages. And when their first son was born, Edward's pride knew no bounds. . . . *He's a strapping boy with his mother's dark hair and blue eyes. . . . I'll*

have him seated on a horse before his second birthday.... But something was missing, the sense of innocent joy that had radiated from the pages of the earlier
volumes. Was the marriage less than satisfactory? she
wondered. Or, like so many things in life, did you simply grow accustomed to paradise?

By the eighth volume she had her answer. ...*She taunts
me with her dalliances... she says if I could satisfy her,
she wouldn't find it necessary, but I fear there is nothing
I could do that would ever be enough for her.... She is
voracious... and our son grows lonelier by the day....*

She wiped away tears as she reached for volume nine.
Her hand trembled as she opened to the first page.

Merriton Hall, 3 January 1872

She has grown careless in her haste to be with him.
She no longer cares if she is seen by our acquaintances or if those acquaintances make certain I know
of her rendezvous.

It is as I thought. I first suspected last year at the
garden party when Nicholas saw his mother, flushed
and disheveled, near the gazebo. But I didn't want
to know. I have been living these years in a paradise
made for fools. Is it any wonder she found it so easy
to make me the cuckold?

To think that my best friend would be the one to
come between a husband and wife. Jonathan
Hughes, the man I—

She couldn't breathe. The room went airless and for an
instant she feared she might faint. Jonathan Hughes! It
couldn't be. Jonathan Hughes was her uncle... her
father's brother....

Heart pounding, she struggled to take a deep breath and forced her gaze back to the leather-bound diary. It took a moment to focus on the handwritten words for her eyes swam with tears.

Jonathan Hughes, the man I had considered close as a brother, is my wife's lover. How they must laugh at me when they are alone together. What a pathetic excuse for a man I must seem to them as they lie together in bed, no more of a man than my young son is. I don't know what gives me the greater pain— my wife's infidelity or my friend's disloyalty. What a fool I have been. . . .

The entry ended there. The rest of the book was blank. Her hands shook uncontrollably, and she placed the volume on her lap and hung her head against the burden of shame. She knew the rest of the story. Thanks to her uncle, Edward St. George had put a gun to his own head and ended his life. How could Nicholas bear to look at her, knowing that Jonathan's blood flowed through her veins?

It was no wonder he didn't want a child with her.

She sat there, tears streaming down her cheeks, as she replayed her time with Nicholas. From their very first meeting in the lobby of the Pem there had been something propelling him, an anger that she didn't understand. He'd said that he had come to Cape Charlotte to see to it that Jonathan's young niece was cared for, but she no longer believed his motives had been that simple. One of the few things she knew about her husband was the fact that he had run away from a boarding school and signed on to a merchant ship in order to see the world.

Had her uncle been the one to send him away from home, to some cold and dismal school that turned young hearts into stone?

"Ma'am," called a voice from the third floor. "Dinner is being served."

"I'll be there shortly," she called back. It startled her to realize so much time had passed.

In due time she went down to dinner, but found she could not eat. Her stomach was coiled into a knot and just the smell of the roast beef made her queasy. Begging fatigue, she requested a pot of tea be delivered to the master bedroom, and she retired for the night.

It was wrong, and she knew it, but Molly spent the night rereading each and every word of Edward's diaries. His transition from happy young boy to desperate husband tore at her heart for she saw much of her own husband reflected in those pages. Dawn was beginning to gild the sky when she finished reading the painful final entry in volume nine. She wanted to reach through the pages and hold Edward in her arms, tell him that life was a wonderful gift, one not meant to be squandered. He had a son who needed him more than he could ever know.

But of course she could not. Edward was gone these fifteen years past, his life snuffed out by that one fatal gunshot. How terrible for Nicholas, to see the dark side of love before he was old enough to have experienced its wonder.

Exhausted, she put down the book and was about to extinguish her gas lamp when volume ten, its pages blank, fell to the floor and a yellowed piece of newsprint floated across the bare wood.

Curious, she reached down to retrieve it, then gasped as she saw the headline. "Master Nicholas St. George Lone Witness to His Father's Suicide." The story was as horrifying as it was heartbreaking. "'I begged Papa not to do it,' said the thirteen-year-old lad, 'but he said life was no longer worth living.' Mrs. Cynthia Stanton St. George was reached at the home of Jonathan Hughes, wealthy scion of the London Hughes family. Mrs. St. George expressed her shock but made no other comment."

Molly didn't need news clippings or diary entries to figure out the rest of the story. A thirteen-year-old boy was a hindrance, a living, breathing reminder of the tragedy Cynthia and Jonathan had brought upon the family. Nicholas had no doubt been shipped off to boarding school at the first possible moment, his young heart and soul shattered and in need of repair.

She was no better than Jonathan Hughes. He had turned away from a young boy in great pain and desperate. And she had put her own needs before anyone else's, tricking Nicholas into marriage to further her own cause. He must think her a conniving monster, as devoid of compassion as his stepfather had been. Nicholas's reaction to her inheritance had been fueled by more than simple anger. It was his way of seeking revenge against the man who had ruined his life.

And she could no longer entirely blame him for feeling that way.

"I cannot stay here," she said aloud to the empty room. There could never be a future with Nicholas, not with the history that existed between their families. Now that she knew the terrible truth she could no longer hang on to her dreams.

Today was the day Mona Tompkins had promised to return. Mona had urged Molly to consider a visit at the Tompkinses' London home. Molly would be packed and waiting when she arrived.

Chapter Seventeen

Liverpool had grown considerably since the day Nicholas had signed on to the merchant ship *Wetherby* some fifteen years ago. With more people, bigger buildings, Liverpool resembled London on a smaller and earthier scale. His associates took him to some fine restaurants and kept him amused with humorous stories and clever talk, but Nicholas found himself longing for his wife.

And, to his surprise, not only in the bedroom. He missed the throaty sound of her laughter, the way she made a room come alive with her smile. She embraced life with both arms in order to wring every last drop of happiness from each and every day.

Some might call it love, but not Nicholas. He was too much in control of his emotions to fall in love. He'd spent too many years training himself not to be like his father—a man destroyed by emotion. He was infatuated with Molly... intrigued... more than a little enchanted. But he didn't love her. He couldn't love her. He simply didn't know how.

But still he missed her. The double bed in his hotel room seemed huge without her slender form pressed up against him. Who would have imagined that a few weeks of married life could so quickly turn an inveterate loner into a contented husband?

There were times when he looked at his wife and wondered how it was he had lived before she came into his life. The pleasures of the marital bed were beyond compare, but the simple joy he found in talking with her, late at night while the rest of the world slept, still caught him by surprise.

His business took him longer than anticipated. By the time he boarded the train for the return trip to London, he was anxious to see her beautiful face again. As the train rattled along the tracks he wondered what manner of surprises she had waiting for him at Merriton. Somehow Mona Tompkins's visit had made Molly catch fire. She'd been filled with enthusiasm for her new home, determined to whip both house and staff into shape or know the reason why. Woe betide anyone—or anything—that got in her way!

Smiling to himself, he leaned back in his seat and closed his eyes.

In Southampton, Mona Tompkins was doing her best to dissuade Molly from her chosen course.

"There's no use trying, Mona," she said, forcing a weary smile. "I have made up my mind. There can be no other way."

Mona took Molly's hands in hers. "Running away from a problem is never the answer. Go back to Merriton, Molly. Speak with Nicholas. Find out what he thinks. Listen to his point of view."

Molly sighed and withdrew her hands from the woman's grasp. "It no longer matters what he thinks. It matters what *I* think, and I know I could never live in that house again."

Mona dabbed at her eyes with the corner of a well-worn linen handkerchief. "I am to blame. If only I hadn't told you what I did about Nicholas's father."

"Stop it, Mona. I needed to know. If you hadn't told me, I'm sure one day Lady Arabella would have—and she would not have spared me the full story."

"Please reconsider, Molly. You mustn't blame yourself for the actions of your uncle."

But Molly's mind was made up. Any moment the call for visitors to depart would sound and she would be on her way back home to Cape Charlotte. She reached into her drawstring pouch and withdrew a velvet envelope. "I want you to have this, Mona, in payment for my passage on this ship."

Mona shook her head. "I refuse to take payment for aiding you in this foolish endeavor."

Molly pressed the packet into the older woman's hands. "You must. I cannot and will not take charity, not even from a friend." That morning she had sold her remaining jewelry to a goldsmith in town and that money would help her make the journey from New York to the Pem.

With great reluctance Mona accepted the packet. "And what do I say when Nicholas comes pounding at my door, demanding to see his wife?"

"The truth," said Molly. She handed Mona an envelope bearing her husband's name. "Would you do me the favor of sending this to him tomorrow?"

"He loves you, Molly. I beg you one last time to give your union another chance."

But it was better this way, of that Molly was certain. Nicholas wanted to make a life for himself at Merriton and her presence would make it impossible for him to banish the past once and for all. She would be a living, breathing reminder of her uncle's treachery and she would rather die than bring any more pain upon the man she loved.

"You're a good friend, Mona. I wish we'd had more time together."

"Godspeed," said Mona, kissing her on one cheek and then the other. "I only pray you've made the right decision."

Merriton Hall rose up before Nicholas out of the gathering darkness and for the first time the sight of it didn't make him recoil. Molly waited inside that forbidding structure, and that made all the difference.

The driver seemed to take forever to guide the horses up the driveway and Nicholas waited impatiently for him to bring the coach to a halt. Tossing money at the man, Nicholas grabbed his valise and leaped from the coach, eager to see his wife.

"Molly!" His voice rang out in the empty hallway as the door swung shut behind him. "I'm back."

He hooked a finger in his tie and slid it open, then quickly shed his coat as he checked the sitting room. No sign of his wife. She wasn't in the library or the dining room or the solarium. He took the stairs two at a time, a wicked grin spreading across his face. The bedroom, he thought, as the image of his beautiful and passionate wife teased him. But she wasn't there either. Indeed, the room looked as if a tornado had touched down inside. Her clothes were scattered everywhere. Books were stacked up on the chaise longue. A pair of shoes lay on the floor near the wardrobe. A hairbrush rested in the middle of the bed.

A sense of foreboding descended on him.

"Molly," he started to say, heading for the bath, "are you in there?" His heart pounded wildly. She might have slipped and hit her head on the marble floor. If anything happened to her he'd never forgive himself.

She wasn't in the bath.

Foreboding darkened into dread.

He raced down the stairs, nearly breaking his neck in the process. "Henry!" he roared at the top of his lungs for the new head butler. "Immediately!"

Moments later the man appeared. "Yes, sir?"

"My wife," he said without preamble. "Where is she?"

Henry, a pleasant-looking chap, glanced away. "Madam left with Mrs. Tompkins, sir." The fact that Henry hated breaking such news to his employer was written all over his face.

"When did this happen?"

"The morning after you departed for Liverpool, sir."

"Did she leave a note?"

"Not that I am aware of, sir."

"A message?"

"Only that she has gone with Mrs. Reginald Tompkins."

"When will she be back?"

"She didn't offer that information to me, sir."

He turned away from the look of pity on the butler's face. He'd seen that look years before on the faces of the staff in residence when his father took his own life. He'd hated it then and he hated it now. Pity was for men who couldn't hold on to their wives, men who—

He banished the thought with an angry shake of his head.

This didn't make sense. There was no reason for Molly to leave. They'd managed to smooth over the rough patch they'd encountered when he told her how he felt about children; indeed she had been more passionate and loving than ever before. When he left for Liverpool, she had been aglow with ideas on how to restore Merriton. What in hell could have happened to make her change so abruptly?

He paced the floor, trying to outdistance his apprehension. Mona Tompkins must have a problem, that was what it was. Molly's heart was wider than the Thames, and he had no doubt she was a soft touch for a friend in need. Maybe one of Mona's children was ill. Yes, that had to be it. Mona had thrown herself at Molly's feet and begged her assistance and Molly, being Molly, had put aside everything and gone off with the older woman. He knew his wife had been lonely these past few weeks, trapped out here in the country without friends or her makeshift family. With him away she must have leaped at the chance to spend time with a real family.

Yet a buzz of dread settled itself inside his ear and wouldn't be stilled. *She's left you for good,* whispered his darkest inner voice. *Happiness is an illusion. Why didn't you listen?*

"Not this time," he said out loud. Molly was different. He'd seen her loyalty at work from the first moment they met as she struggled to save the Pem. When she loved, she loved with her entire being and she would do anything to help a loved one in need.

Even marry a stranger?

He brushed away the doubts. Once she knew he was back, he had no doubt she would return to him immediately. He could hire a coach in the morning and she would be in his arms two hours later. The idea went far to soothe his fears.

Now all he had to do was get through another night without her. Dinner would help. He was about to bellow again for Henry when the man appeared at his elbow.

"Dinner," said Nicholas. "I'd like something brought to me in the library."

Henry, his expression once again impassive, bowed slightly. "As you wish, sir." Nicholas suddenly noted the silver salver the man extended toward him. "These arrived for you moments ago, sir."

A parchment envelope with his name written in his wife's hand and a velvet pouch tied with a ribbon.

"Where did they come from?"

"Mrs. Reginald Tompkins."

Nicholas nodded. "That's all, Henry." So Molly hadn't forgotten after all. This letter probably explained her sudden disappearance. He tore open the envelope and extracted a sheet of paper. At first the words had no meaning. He felt as if he were staring at Sanskrit or ancient Greek. The bitter taste of loss filled his mouth as the words settled into a recognizable form and pattern. ...*It's better this way*.... *We do not belong together*.... *I only wish I had never tricked you into this marriage*....

He remained deadly calm, despite the roar of his blood pounding in his ears. He tore off the ribbon with his teeth and reached into the velvet packet. Molly's heirloom necklace lay inside, along with a folded note on tissue-thin blue paper. "She wished to reimburse me for her passage home but I cannot take her precious belongings. Please, Nicholas, return this to her with my love. Mona."

Gone.

She was gone.

His heart cracked open wide, splitting his rib cage, forcing the air from his lungs. Rearing back, he threw the necklace across the room, not even hearing the sound it made as it crashed into the dressing table mirror and shattered the glass.

Why are you so surprised, Nicky? It happened to your father and now it's happening to you. Your wife has found somewhere else she'd rather be....

But he wasn't his father. He was made of stronger, better stuff. He wouldn't turn a pistol on himself and he wouldn't beg her to return.

If you didn't love, you couldn't be hurt. And he didn't love her. He didn't love anyone. He would drown himself in the best whiskey he could find and when that was over, she would be nothing more than a faded memory, like all the other women he had known.

"Ma'am?" The deckhand stood in front of Molly, a worried expression on his young face. "Is something wrong?"

Molly, her stomach roiling, shook her head. "Nothing's wrong. I'm fine. It's just—" She swallowed as the nausea once again asserted itself. "It's a rough crossing, wouldn't you say?"

"Well, no, ma'am, not really. The gents was just sayin' how they ain't been out on such a glassy sea since 1856."

Molly hadn't been born in 1856, so she couldn't say anything about that year, but she certainly could say something about the seas of 1887. Terrible, was what they were. Turbulent, hostile, enough to keep a woman land-bound for the rest of her life.

The deckhand bade her a better journey and disappeared below to get on with his business. Molly, relieved to be alone, rested her elbows on the deck and breathed deeply of the salty air in the hope that it would settle her stomach. Four days into the journey and this was the first morning she'd managed to make it from her cabin and into the open air. The only souls she'd met on this journey were her cabin steward and the deckhand who'd just informed her that the seas were calm.

The only good thing she could say about feeling so dreadfully ill was that it made thinking most difficult. She didn't want to think. She couldn't bear the memories that came back to her in moments like this—memories that would have to last forever.

"It's better this way, Nicholas," she said out loud with only the endless ocean to bear witness. There could be no future for them, not after the way she had played with his life. And certainly not after what she had learned from his father's diaries. Her uncle had wrecked a marriage and destroyed two lives in the process: driving Edward St. George to suicide and Nicholas to a lifetime of loneliness.

Three days from now she would be back where she belonged, in Cape Charlotte surrounded by people who loved her and needed her. Once upon a time that was all she'd asked of life.

It would have to be so again.

On the last day of the longest drunk of his life, Nicholas finally looked into what remained of the dressing table mirror. If hell had a face, it would be the face that looked back at him. His eyes were redder than the fires of Hades. The dark circles beneath them extended halfway down his face. His cheeks were sunken and stubbled with a thick growth of beard.

His head pounded from the accumulated effects of whiskey, bad food and little sleep, and he knew it was time to either return to the living or give up the ghost. He looked toward the bed where Molly's nightgown still lay across the pillow. She was gone and she wasn't coming back.

It had taken five days of concentrated effort to drum that fact into his head, but at last he believed it. She'd walked out on him the way his mother had walked out on his father. In Nicholas's case there wasn't another man involved, but his soul felt every bit as empty.

He'd come very close to letting a woman into his heart, and see where it had gotten him. Molly was as faithless, as cunning, as his mother had been. Only he had been prepared for it in a way his father never had.

The worst had happened and his heart still beat inside his chest.

It wasn't much to be happy about, but it was something.

The thing to do now was figure out how he would get on with his life.

He took another look at himself in the mirror and shuddered. A bath and a shave would be a good start. Stripping off his shirt, he started for the bath, only to find his attention drawn to a stack of leather-bound books on the chaise longue. He vaguely remembered seeing them there the night he'd discovered Molly had walked out on him, but the liberal consumption of whiskey had quickly pushed that observation aside.

Pausing, he bent down to inspect one of the volumes. The Roman numeral ix was embossed on the spine in gold leaf. He flipped open the cover and flyleaf, idly curious about her choice in reading matter.

Merriton Hall, 25 December 1870

Christmas Day. Cynthia told me she wished to visit family today but that held little appeal. Jonathan Hughes is holding a dinner party at his estate later this afternoon and I have accepted that invitation. Cynthia begged me to send our regrets but I find her request both childish and peculiar. It is almost as if she wishes to put as much distance between herself and Jonathan as she can.

His father's diaries.

A flood of memories washed over him. Every night his father would sit at his desk, dip his gold-nibbed pen into the inkwell and record his diary entry. On Nicholas's tenth birthday his father had presented him with his own set of empty books and the exhortation, "Life is meaningless until it is recorded."

Nicholas was an active, extroverted child, and the idea of spending precious hours hunched over a desk when he could be racing across the open fields held little appeal. To his father's dismay, he'd declared he'd rather have a pony.

He flipped the pages, dark with his father's precise handwriting. ... *The arguments grow more intense. There are times I believe we have not been happy since Nicholas was an infant. Those were such hopeful days....*

It wasn't that he cared what was in his father's diaries. There couldn't possibly be anything in them that could explain away his mother's infidelity or his father's weakness. He didn't want to know Edward St. George's deepest secrets. He didn't want his parents to seem like living, breathing people instead of shadowy memories from the past. And certainly there was nothing he could find in these volumes that could ever explain away the callous indifference Jonathan Hughes had shown toward Nicholas and toward Molly.

But the story was so compelling that he sat down on the edge of the chaise longue and reached for volume one.

Merriton Hall, 15 April 1842

Today I am ten years old. Granny says that great men keep diaries so that when they are famous...

Day turned to night. Nicholas read on. It wasn't often that one saw the entire fabric of a man's life spread out before one—warp and weave and imperfections.

He saw his parents as they had truly been, not the way time and memory had distorted them. He remembered the arguments behind closed doors. The sound of voices raised in anger. His mother's tears . . . the way his father retreated to his study whenever the harshness of life grew too difficult to bear.

Cynthia's tempestuous nature had overpowered Edward's more introspective temperament. She lived for excitement; he lived because it was expected of him. They were two people who should never have married.

Jonathan Hughes hadn't destroyed a happy marriage; he had only hastened the destruction of one already in trouble. Edward and Cynthia's union had been a mistake from the moment they took their vows, and Nicholas only wondered that it had taken him so many years to realize it.

The shame of it was that they hadn't realized it before tragedy changed the course of so many lives.

His eye was caught and held by a yellowed newspaper clipping. He read about his thirteen-year-old self and felt compassion for the boy but nothing else. He waited for the pain to come, for the familiar black cloud of anger to descend, but it didn't happen.

After a decade and a half, it was finally over.

It no longer mattered who was to blame. Merriton Hall was only a house, not a trophy to be won in battle. He had vanquished the last of his ghosts and laid the memories to rest.

He thought of Molly, of her courage and resourcefulness, the way she faced each day with optimism and hope. Her beauty had drawn him to her side, but it was her spirit that held him fast. She was everything he could ever want in a woman, and the fact that she was on the other side of the ocean made no sense to him at all.

She was his wife.

They had a future to plan.

And the sooner they got started, the happier he would be.

"You okay back there, Molly?" Old Jake twisted around on his bench until Molly feared he would topple onto the road and get run over by the carriage wheels.

"Jake, please! I'm absolutely fine, I promise you."

"Don't look fine," he said, sneaking another look over his shoulder. "Real peaked, if you ask me."

"I didn't ask you. Now mind the road or we'll both end up under the horse's hooves."

"Mind your tongue, girl," Jake retorted as he guided his horse around a ditch. "Just because you married an Englishman don't mean you got to give yourself airs here in Cape Charlotte."

Leave it to Jake to put her in her place. Her days as Mrs. Nicholas St. George were over. Vanished like her dreams of happiness.

"Gotta say I'm right surprised to see you back this ways so soon."

"So am I," she muttered.

"You leave your mister up in New York or something?"

"Or something," she said.

"Can't say I'd relish leavin' the missus by herself too long."

"You don't have a missus, Jake."

Again he twisted around in his seat and fixed her with a look. "Don't Fritzie write you none of the doings around here? I got myself a new wife two weeks ago Friday, and a fine one she is, if I do say so."

Molly offered Jake her congratulations, all the while feeling as if her heart would break. Happiness was such a simple thing. Why on earth couldn't she and Nicholas have been happy together?

Jake rattled on, extolling the virtues of his wife's apple pie and her way with horses, while Molly fought a wave of nausea. It wasn't Jake's words that caused the nausea, rather it was the dreadful swaying motion of the carriage. She found herself gritting her teeth and counting the minutes until they arrived at the Pem.

Finally Jake brought the coach to a shuddering halt and helped her down. The sun blazed high in the sky, blisteringly hot for a day in late September. The Pemberton Arms stood there in all its glory, freshly painted pristine white with jet-black shutters jauntily framing the brand-new windows. Gardeners fussed about, trimming hedges and such, while from inside she heard the sounds of carpenters plying their trade with zestful abandon. It was all happening, everything she had ever dreamed of for the Pem, and she was too tired and too sick at heart to care.

"You sure you feel okay?" asked Jake as he struggled with her valises. Normally she would have given him a hand, but she was feeling a trifle unsteady on her feet.

"It's so hot," she said, passing her hand across her forehead. "The sun never shines in England. I'd forgotten how strong it can be."

"Ain't all that hot," said Jake, staring at her curiously.

She resisted the urge to kick him in the shins, but only because she feared she might topple over if she did. Slowly she walked up the path with Jake bringing up the rear, as he dragged her valises along the sandy flagstones. The steps were level and they no longer squeaked, while the porch boasted a fresh coat of paint and a new set of chairs. The words Pemberton Arms winked at her from a hand-painted sign that hung over the front door.

"You can leave my bags here," she said to Jake, gesturing to a spot near the door. "Someone will bring them in later." She went to hand him his fare but he shook his head and backed away.

"That Englishman you married paid me real fine, Molly. This one's from me to you."

She wished him well again on his marriage, then stepped inside the cool foyer. After the intense glare of the sun, the dimly lit room seemed plunged in darkness. She felt disoriented, as if she had been blindfolded and taken to a strange place.

"Fritzie!" she called out, her voice sounding unnaturally thin and weak. "Fritzie, it's me!"

From the kitchen she heard a clatter as a pot hit the floor, followed by footsteps hurrying toward her. Fritzie, hair piled atop her head, crisp apron wrapped about her waist, enfolded Molly in a bear hug.

"Saints be praised! It's a vision you are, standin' there so pretty and ladylike in your fancy dress! And where's the mister? Is he walkin' from the railway station?"

Molly blinked, struggling to retain her equilibrium. "Oh, Fritzie. I'm so glad to see you." She sounded as if she were submerged underwater.

Fritzie held her at arm's length. "You're pale as a ghost." She touched Molly's forehead with her fingertips. "And clammy, as well."

"I'm f-fine," Molly stammered as Fritzie led her toward a seat. "The sun ... the heat ... I—"

When Molly opened her eyes, she found herself stretched out on a brand-new divan in the refurbished lobby with a score of familiar—and very concerned—faces peering down at her.

"Thank the good Lord she's comin' around," said Stella, plump fingers working her rosary beads.

"Still looks mighty pale to me," said Arthur, his brow more furrowed than usual.

Fritzie bent down next to Molly and handed her a glass of lemonade. "Drink this down," she said in her no-nonsense way, "and Dr. Crawford will be here before you know it."

"Doctor?" Molly struggled to sit up. "I don't need a doctor."

"When a body faints dead away like the Almighty has called her home, I'd say she'd be needin' a doctor."

"For heaven's sake, Fritzie." Molly felt suddenly cross and irritable. "Don't make more of this than necessary."

"Well, we'll be seein' what your husband has to say about that."

Molly glanced toward the others. "Fritzie, I—"

Bless her soul, Fritzie immediately understood. "And what would all of you be gapin' at with your mouths flappin' in the breeze like fresh-washed sheets? Go about your business and I'll be seein' to our girl."

"Thank you," breathed Molly after the others grudgingly returned to their duties.

Fritzie fixed her with a stern look. "And where is your husband, missy?"

Molly felt herself stiffen. "He isn't here."

"Is he in New York then?"

"No, he isn't in New York."

"Philadelphia?"

"No, he isn't in Philadelphia, Fritzie. He's at Merrion."

"And why are you here?"

"Because this is my home."

"A wife's place is with her husband."

"I don't have a husband. Not really."

"I witnessed your vows with my very own eyes, missy, and I say you have a husband."

"Not any longer."

"Has he thrown you out?"

Molly glowered at the woman. "No, he hasn't thr[own] me out. I left."

"You left," said Fritzie, as if the words were foreig[n] to her. "You'd be breakin' your sacred vows."

"Sacred vows?" Molly tried to laugh but her emo tions were too close to the surface. "You know the trut[h] of the matter, Fritzie. There was precious little sacre[d] about our union."

"You're being cagey with me."

Molly managed a smile. "And you're being nosy."

Fritzie's mouth curved in an answering smile. "The[n] I'd be sayin' things are about the same as they alway[s] were."

"No," said Molly, ducking her head to hide the sud den sting of tears, "nothing's the same as it was, Fritzi[e]. Especially not me."

Fritzie made a show of inspecting Molly's sea-gree[n] traveling costume and elaborate coiffure. "Except fo[r] some fancy clothes, you'd be the same girl I watche[d] grow up."

"I wish that were true," Molly whispered. "I wish [I] could undo everything."

Fritzie sat on the edge of the divan and enfolded Moll[y] in her arms. "Married life wouldn't be for everyone," sh[e] said, smoothing back a stray lock of Molly's hair. "Di[d] he hurt you, lovey?"

She shook her head.

Fritzie's round cheeks reddened slightly. "Would he b[e] askin' you for more than you wanted to give?"

"No." In truth she only regretted the nights they ha[d] let slip by without knowing the pleasures of the ma[r] iage bed. "Fritzie—" She stopped abruptly. How did you tell someone you dearly loved, a woman who had raised you like her own child, that there were parts of our life that you could no longer share?

A bittersweet look of understanding shadowed Fritzie's beloved face. Molly wished she could lay her head against the kind woman's ample bosom and pour out her sorrow. Those days, however, were gone, vanished with her innocence and the youthful certainty that life would always go her way.

"Doc's here," called Stella from the dining room. "He's comin' up the walk right now."

"About time," muttered Fritzie, rising to her feet.

"This is ridiculous." Molly sat up and tugged at the bodice of her traveling costume. "I'm fit as a fiddle."

"We'll see about that," said Fritzie with a sniff. "A body doesn't faint without a reason."

"I was tired and hungry."

"We'll just let Dr. Crawford be the judge of that."

As it turned out, Dr. Crawford agreed with Molly. She *was* tired and hungry. A good night's sleep and a hearty meal would set those problems right.

But there was something else happening inside her, something both wonderful and terrifying and so unexpected that it stole Molly's breath away.

Molly Hughes St. George was pregnant with her husband's child.

Chapter Eighteen

Fall came early to Cape Charlotte. In the blink of an ey
the blazing heat of summer gave way to the crisp chill
October. The smell of apples and wood smoke was in t
air, foretelling the coming of the first frost. Vacatione
returned to their city homes, taking with them the strip
cabanas that had dotted the beach. In the past Molly ha
hated to see the end of summer. She'd always doted
the crowds and excitement the holiday revelers broug
to the sleepy seaside town.

This year, however, she was glad to see them go. Th
lonely, windswept stretch of beach suited her mood, an
in the weeks that followed she spent endless hours wall
ing the length of the boardwalk in an attempt to outdi
tance her thoughts.

But she couldn't outdistance the truth.

She was with child. Her hands instinctively went to h
still-flat stomach. Inside the cradle of her body, the bal
was growing bigger and stronger with each day th
passed. The image of an infant with Nicholas's vivid bl
eyes appeared before her, and a wave of longing for bo
father and child tore at her heart.

She tried to imagine herself six months from now wh
she was great with her husband's child. Or in a year wh
she cradled their infant in her arms. She wondered wh

would she say six years from now when a little boy asked why his father lived across the sea.

It all seemed so unreal, almost as if she were reading about some other woman's life. Since leaving Merriton, she had felt disoriented. Her body had become alien to her. Her breasts were fuller, more tender to the touch of her clothing. Her dreams were vivid, filled with strange images that left her feeling tired and irritable come morning. How she envied women with husbands who welcomed the advent of a child. A husband who would share in the miracle created by their love.

But then love had never been part of the equation for them. She'd let her romantic imagination convince her of something that had never existed.

Nicholas didn't want a child. He had made that fact abundantly clear that night he returned from London; once she'd read Edward St. George's diaries, she understood why. Fritzie had begged her to write to Nicholas and tell him about the baby, but Molly was steadfast in her refusal. At the very least, she owed him a clean break.

Her eyes burned with tears. She leaned against the railing and looked out over the ocean. The pungent smell of burning leaves mingled with the salt air, reminding her of autumns past when she'd believed the world was hers for the taking.

Fritzie had embraced her when she told the older woman of the baby. "Please," Molly had begged her, "don't tell anyone else yet. I—"

Fritzie had nodded, eyes warm with compassion. "I understand, lovey. You just leave everything to old Fritzie."

Fritzie explained away Molly's morning sickness, her irritable moods, the way she fell asleep at the drop of a feather duster. Fritzie also never asked questions Molly couldn't answer and for that she was deeply grateful.

There had been a time when a hug from Fritzie and a walk along the beach had been enough to ease her woes. She was home where she belonged, with people who cared deeply for her. The Pem was on its way toward claiming its place among the finest hotels in Cape Charlotte, and before too long she would begin to reap the returns of her investment. Still, the emptiness in her heart seemed as deep and wide as the ocean that separated her from the man she loved. If she'd believed returning home would solve everything, she had been terribly mistaken.

You have everything you need, Molly. The Pem is a tremendous success. You have money and freedom and health. And a baby on the way. What more can you ask?

She knew the answer to that question as well as she knew her own name. *Nicholas.* She longed for his smile, his touch, the sound of his voice. In the blink of an eye he had captured her heart and soul and she knew that no matter where life took her, he would be the only man she would ever love.

But there was no hope for them. She knew that and was struggling to accept it. With each lonely day that passed, she thanked the Almighty for blessing her with the baby who grew inside her womb. She would never again be part of Nicholas's life, but she would have his child and she would see to it with her dying breath that his child never knew a moment of unhappiness.

Old Jake, teeth clamped down hard on a cigar, craned his neck around to look at Nicholas.

"Sure brought a lot of stuff with you this time," he said, eyebrows waggling. "Plannin' to stay awhile?"

"I hope so."

The moment his ship docked in New York yesterday afternoon, Nicholas had felt as if he had finally come home. The feeling he had searched for for the past fif

en years was waiting for him not in England, but right
ere in the United States of America. This was where he
:longed, the place where he could most be himself, a
untry large enough and young enough to accommo-
te his dreams. From the frenetic bustle of Manhattan
land to the friendly shores of Cape Charlotte, he loved
all.

"The missus know you're comin'?"

He shook his head. "It's a surprise."

"Don't know if that's such a swell idea," said Jake
ith a baleful look. "Seems to me most women don't
tton much to surprises."

"I'm certain Molly won't mind."

"They worry about their hair," Jake went on, obvi-
isly taken by the topic. "You catch 'em at the wrong
ne and they're just as likely to box your ears as give you
e time of day." He gave Nicholas another one of those
eaningful looks over his shoulder. "'Specially when
ey're in the family way."

Nicholas, who had been admiring a fine stretch of
:achfront property, was caught by the man's words.
What was that?"

"I said they're mighty fussy when they're in the fam-
y way."

"Is your wife pregnant?"

Jake laughed so hard he dropped the reins. "Rita's
:aring sixty," he said, wiping his eyes. "I'm talkin'
out our Molly."

"You mean, *my* Molly?"

"Been *our* Molly so long I keep forgettin' she belongs
you now."

"Somehow I don't believe Molly belongs to anyone."

"True enough," said Jake. "By the way, I hope you
dn't mind me shootin' off my mouth about the baby. I

just happened to overhear Doc Crawford talkin' to Fr
zie the other day and—"

A baby... Molly was having his baby....

Nicholas faced Fritzie in the lobby of the Pem a fe
minutes later. "Is it true?" he asked without preamble

Fritzie didn't feign ignorance. "'Tis true." She na
rowed her eyes as she regarded him. "She didn't t
you?"

He shook his head. "She didn't tell me."

"The notion takes some gettin' used to, don't it?"

"Less than I would have thought." He was still su
prised, but something else was happening inside him.
primitive, urgent sense of coming full circle, back to t
beginning when all things had been possible.

"Not every man is cut out to be a father."

"I know," he said, meeting her eyes. "Not every m
is cut out to be a husband."

Her eyes narrowed further. "You hurt my girl a
you'll have me to answer to."

He glanced about the refurbished lobby. "Where
she?"

"Walkin'," said Fritzie. "Every day she heads out
the boardwalk. Says starin' at the water helps her think

He kissed Fritzie on the forehead. "Thank you."

Her expression softened noticeably. "You take go
care of her. That'll be thanks enough."

If only things had been different, thought Molly as s
watched the waves crash against the shoreline. Perha
if they'd met under more propitious circumstanc
Nicholas might have come to love her in time. The
wasn't a soul in Cape Charlotte who didn't have a ki
word to say for Molly. In her whole life she had know

nothing but the love and approval of others. Everyone, that was, except her husband.

Sighing deeply, she leaned back and closed her eyes. Strange, but for an instant she thought she heard someone call her name, but she knew it was only the sound of her heart beating—and her own bone-deep loneliness echoing deep inside.

"Molly."

She tilted her head to the side. What a cruel trick of nature, to make her think she heard that familiar voice, low and intimate and so thrilling. She remembered the first time she'd heard that voice as she'd peered out the front window of the Pem to get a glimpse of the handsome stranger. Bigger than life he'd seemed, larger than her dreams. The man she'd never dared to believe existed beyond the boundaries of her heart.

"Molly."

It couldn't be—it simply couldn't. He was thousands of miles away in England.

Wasn't he?

She felt a hand on her shoulder and a warmth more powerful than the sun spread through her body.

"It can't be," she whispered. "You're not really here."

Nicholas sat down next to her on the bench, and it was as if she were seeing him for the very first time. That thick chestnut hair. Those sailor's eyes, bluer than any ocean could possibly be. His shirt was unbuttoned at the throat and his sleeves rolled up to the elbow, as if the sheer force of his nature could not be contained by civilization or cowed by the elements.

She yearned to trace his cheekbones with the tips of her fingers. She wanted to press her lips to the pulse beating at the base of his throat. She wanted to disappear into the safe haven of his embrace.

It wasn't her imagination. Her husband was there beside her, conjured up from her dreams. She struggled to control the elation and the hope that surged through her veins.

"Why are you here?" she managed, steeling herself for the inevitable. *A divorce. He has come here to obtain a divorce.*

He said nothing, simply touched her cheek, and that one gesture was her undoing.

"Don't," she said, her control snapping. She straightened her shoulders and fixed him with a look of defiance. "If you have come here for a divorce, then let's get on with it." *Just don't make me remember how it felt to lie in your arms.* "I will not fight you on this."

"I am glad to hear that."

She lifted her chin, pain veering sharply toward anger. "And you can have the fancy dresses and the jewels."

"As you wish." Was that a *smile* she saw on his face? Had the man no heart?

"All I ask for is the Pem. Tell me the price and I'll—"

"Done."

She started to rise from the bench, but he put his hand on her shoulder to keep her in her seat. "Are you finished?" he asked.

She glared at him. "I'm finished."

"Good, because now I have something to say."

"What on earth is there for you to say? I am returning your property and you are returning mine, although you are making me pay for something that by rights should belong to me. If you have any arguments with that, then I'll—"

"I love you, Molly."

Her breath left her body in a violent rush.

"I love you," he repeated, sliding closer to her on the bench. "I have from the first moment I saw you, only I was too bloody stubborn to realize it."

"I—I don't know what to say." She'd expected anger, recriminations, the cold sting of divorce. Anything but this. *The baby... tell him about the baby before this goes any further....*

"Say you love me, too."

"Nicholas, I—"

"Say it, Molly."

"I can't. You don't understand. There are things you don't know... things that would change everything."

He waited, watching her.

"I know how you feel about children," she began, "but nature had other plans...." *Wonderful plans. Miraculous plans.*

"You're with child." It was a statement, not a question.

"Yes," she whispered. "I'm carrying your baby."

Was she mad or did she see the glitter of pride in his blue eyes?

"You don't want children," she reminded him. "You said children force you to think of the future and the future was something you didn't believe in."

"Let's say I've seen the error of my ways."

"I read your father's diaries," she said bluntly. "I know what happened. Jonathan Hughes was my uncle. Can you live with that?"

"Can you?" he countered.

"When I think of what he did to your father, I could die of shame. To know that his blood—"

He placed a finger against her lips. "You're not Jonathan Hughes. I'm not my father. It doesn't matter what happened between them. All that matters is that we love each other." Later on he would tell her about his childhood, fill in the blank spots left by his father's diaries. This moment, however, belonged to the future and he was eager to take the first step. "Marry me, Molly."

He dropped to his knee right there in the middle of the boardwalk as a wild burst of hope blossomed inside her heart.

"Nicholas! Stand up. Someone might see."

"I want them to see. I want everyone to see. Marry me, Molly, in a church with flowers on the altar and a priest saying the words this time, instead of a gun-toting sheriff. You deserve the wedding of your dreams."

"You're teasing me." She paused. "Aren't you?"

"I've never been more serious." He pulled her down to sit on his knee. "We'll have the biggest wedding in Cape Charlotte's history. We'll bloody well invite the whole town."

She wanted to believe him. Dear God, how much she wanted to believe. . . .

"You're forgetting one very important thing," she said. "We're already married."

"In the eyes of the law. This time it will be in the eyes of God."

She ducked her head, pressing her forehead against the side of his neck. "Say it again," she whispered. "Say it once more so I know it's real."

"I want to grow old beside you. When I die, I want yours to be the last face I see, the last voice I hear. I don't want to go through this life without you by my side."

"When I found out about the baby, I thanked God would have a part of you with me always."

"There's no turning back this time, Molly."

"And no secrets?"

"No secrets."

"This is a big decision," she said, a smile playing at the corners of her mouth. "You mustn't rush me."

"I'm not a patient man." He'd spent too much of his life waiting. He wouldn't make that mistake again. He pulled her close, his body hard and insistent against hers. "Marry me, or do I have to hire a sheriff in a candy-striped nightgown to help convince you?"

"No one has to convince me." Her voice was soft with love as she placed his hand against her belly. "I don't care where we live or how. I don't care if we're in England or Cape Charlotte, in a shack or a mansion. All I care about is that I'm with you."

He waited, not saying a word, and Molly knew what it was he wanted to hear.

"I love you," she said, amazed by the power of three simple words. "More than you'll ever know." Rich or poor, through good times and bad. This was the man of her dreams, the man who had claimed her, heart and soul.

Nicholas threw back his head and laughed with joy. Years from now Molly would remember this moment, hear that laugh again, and be reminded that fairy tales sometimes came true. Somehow a miracle had happened and a marriage born of deceit had turned into the most precious wonder of all: a match made in heaven.

Oh, what a story they'd have to tell their grandchildren!

* * * * *

JAYNE ANN KRENTZ

A two-part epic tale from one of today's most popular romance novelists!

Dreams
Parts One & Two

The warrior died at her feet, his blood running out of the cave entrance and mingling with the waterfall. With his last breath he cursed the woman— told her that her spirit would remain chained in the cave forever until a child was created and born there....

So goes the ancient legend of the Chained Lady and the curse that bound her throughout the ages—until destiny brought Diana Prentice and Colby Savager together under the influence of forces beyond their understanding. Suddenly they were both haunted by dreams that linked past and present, while their waking hours were filled with danger. Only when Colby, Diana's modern-day warrior, learned to love, could those dark forces be vanquished. Only then could Diana set the Chained Lady free....

Harlequin Supermance ®

Come to where the West is still wild in a summer trilogy by Margot Dalton

Sunflower (#502—June 1992)
Robin Baldwin becomes the half owner of a prize
rodeo horse. But to take possession, she has to travel
the rodeo circuit with cowboy Matt Adams, living
with him in *very* close quarters!

Tumbleweed (#508—July 1992)
Until she met Scott Freeman, Lyle Callander was about
as likely to settle in one spot as tumbleweed in a
windstorm. But who *is* Scott? He's more than the
simple photographer he claims to be . . . much more.

Juniper (#511—August 1992)
Devil-may-care Buck Buchanan can ride a bucking
bronco or a Brahma bull. But can he win Claire
Tremaine, a woman who sets his heart on fire but
keeps her own as cold as ice?

**"I just finished reading *Under Prairie Skies* by
Margo Dalton and had to hide my tears from my
children. I loved it!"** —A reader

Harlequin Historicals

COMING NEXT MONTH

#139 BOSTON RENEGADE—June Lund Shiplett
After inheriting a ranch from her nefarious brother, spinster
Hanna Winters was threatened by outlaws searching for a missing
cache of stolen money. Yet the biggest threat of all came from
drifter Blake Morgan, who threw her well-ordered life into chaos.

#140 BODIE BRIDE—Isabel Whitfield
Spinster Margaret Warren believed she had everything she needed.
But when her father brought good-natured John Banning into their
home, Margaret was forced to recognize her loneliness—and her
undeniable attraction to the one man who infuriated her the most.

#141 KNIGHT DREAMS—Suzanne Barclay
Lord Ruarke Sommerville was drunk when he rescued French
noblewoman Gabrielle de Lauren from marauding soldiers and
impulsively wed her. Although the morning after brought
surprises, haste doesn't always mean waste—especially when the
courtship begins *after* the wedding.

#142 GYPSY BARON—Mary Daheim
Lady Katherine de Vere had always been loyal to king and country.
Nevertheless, when mysterious half-Gypsy Stefan Dvorak drew her
into a web of political intrigue, she began to doubt not only her
politics, but her heart, as well.

AVAILABLE NOW: